MARS NATION 3

Hard Science Fiction

BRANDON Q. MORRIS

D1500544

BRANDON Q.
MORRIS
HARD SCIENCE FICTION

Contents

Mars Nation 3

Sol 314, MfE Base

"Push," Theo said, "and be careful!"

The triangular object began slowly moving toward him. He let the leading edge slide onto his gloved hands. The structure, created from panes of glass attached to a base, was surprisingly heavy. He took a small step backward, securing his grip on the base before the whole thing could slip off the bed of the rover's cargo area.

"Okay, stop," he said. "Now I need you over here,"

"Sure," he heard Rebecca reply over the helmet radio. She leapt elegantly from the cargo bed and reached for the other end of the structure. The base, a thick plastic panel about three meters long and just as wide, could be carried quite easily by two people. On top of it, though, two rectangular panes of thick glass had been leaned against each other, forming opposing faces of a wedge-shaped structure that had been closed by attaching two triangular glass panels to the sides.

"Do you see the set-up area?" Theo asked.

"Yes, I do."

They had leveled the area yesterday, and today they'd positioned the rover close to it. They were on the summit of the hillside that towered over their small settlement. The glass prism was going to sit up here like the jewel on a crown.

"And heave!" he commanded. In perfect unison, they lifted it clear of the rover and sidestepped the short distance from the vehicle to the chosen spot. "And down," he said. They maintained level as they squatted to lower the structure to the surface. They laid it down as planned and straightened back up.

Theo took a step back.

Rebecca looked down the hill and waved. She'd seen someone watching them. The presence of the settlement was only apparent at second glance, since the majority of it was located underground.

"I'll bring the first canister," Theo declared.

This was the weakest part of his plan. They'd brought containers of water along, keeping them inside the heated rover. They were going to fill the glass structure with the water—quickly, considering the air temperature was minus 40. They didn't have much time before the water would freeze.

"I'll open the fill valve," Rebecca said. This was the 'division of labor' they had planned.

Theo walked over to the rover and removed the first canister from the cargo area. He rushed over to the glass wedge, opening the container's seal en route, and poured the water into the structure.

"It worked!" Rebecca declared. "Congratulations!"

"Thanks."

The contents of the first canister had covered the bottom of the structure. He hurried back and forth between the structure and the rover, eight more times. He had calculated, of course, how much water they would need to fill it. The water level rose proportionately higher with each addition because the structure tapered from bottom to top. Theo wasn't fast enough, however, with the last canister. The water froze before he could pour it, and he huffed in frustration.

"That should be okay," Rebecca said. "Look—we're only short by a couple centimeters at the top."

"True," he replied, glancing up at the sun. It was early

afternoon, but its position was already fairly low. "Let's drive back down," he urged. He was excited. Nothing depended on this structure, neither their survival nor the fate of humanity. And this fact was precisely what made it so special. It was pure luxury.

They jumped back on the rover. Since she reached the vehicle first, Rebecca took the driver's seat. They sped down the hillside. They had to take a long detour since the crater wall was too steep for a straight route. Theo held tight to Rebecca from behind to keep from being hurled from the bucking rover. It was a lot of fun being out and about with Rebecca.

She was also the inspiration behind his idea for the water-filled glass wedge. She had been speaking wistfully about the fact that they would probably never see a rainbow again. This structure should change that.

They reached the base of the crater.

"Please stop," Theo said.

Rebecca brought the rover to a standstill.

Theo leaned forward and tapped the map screen beside the control panel. "It should be about here," he said.

Rebecca restarted the engine. She drove slowly to the spot that Theo had marked on the map. "This must be it," she said.

Theo checked the time. "Twenty minutes to go," he said.

They stood side by side, their upper arms brushing against each other. It was impossible for them to feel each other's warmth through the thick fabric of their spacesuits, but it felt to Theo as if he could. They watched the edge of the crater wall.

"Now," Theo said.

The sun was on the verge of disappearing behind the crater wall. This was the moment. Its rays reached the glass wedge, which, functioning as a prism, split the light into its various components and a rainbow appeared, small but clearly visible. The sun's light was much weaker than on Earth, but as twilight settled around them, the rainbow became all the more distinct.

"It's beautiful," Rebecca exclaimed.

"Just like you," Theo replied softly.

"Thank you," she said. She gazed unwaveringly at the prism-generated colors.

Theo stepped behind her and wrapped his arms around her waist. "Imagine that we're standing on some Caribbean beach after a tropical storm," he said.

"I'm there with you now. The sand is warm and soft under my feet. The air smells like the sea."

Sol 316, NASA Base

"LANCE?"

"Yes, Sarah?"

"What do you get when you multiply 268 by 24, divided by 24.66 plus 56?"

He looked over at his girlfriend, who was sitting across from him at a computer. *Why doesn't she just plug the numbers into the computer?* he thought. However, what he was doing right now was so dull that he didn't mind the distraction. He was supposed to be comparing the water and fertilizer quantities used over the past two weeks to the amount of food that had been harvested. This was actually Sarah's task, since as the crew biologist, she was responsible for the garden, but he was helping her. Lance mentally ran the calculation she'd posed. Since Sarah hadn't mentioned any parentheses, 268 times 24 divided by 24.66 came to roughly 260, plus 56, came to 316.

Today's date! Lance jumped up. Of course, on Sol 56, they had... He walked around his desk and up behind his girl-friend, starting to rub her shoulders.

"Is it starting?" he asked.

"I think so. I've never been through this myself, but if another woman told me, as her doctor, that she was having pain like this, my diagnosis would be obvious. He seems to be super punctual."

"We have to tell Mike and Ewa," Lance said. "Hurry, let's get you to sickbay."

But Sarah remained in her seat. "No need to rush," she replied calmly. "I can still walk on my own."

"Then I'll head out," Lance said, "and get Ewa."

Besides Sarah, there weren't any other doctors at the base, which was why Ewa had gone through childbirth training. As a trained farmer, she knew how to bring calves into the world. Sarah had laughed loudly at that and said that she felt like she was in the best possible hands.

Ewa wasn't on shift at the moment, so Lance tracked her down in her quarters. This part of the subterranean structure still smelled like fresh paint. The rooms along here hadn't been move-in ready until two weeks ago. Until then, Ewa had more *lodged* than *lived* in a storeroom.

He knocked on the door, and she invited him in. Ewa was lying on an improvised bed, the frame for which she had welded together. A large, flat sack stuffed with dried grass from their own garden was functioning as her mattress, causing her room to smell a little like hay.

"It's starting," Lance said without any other greeting.

Ewa sat up. "Just stay calm," she said.

Sweat was trickling down his back although Ewa's room was barely twenty degrees. What in the world was she talking about? What was happening now was the greatest miracle that the universe had to offer! And he was supposed to stay calm? "Easier said than done," he said, rubbing his chin.

"We'll get through this," Ewa answered. "Everything looks really good. The baby has developed extremely well."

Ewa was right. Neither the low gravitational force nor the higher radiation seemed to have harmed the fetus. The ultrasound pictures revealed a little boy who was well-developed in every possible way.

Lance was nevertheless worried. No human had ever been born on another planet. And their medical capability was limited. The NASA expedition had been provisioned for a visit to Mars, not for a permanent settlement. In contrast to the members of the privately funded Mars City space project, which was also located here on Mars, his son wouldn't be receiving any vaccinations or even the vitamin K shot that was customarily given to newborns right after birth. The relations between their base and Mars City were tense at the moment, since they had refused to pledge allegiance to the administrator there.

"Are you coming now?" Lance asked.

"In just a minute," Ewa said. "I'll change clothes and wash up well. You should do that, too, if you want to be present for the birth. Do you?"

He nodded. Of course he did. He was going to be the first person to greet his son's arrival on Mars.

THE BIRTH WAS NOISY, stressful, and bloody. And it stank. Lance was drenched in sweat. He sat on his heels supporting Sarah on the plinth as she grunted and pushed. Tears ran down his face, but the only reason he noticed was because of the salty taste in his mouth. He felt responsible for Sarah's suffering while all he could do was watch. He was glad when she squeezed his hand so hard that it hurt, and when his legs fell asleep and started to burn under her weight. Maybe this way he could reduce her burden at least a little.

Sarah was breathing at the rhythm that Ewa set for her. She was an exemplary mother already in these first moments of their son's life. One final shout and they were done. Sarah's muscles went slack, and Lance had to hold her firmly to keep her from sliding onto the floor. Her strength seemed to drain out of her body. He held her tightly.

"Do you want to do it?" Ewa was handing a pair of scissors to him.

What was he supposed to do with it? He shook his head.

"The umbilical cord," Ewa said. "It isn't difficult." She put the scissors into his right hand and told him what to do. "Now," she said.

He manipulated the scissors with his right hand, still stabilizing Sarah between his left arm and his body. The umbilical cord offered little resistance. He had now separated his son from his mother. Lance suppressed a sob. It was a farewell and a hello. He never would have thought that this would be so... so dramatic.

"Can you help her onto the cot?"

Ewa took a few steps to the side to take care of the infant. Lance didn't think he could stand up to take Sarah to the cot, but he somehow managed it. When she was finally lying down, he brushed her hair out of her face with his index finger. She looked utterly exhausted, but nonetheless beautiful. Her eyes opened, and she shot him a little smile.

Ewa brought their son over and showed him to Sarah. He was wrapped in a white towel, and when Ewa held him up to Sarah's face, he started to cry. Sarah smiled as she reached up to take her newborn son.

"He doesn't mean it," Lance said quietly.

"I know," she whispered, wrapping her arms around their son.

A ringing sound went off in the background. Lance ignored it. His son was simply too amazing. He would never stop gazing at him. Someone touched his shoulder, and he spun around in surprise.

"Mike needs you on the bridge," Ewa said.

"Is it—"

He didn't finish the question, since Ewa's face provided the answer. A horrible fear washed over him, such as he had never known before. He suspected this reaction was the result of now being a father. Would it always be like this? He straightened up. "I have to go see Mike," he said.

Sarah just nodded.

"I have no idea what he wants from me," he said, although Sarah hadn't asked. With that, he turned around and left the room.

"WHAT'S GOING ON?" Lance asked as he stepped through the door.

Mike whipped around to face him as Sharon leaned against the right-hand wall, fiddling nervously with her belt. "We've received an emergency signal from the MfE," Mike replied.

"'An emergency signal?'" Lance echoed, afraid he could guess what he was about to hear. As terrible as it sounded, he found himself wishing a meteorite had hit the MfE base, or that perhaps an epidemic had broken out there. It would be horrible, but it wouldn't affect his newborn son.

"An attack. Ten armed assailants from Mars City. Summers sent them."

"Were there fatalities?" Lance felt himself growing cold and clammy. The sweat on his back felt disgusting. He needed to shower and change clothes.

"No. Ellen decided not to put up a fight. They wouldn't have stood a chance. The entire MfE base is now occupied."

"That was prudent," Lance said. Mike was involved with Ellen, and now he'd learned the woman he cared for was in the hands of a ruthless enemy. Lance wiped his forehead with his bare hand, rubbing the perspiration onto his pants. "Is there anything we can do?" he asked.

"No," Sharon said, shaking her head. "They're too far away."

"We have to consider how we'll respond to the attack," Mike declared.

"We'll fight," Lance said. However, as he uttered these words, they seemed to lose their force. What would they fight with? There were just the five of them. *No, make that six.* And that fact made the decision all the harder.

"I don't know if that would be smart," Sharon said.

"My first impulse is that we'd need to defend ourselves, too," Mike said. "But imagine what would happen if Summers' people show up at our base. He might send fewer of them, but if we fight back, there would be losses."

"He'll send more than he did to the MfE," Sharon said.

"We have forewarning. Summers will be reckoning on countermeasures. He made a smart call to take out the MfE first. They have three times as many people as we do. The element of surprise was a bigger factor where they were concerned."

"Summers is an asshole," Lance said.

"A powerful asshole," Mike corrected him.

"Boys, this isn't helping us," Sharon cut in.

"How much time do we have?" Lance asked.

"Hard to say," Mike declared. "If Summers sends the same people here that he used against the MfE, we might have a few days."

"But he might have sent us our own attack team," Sharon interrupted. "It could show up here at any moment."

"You're forgetting about our surveillance drones," Lance said. He had stationed three automated drones at a distance of 20 kilometers from the base to notify them about unusual incidents. "They will give us about two hours to react."

"If they pick up on the enemy," Mike said.

"I'm assuming that they wouldn't come on foot. And every vehicle produces a clearly visible trail of dust."

"That's true," Mike admitted.

"I suggest that we give ourselves until tomorrow to consider if we want to defend ourselves or not," Sharon said.

"And in the meantime, we should go ahead and prepare our defenses," Lance said.

"Agreed," Mike replied.

Sol 316, MfE Base

"ALRIGHT NOW, you men need to calmly climb in," said one of the men in the modern *Spaceliner* spacesuits, pointing at the airlock on one of the enclosed rovers.

Theo glanced back. Rebecca wasn't in sight. He hoped that she was doing okay. He recognized Andy and Ellen. Her arm was wrapped around his shoulders. She was probably trying to convince him to not fight back. Her decision to raise the white flag hadn't met with everyone's approval. Theo had supported her. They wouldn't have stood any real chance against ten armed attackers. But what would happen next?

Somebody suddenly shoved him from the side.

"Hey! You're supposed to get in there. Didn't you hear that?"

Another of Summers' men. Theo had to restrain himself —it was tempting to beat the arrogance out of the man. The guy was armed, but holding his gun so awkwardly that Theo could have easily overpowered him. However, there were seven other men here who could put him out of commission. Two of their gang seemed to be down with the women in the underground quarters. He waved at Andy before turning around and climbing into the airlock.

The rover smelled unpleasant. *Not surprising, considering that five men had spent several days in here*, he thought. One of them was waiting for him inside. He signaled for Theo to take off his spacesuit. If only the guy wouldn't wave his gun around so much!

"Man, that's dangerous!" Theo couldn't stop that from slipping out. If a bullet was fired and went through the external wall, they would both be toast!

"That's my business," the man said in a thick Texas accent.

Some people never learned how dangerous guns could be in a world without breathable air. He preferred to not be around that kind of behavior.

The man pushed him toward the back of the cabin. *Why doesn't he just say what he wants, and why?* At the rear of the vehicle was another airlock that led to the second rover. Theo was about to lean down and reach for his spacesuit when the Texan shoved him again. *Got it. You don't want me to take my suit along.* Theo had to acknowledge that the rationale behind this was quite clever. If they stuck all the MfE men in the second rover and removed the airlock, they'd be cut off from every possible escape route. No one could leave the rover without a suit. They would be able to transport them across the Mars desert without any kind of security watch.

But this would be torture for the prisoners. The trip would take at least four days, or five, and maybe longer. They would have to spend the time together in cramped quarters, without any privacy whatsoever. And the sanitary facilities would be primitive. Would they provide them with enough food and water? Of course they would. The administrator was following a specific strategy. Every life had a role to play. The larger the gene pool was for his colony, the easier it would be for it to survive. If the man wasn't such a big asshole, they might have agreed to join him before now. It would have been reasonable. It didn't make sense to maintain three separate human settlements on the planet.

"Can't you hurry up?" the man behind him called.

Theo didn't let this ruffle him. He was about to exit the tube when he heard Andy's voice.

"Don't touch me!" Andy shouted.

"I'll touch you whenever I want to," the Texan replied.

Theo stopped. He knew what this expression really meant. The man wanted an excuse to pick a fight, and he was just waiting for the right opportunity to hit Andy. The delicate Georgian probably looked like easy pickings to him.

"Don't even think about it," Theo yelled. He could be at Andy's side in three seconds.

"Keep out of this," the Texan said. "It doesn't concern you. Have you already forgotten who's got the gun here?"

That did it. Theo strode back down the tube. The man was aiming at him, but he didn't stop. "You'd be a dumb ass to fire," he said. "But hopefully you already know that."

The guy lowered his weapon. "Fine," he said. "Just go! Into the other rover. We're about to leave."

REBECCA WAS WAITING on the bridge, but she didn't know why. What was happening on the surface? What was the administrator going to do with the men? Nobody was answering her questions.

Two armed guards were stationed down here with the women. They were strolling down the corridors, making lewd, immature jokes as if they had never seen a woman before. Regardless of their weapons, if they wanted to, the women could take out the two jokers any time they chose.

But that might put the lives of the men at risk! That had probably been the administrator's idea to begin with. If he separated the two groups, he could use the one as a pawn against the others. Rebecca was afraid that his plan might actually work.

The two strangers had shown up on the bridge just now, unexpectedly. It was evident that they were listening to orders via the small button speakers in their ears. "Alright, people," one of them finally said. "We're going to leave you on your own. Twice a day, you'll need to contact the office of the administrator to receive your daily duty roster."

"And what'll happen to our men?" Ellen asked.

"We're taking them with us. They will be put to good use in the city."

"But you can't...," Rebecca started, then stopped as she realized what she was saying. *Of course they can.*

Ellen grabbed Rebecca's upper arm.

"Good, ladies," the other man said with a nod at the two of them. "And if any of you ladies find yourselves needing a real man, just call for Jack."

The first man slapped him on the back. "You're married, bro," he said.

Jack gave a 'whatever' shrug.

The men fastened up their suits before leaving the bridge through the airlock. As soon as the light attached to the lock chamber glowed green, Rebecca followed them in her space-suit. She was too late. A trail of dust indicated that the three vehicles had already driven out of the crater, heading eastward. She waved after them in the crazy hope that maybe Theo could see her through a telescope. Then colorful flecks of light surrounded her.

She turned around and saw the daily rainbow. Her promise that she would see Theo again. *No question,* she told herself firmly.

Sol 317, NASA Base

"Good morning!"

Lance set the tray holding fresh coffee and muesli down on the table. Sarah sat up in her bed. He picked up the pillow from the foot of the bed and handed it to her. She stuffed it behind her back so that she could lean against the wall.

"Did you sleep well?" he asked.

Sarah smiled. "Mostly. He only woke me up every four hours or so." She pointed next to her, where their son was sleeping in his little basket.

Lance stood beside the bed and watched him. He was beautiful, but he also looked quite fragile.

"You could change his diaper," Sarah suggested.

He stared at her.

"You do know what diapers are, right?"

"Yeah, uh, I can do that?"

"Give it a shot. It's just as new for me as it is for you, or do you think that women are somehow born with this special knowledge?"

"I... No, of course not." Lance leaned over the basket and carefully picked up his son. The baby opened his eyes and stretched. "Amazing," he said.

He lifted him up to his face and touched his soft skin with his cheek. The baby smelled sweet. Lance then set him carefully down on the end of the bed before unbuttoning the tiny sleeper. Lance remembered how Sarah had sewed it from spare clothes at the base. At that time, everything had still seemed so far off. Now a diapered bottom was right in front of him. The diaper was made out of thin cotton fabric. He tried to memorize how it was wrapped around his son's lower body. He would have to recreate it somehow.

"Who diapered him like this?"

"Ewa," his girlfriend declared.

"Ah, she seems to have mastered it."

"It's not hard," Sarah said.

Maybe, maybe not. He removed the used diaper. The blackish smear in it smelled slightly sweet, not at all unpleasant. He folded up the diaper. Someone had set a bowl of warm water beside the bed. A rag hung over its edge. "The water?" he asked.

"Ewa brought it by right before you came with breakfast."

"Oh, the coffee!" Lance exclaimed. "Please serve yourself, or it'll get cold."

"I'm hungry," Sarah said.

"Enjoy!"

Lance cautiously cleaned his son who suddenly screwed up his face and began to screech. Lance flinched. "Did I do something wrong?"

"Who knows?" Sarah said. "The rag might be too cold for him."

Lance dried the damp skin with a towel, pulled out a fresh diaper from the container under the bed, and tucked it under his son. He did his best to replicate the wrapping technique. It worked. The baby looked just like he had before the soiled diaper had been removed. "Look," he said proudly. "Freshly diapered. And, he isn't crying anymore."

"That's good," Sarah said. "Now we just need to do that a thousand more times, and he'll be in the clear."

"Sounds promising," Lance replied wryly as he juggled wiggly little arms and legs back into the sleeper. "By the way, we haven't discussed names yet. Why not?" Had he been trying to suppress thoughts of the impending birth? Lance was surprised at himself.

"That's true," Sarah said. "I also don't know why we didn't. Maybe because I've always had a name in mind and didn't want you to try to change my mind."

Lance laughed. "What made you think that I'd try to change your mind?"

"Well, you might not have liked it."

"You'd have to tell me what it was before I could do that."

"Okay. I came up with Michael. The name sounds good in German and English. And—"

"And what?"

"It's a little crazy."

"Out with it."

"After the first moon landing," Sarah continued, "everyone focused on Neil Armstrong and Buzz Aldrin. But no one gave any thought to the poor man who spent all that time up in the *Apollo* shuttle, circling the moon by himself."

"Michael Collins," Lance said. "I remember it as if it were yesterday." He laughed. The first moon landing had been over seventy years ago. Would the history books someday tell the story of the first Mars landing? At this moment, it didn't look like there would be any more history books written.

"Good, you even know his name."

"That was part of our training. History of NASA 101."

"So… what do you think of Michael as a name?"

He spoke the name several times out loud. "What does it sound like in German?" he asked.

"Michael," Sarah said.

"Mikhael."

"Something like that. A soft *ch* sound, you know?"

"Soft is good. I'd prefer that he not turn into one of those hardened men."

"He shouldn't turn into a hardened man?"

"Of course he'll become a man. But not so callous, you know?"

"I think I know what you mean. So we agree on Michael?"

"Yes, he should be named Michael for the man who never got to land on the moon," Lance said.

"Did you know that Collins was later offered the opportunity to walk on the moon with the *Apollo 17* mission?" Sarah asked. "He turned it down."

"Good call. He wanted to stay alive. The missions were just kind of cobbled together back then."

"Probably. But I prefer to interpret that as his decision to remain the man in the background. He always spoke with such unbelievable humility. I really liked that about him."

"Yes, that suits you," Lance said.

THEY GATHERED on the bridge around noon. Sarah brought Michael along in his basket. He stayed fast asleep as she carried him through the base's corridors.

"I would like to introduce you to Michael," Lance said once they were all there.

"We know each other already," Ewa said with a smile.

"Pleased to meet you," Sharon said. "I'm Sharon, but you may call me Aunt Sharon."

"I'm Mike. You may call me Boss."

Sarah laughed in response.

"For real, it's a nice name," Mike stated. "In honor of Michael Collins, I assume?"

"My NASA hero," Sarah said. "Besides, I like how the name sounds in German."

"Michael," Mike said.

Sarah looked at him with appreciation. "That was perfect. Where did you learn to pronounce the soft *ch* sound?"

"Kiss-up," Lance said.

"At school," Mike replied. "We had a very pretty German teacher, so all of us guys worked harder than usual."

"You had German in school?" Sharon asked. "I hadn't heard about that."

"It was totally normal when I grew up in North Dakota. There were a ton of German Americans up there."

"But your mother was from Italy, right?"

"That didn't mean the German teacher wasn't really pretty, which was why that language interested me more than my mother's native one."

"That's great. You can speak a little German with Michael sometimes," Sarah said. "It would be good if I wasn't the only one he heard speaking it."

"Unfortunately, I've pretty much forgotten everything I learned."

"Then I'll refresh your memory."

"Maybe later, after we've solved the Summers problem," Mike said.

All of a sudden, the mood on the bridge darkened. *What a shame*, Lance thought. Reality had returned.

"How should we respond to an attack?" Mike asked.

"We should surrender," Sharon replied spontaneously. "I don't see that there's any way we could defend ourselves."

"Our base should actually be pretty easy to defend," Lance said.

"Yes, but for how long? If we can't get out, we'll run through our resources. Our enemy would definitely last longer than we could."

"Do we have any aces up our sleeve that we don't know about?" Mike asked.

Sarah spoke up. "What do you mean by that?"

"I don't know. Something that we could use to surprise them. Something that might make us unassailable."

"I... I could—" Ewa didn't finish the sentence.

"What could you do?" Mike asked.

"No, that's ridiculous. I can't do anything."

"Just say what you're thinking. What could you do?" Mike asked again.

"Forget it. We should surrender when they get here."

"I can't agree to that. We shouldn't make it so easy for them. Maybe our ditch will hold," Lance said. "Our odds might not be high, but if we don't even try, we've lost everything anyway."

"Then I suggest that you and Sharon remove the bridge and inspect the ditch," Mike said. "Not that it's collapsed already, or anything."

The others nodded. Lance studied Ewa. What had she been about to propose, and why was she now so reluctant to tell them about it? She could be really stubborn sometimes.

"I'LL BE RIGHT THERE," Sharon said over the helmet radio.

"Take your time. You haven't missed anything," Lance replied.

He examined the sky. The thin air was full of dust, as if a storm had moved through the day before. But it had been dead calm here for the past few days. Maybe this was caused by a spin-off from a dust storm farther to the north. Here, close to the equator, the weather was more stable than to the north and the south, where the seasons changed.

The hatch in the floor opened, and Sharon's head appeared. They should have expanded the airlock long ago so that more than one astronaut at a time could exit onto the surface. However, they'd had so many other things to do that they hadn't gotten around to this.

"Sorry you had to wait," she said.

"I enjoy taking in the sights around here. Every day, there's something new to discover," Lance replied.

"Very funny!"

Nothing except for the quantity of dust in the air ever changed from day to day around the base. The turbine he had built shortly after their landing sometimes turned slower and sometimes faster. By this point, they were extracting energy from the temperature changes in the planet's surface. Since locating a water source, tricks like this were now possible. But he still hadn't disassembled the turbine. After all, it was the only thing that conferred a degree of vitality on their base.

"Let's go," Sharon said, reaching for his arm.

Lance brushed some red dust from the shoulder of her suit.

"Thanks," she said.

It was a good 200 meters to the outer base boundary. The ditch was definitely visible. Lance checked to see if the edge they had reinforced with ice was still solid. To do that, he had to balance on the large stones they had deposited all around to shield the ice from the sun.

"Just be careful," Sharon said. "A five-meter fall is nothing to laugh at."

Lance knelt and peered down. The ground there was stone hard. If he fell, his suit wouldn't survive the impact. Sharon would have to quickly drag him to the airlock. He stood back up and climbed from rock to rock. He felt a little like a knight at a castle. The ditch walls seemed to be well-preserved from up here. "Should we take a look at them from down there?" he asked.

"Sure. We have no idea how long it'll be before we'll be back out here."

He turned to face her and leapt forward with all his strength from the rock he was on to the solid ground. Something behind him crashed. The rock, which weighed at least 50 kilograms, had absorbed his momentum, rolled backward, and tumbled off the wall. He hoped the damage was limited to this. The collision was audible despite the thin Martian air. Lance memorized the spot in question.

They crossed the bridge they'd made from two steel girders left over after the reconstruction of the drill tower, over which they had laid sturdy panels. They wouldn't be able to manually remove the beams—they were too heavy for that. After all, the bridge had needed to bear the weight of an enclosed rover. The structure was dusty, just like everything else that sat out in the Mars atmosphere for an extended period of time. On the other side of the bridge, they turned to the right. From the outside, the ditch's slope didn't look very steep. Any vehicle that reached the ditch would have to drive down a 30-degree slope before coming to a stop in front of a smooth, five-meter wall.

Lance and Sharon climbed down into the ditch. Sand and a few small rocks were scattered across the ground. Lance stepped very close to the wall. It wasn't as pristine as it had seemed from the top of the ditch. Erosion had already started to work on it, but now wasn't the time for improvements. Their enemy could show up at their door at any time.

He looked up. The damage to the wall was superficial. The outer layer of ice hadn't been penetrated. For an average climber, it would still be impossible to scale the five meters. Even if you drove a rover right up to the wall and climbed on the roof, you would still be short by about a meter. However, if the enemy brought along a crane... but that was unlikely, at least on their first attempt.

Sharon walked to the left. She obviously wanted to circle the base. He followed her. They soon ran into the boulder that he had accidentally caused to crash down. Half of it was buried in the ground. Here, too, the wall was undamaged. What luck! They kept going. It was strange to be down here. He felt like he was in some sort of primitive maze since he couldn't see any of their surroundings. Fortunately, they would eventually reach the bridge. Otherwise, they would just keep circling the base forever. At a diameter of 500 meters, the ring ditch was more than one and a half kilometers long. They needed about 15 minutes to complete the circuit.

"You want to take down the panels? I'll get the rover," Lance said.

Sharon nodded and began to remove the sand-covered panels from the bridge. He walked toward the airlock. The unenclosed, lightweight rover would have to be enough to pull out the steel girders. He walked around to the other side of the rover. The ignition key was sitting in the tool box. He stooped down and was taken aback to see someone messing around with the enclosed rover next to the one he was going to use. He only saw the person from behind. It had to be either Mike or Ewa.

"Mike, is that you?" he asked over the helmet radio.

The person turned around. He recognized Ewa.

"Ah, Lance," she said. She seemed slightly breathless.

"What are you doing here?" he asked.

"I just need a tool. The air conditioner in my room isn't working right."

"We could have brought it to you if you'd just said something."

"I didn't want to bother you."

"Makes sense. I need to get back to the bridge now."

"Good luck, Lance."

The sentence sounded like a goodbye, but he had to be mistaken about that. Or was Ewa up to something? If so, what could it be? He leaned over the control panel on the lightweight rover and activated the vehicle. He then climbed into the driver's seat and drove to the bridge where Sharon was already waiting for him.

"Do you have the tow rope?" she asked.

"In the toolbox on the left."

She walked over to the right side of the rover and hunted for it.

"On the other side," he said.

"So on the right side after all," she replied.

"No, my left."

"Portside then," Sharon said.

"Exactly."

"Just say that next time!" With a chuckle, she walked around the rover and extracted the rope from the toolbox. She tied it to the rear of the rover and carried the other end toward the bridge. "It doesn't reach," she said.

He drove the rover closer to the bridge.

"That's far enough," Sharon said, bending down and attaching the rope's carabiner to one of the openings in the first girder. "Ready."

"Okay," he replied.

He sat down in the driver's seat and steered the rover toward the airlock. He pressed the accelerator, first a little, then more. The vehicle started moving. He looked back. The girder broke free, and its back end crashed down into the ditch. The rover wobbled, but it was appreciably heavier than the girder. Lance steered it straight forward until the beam lay flat on the base's surrounding area.

"When the time comes to rebuild the bridge, we'll have to be creative about it," Sharon said.

She was right. They hadn't considered that. When they had constructed the ditch, they had first installed the girders and then hewn away the stone underneath it. That approach wouldn't be an option the next time around. But, who ever thinks they're about to be invaded?

"We can talk about this later on," Lance said.

"Okay," Sharon replied. She leaned across the girder and loosened the rope. "Your turn," she said.

He drove the rover back to the bridge, and she attached the rope to the second girder. Two minutes later, there was nothing left of the bridge. They now lived on an island. Would that help them? Lance wanted to believe it would, but they wouldn't be able to withstand a long siege. Their enemy would only need a long ladder to infiltrate their base. The first altercation might end in their favor, but the second one most likely wouldn't. Nonetheless, it still felt right to not surrender their base immediately.

They drove the rover back to the airlock. Ewa was gone. She must have gone back inside the base to repair her air conditioner. Perhaps he should go check on her in case she needed help but didn't want to ask for it. He wouldn't put it past her. She was probably still struggling with a guilty conscience. If he were in her shoes, he would probably feel the same.

"You go first," he said to Sharon. "I need another minute out here."

She nodded and vanished into the airlock. He turned

around and thought back to what it had felt like the day they had landed on Mars. The panorama was breathtaking—a completely sterile, even life-threatening environment stretching all the way to the horizon, which still seemed frighteningly close to him. And yet they had been living here for almost a year. Humans had been an astonishing invention on the part of Mother Earth.

Sol 318, NASA Base

THEY WERE SITTING AT BREAKFAST. Lance yawned loudly. The night had been stressful. In order to provide Sarah with a peaceful night's rest, he had taken over Michael's feedings with her pumped milk.

"I just spoke with Ellen," Mike said, his eyes rimmed with red. He was probably really worried right now. Sharon had told Lance at some point that Mike and Ellen were in a relationship. The news still wasn't official.

Lance scratched his right temple.

"And how is she doing?" Sharon asked.

"They haven't heard from the men for two days now," Mike said. "Other than that, it's life as normal. Summers notified them that a transporter will arrive at their base shortly in order to collect all the resources they won't be requiring over the next month."

"Ah, he wants to make them dependent on Mars City," Sharon said.

"I think so," Mike declared.

"You're fairly quiet, Lance," Sharon remarked.

He glanced at her in surprise. He usually didn't say much at breakfast. It was too early to chat, and his powers of concentration barely sufficed to open and close his mouth for eating.

"Not awake yet," he said.

"The baby's doing well?"

"Yeah," he said.

"By the way, where's Ewa?" Mike asked.

"Probably still asleep," Sharon replied.

Lance paused. He hadn't seen her since early yesterday afternoon up on the surface. She hadn't joined them for supper. He had assumed she had lost track of time while repairing her air conditioner. He had decided to offer her his help that evening, but then Sarah had brought the baby over. "She was having trouble with her air conditioner yesterday," he said.

"That can't be true," Mike replied. "I would've been aware of that. It's connected to the central control system."

"Maybe I misunderstood," Lance said. But that wasn't true. She had expressed herself quite clearly yesterday at the rover. His suspicions arose. *Is she up to something?* he wondered. She had tried once before to kill her crew. *Was she back to being manipulated by the AI inside her head?* "Maybe we should go check on her. She might be sick," he said.

"I'll take care of that," Sharon volunteered. "Right after breakfast."

"Thanks," Mike said.

They spent the rest of their meal in silence. *Something's going to happen today*, Lance thought. His appetite disappeared. With difficulty, he choked down his last spoonful of muesli and took a sip of coffee, which tasted like dishwater. They had run out of real coffee a long time ago. Sarah had roasted some kind of plant remains as a replacement. He preferred not to know what the ground-up plant matter was.

Lance set his coffee cup down on the table. He felt nauseous. Standing up, he poured the remaining coffee away and got some water instead. The liquid was clear and didn't smell like anything, but he still couldn't help thinking that his cup might be holding purified urine. This was how the base's life support system functioned, despite the fact that they now had an external water source.

He deposited his cup on the table. "I'm going to wash up and get to work in the garden," he said. He didn't mind tending to the plants. It would keep him from thinking too much, from wondering when Summers' men might show up, or what Ewa had been doing up on the surface yesterday.

LANCE SCOOTED through the dirt on his knees, but he didn't care. The greenhouse ceiling was low, which meant he couldn't stand up in here. The air smelled like fecal matter. It was damp and warm—just the way the plants liked it. Besides that, the carbon dioxide content of the air was five times as high as on Earth, which was why the air pressure was maintained at half the normal level. None of this bothered Lance, who was totally absorbed in his work. Each of the little lettuce plants had to be examined. Did they have enough space and fertilizer? Were they developing well, or were there signs of an impending illness?

The ecosystem had been set up to produce the greatest amount of biomass in the shortest amount of time. In the same period, it could quickly careen out of control. The sheer variety of microflora was significantly lower than on Earth, where many thousands of species struggled for dominance. They had only relatively few species here. They had either been unintentionally brought here by the humans, or had been deliberately selected by the astrobiologists for their ability to promote plant growth. For example, they might promote the recycling of dead plant parts into nutrients.

However, there were still some functions that humans had to handle, including pollination. This wasn't necessary for the lettuce plants, though. A mature plant was growing at the end of the bed. It was already almost a meter tall. Its inflorescences were pollinating themselves, and Lance would soon be able to harvest the seeds that they would need for the next generation of plants. Lots of little miracles were taking place in front of his eyes. Lance could understand why Sarah had volunteered to take care of all the gardening work.

He scooted forward a little. What the soil didn't contain were any organisms that could aerate it. This was why he had accepted the role of earthworm and was digging around in the dirt with a garden fork. Good topsoil was much more valuable here than it was on Earth. The soil they brought inside was sterile at first, so it needed preparation. Lance regularly sprinkled it across the existing topsoil and then turned the Mars dust under.

"Lance, can you hear me?"

What does Mike want now? He already quizzed me earlier about the ditch. "What's going on?"

"I think we have a problem."

"You… think?"

"Ewa's missing," Mike said. "Sharon went to check on her in her quarters, but she wasn't there."

"Is she maybe in the storeroom or the workshop?"

"I wouldn't have interrupted your work if she was. She isn't in the base."

"But where else could she be?"

"No clue. According to the airlock's log, nobody has left the base today."

"Then she has to be here," Lance said.

"Or she left yesterday."

"What does the airlock log say about that?"

"Yesterday, there were several exits. The two of you were outside. The strange thing is that the hatch opened five times to allow for exits, but only four times to let people back in."

"Shit."

"You got that right," Mike agreed. "She must have been the fifth exit, must have followed you outside."

"Now what?"

"I've sent Sharon outside to look around."

"Good idea. Maybe Ewa fell asleep in the rover," Lance said.

"Maybe. I doubt it."

"Me, too. Can I do anything?"

"No, Lance, just keep doing what you're doing. I'll call you whenever I hear something from Sharon."

What had happened with Ewa? Had she been terrified about Summers' people because she had broken into the *Spaceliner* and stolen their drill? The administrator had tried to force them to hand her over to him. He would have probably put her on trial. Lance twisted the garden fork back and forth. Under circumstances similar to hers, he might have chosen to flee as well.

But why hadn't she told someone? They would have tried to help her! Had she been worried that she would run into a lack of sympathy? Or did she want to protect them? She might have expected a different reaction. They could have all run away together, all five of them. It would have been preferable to living under the administrator's thumb. Lance would have suggested this course of action under normal circumstances. But the baby now shut the door to that option. He could never put Michael at risk, even if that meant that eventually they had to wave a white flag.

"LANCE, Sharon is now outside. I'll switch you over to our channel."

"Thanks, Mike."

"There's no trace of Ewa up here," Sharon said. "More than that, our heavy rover is missing, too."

"She took off with that?" Sarah asked. "I never would have thought she'd do that."

"Looks that way," Sharon said.

"But we took down the bridge yesterday. I saw Ewa around that time," Lance said.

"Just a second," Sharon said.

All they could hear for a few moments was the sound of her breathing.

"I'm now at the ditch at the end of the bridge," Sharon said. "The former bridge," she corrected herself.

"And?" Mike said.

"Ewa must be insane. She apparently drove the rover right down the perpendicular wall."

"Did she smash it?" Mike asked.

"Surprisingly, no," Sharon declared. "The ground at the bottom looks all churned up, and I think I can see a piece of sheet metal, but the rover must have survived the fall."

Lance recalled Ewa's story about stealing the crane from the *Spaceliner*. She had simply driven it straight down to the ground.

"That would be just like her," he said. "She's crazy."

"Or simply resolute," Sarah offered, "once she has gotten something in her head. But what does she want to do out there? We have to try to reach her by radio."

"Already did," Mike said. "No reply."

"Could this have something to do with the software inside her brain?" Sharon asked.

"Hard to say. I don't think so," Mike said. "This is just how she is. Nobody would have to force her to do something like this. Just think about the hole she smashed into the mountain by making the drill tower tip over."

Lance remembered that all too well. One of the drones Mike had flown to the site had filmed Ewa doing that. "I have an idea," he said.

"Spit it out," Sharon demanded.

"Couldn't we use one of our drones to search for her?"

"I could send it out," Mike said. "If we're lucky, she's left a trail behind her in the dusty terrain. However, the drone's range is limited. We would actually need to drive out ourselves. Do you want to take the open rover and crash it down the slope of the ditch?"

"No, thank you," Lance said.

"Thanks, Sharon. You can come back inside," Mike said. "By the way, I've been going through our inventory."

"And?" Sarah asked.

"Considering the quantity of provisions she took along, she must be planning to spend the rest of her life out there. She could live just fine for the next six months on the quantity of food, oxygen, and water she took with her."

"Good for her," Lance said.

"But how did she manage that without any of us noticing?" Sharon asked.

"Were you paying attention to what she did with her days? I wasn't," Lance said.

"You think that she prepared all this under our noses?"

"Yes, Sharon," Mike said. "That's exactly what it looks like. She didn't even attempt to conceal her forays into our supplies."

"Because we trusted her," Sarah declared.

"Exactly," Mike said. "And I'm still not sure if our decision to do that was unbelievably stupid or surprisingly shrewd on our part."

Sol 319, NASA Base

FIVE STEPS TO THE LEFT, turn around slowly, five steps to the right. Lance was watching Michael's face. The baby's eyes seemed to be closing, but he couldn't stop pacing yet. He slowly turned to the left and walked as far as the cabin allowed him. About-face, and then five steps back. Michael breathed calmly and evenly. His nostrils flared a little as he exhaled. That looked so sweet! He wanted to cuddle him, but that would wake him up. Lance had to keep walking. His son slept his deepest when he carried him and walked around. If Lance stopped for more than 30 seconds, Michael would open first his eyes, then his mouth—almost always to start crying.

A ringing sound disturbed the silence. It was the bridge. *Shit! Michael is going to wake up now.* He had told Mike not to bother him!

As expected, it was Mike. "Lance, can you hear me?"

"Man, you woke him up now." Lance gazed at Michael. His son was asleep, as astonishing as that might seem. To be on the safe side, he kept pacing.

"Sorry about that, but one of the drones has reported movement. They're coming from the north."

"How long do we have?"

"They'll be here in two hours."

"Alright. I'll try to lay Michael down."

"See you in a minute," Mike said.

Lance looked down at his son. Michael was still asleep. Amazing. Hopefully, he could put him in his crib without waking him up. That wouldn't be easy. Lance walked to the crib at the foot of the bed. He cautiously leaned over, holding his breath as he set Michael down. The baby moved his arms a little, and then his legs twitched.

No, please…

The infant slowly opened his eyes. They were dark, deep, and bright. Lance was captivated. Michael looked at him, opened his mouth and began to wail.

Lance heaved a sigh. This was not going to work.

Sarah was in the garden, and neither Sharon nor Mike would want to be taking care of a baby with an enemy about to reach their base. He would have to take his son along. Lance lifted Michael up to his chest so he could cradle him with one arm and walked out of his cabin. Michael immediately settled back down as father and son headed toward the bridge.

ALL THREE OF his teammates were gathered around the screen when Lance entered the bridge. Sarah had gotten here quickly from the garden. She glanced at him and motioned for him to join them. The monitor showed three enclosed rovers plus a tracked vehicle driving one behind the other across the Mars desert, staggered slightly to avoid each other's dust clouds. The image wobbled slightly.

Lance guessed that it was filming the scene from a height of about 50 meters. "How fast are they moving?" he asked.

"According to our calculations, the rover can do about twenty kilometers an hour, but the tracked vehicle isn't as fast, and it's slowing down the column," Mike explained. "The drone is following them. They are about twenty-eight kilometers away."

"Still about two hours off," Lance estimated.

"Yes," Mike agreed.

"They didn't bring a crane along," Sharon said. "Do you think the tracked vehicle poses a threat to us?"

Lance studied it. It was significantly slower than the enclosed rovers and seemed to be optimized for freight transport across uneven terrains. It could presumably scale hills, but a 90-degree wall would obviously be too much for it.

"I don't think it'll be able to get out of our ditch," he said.

"I agree," Mike said.

"Alright, you experts, let's just wait and see what they do," Sarah said. "How large of a contingent do you think they sent?"

"Five men per vehicle?" Mike replied.

"They only sent ten men to attack the MfE base, but if you're right, that means they'll outnumber us five to one." Sharon asked.

"They clearly think we're more dangerous because we're professionals," Mike said.

"We're professionals?" Sharon laughed. "NASA didn't even provide us with a single gun."

"Under normal circumstances, we would've left for home a long time ago," Mike said.

"And what'll happen if they get to our side of the ditch?" Sarah asked.

"If they follow the pattern they set at the MfE base, they will take Lance and me as collateral," Mike replied.

"You think so?" Sharon asked.

"Absolutely. They'll discover that we have a water source, and that alone will make our base invaluable to them. Our facilities will need to be maintained, which means they'll have to leave someone here," Mike said.

THEY FOLLOWED the convoy's progress on the screen for a few minutes. Then it became tiresome. Lance was frustrated.

They couldn't do anything. The ditch, their version of a city wall, was their only defense besides the mines. But was it secure? Lance shook his head. The ice wall would hold up against a random rambler who came upon them, but not against 20 assailants who were determined to overcome it. They wouldn't even need a crane.

"LEFT OR RIGHT?" Sarah asked.

"Right," Lance replied, tapping her on the right arm.

They hadn't come to an agreement yet about who would take care of Michael when the enemy arrived, so they were drawing straws, proverbially speaking. Sarah had been holding both hands clenched into fists behind her back. She slowly brought her right arm forward and opened it—empty. Lance stamped his foot in frustration. He was supposed to watch from inside while the others defended the base?

"Show me your other hand," he said. Sarah opened her left fist. He saw the hair pin.

"Sorry about that," Sarah said. "Just take good care of Michael for me."

"And you take care of yourself! Michael shouldn't have to grow up without his mother."

"Don't worry about that. I want to see him grow up." Sarah stood up on her tiptoes and kissed him. "I won't take any unnecessary risks," she said.

"Waaaah."

There it was again, that unmistakable sound. Michael needed his parents close by. Lance gently brushed his fingers across Sarah's right cheek before turning around and entering their joint quarters, where Michael had just awakened.

"SHHHH-SHHHH-SHHHH," Lance said softly before starting to hum an old melody—the lyrics for which he could no longer remember—while rocking Michael in his arms. He was sitting in front of the large screen. He and his son were the only people still inside the subterranean bunker they so proudly called their base. Mike, Sharon, and Sarah were planning to defend their outer perimeter. Lance had so wanted to join them, and until the last second, he had tried to first convince Sharon and then Mike to agree to watch his son.

The attackers' vehicles were no more than a kilometer away. Nobody had tried to contact them yet. The NASA crew had likewise maintained radio silence. Mike had recalled all three of their drones, which were now patrolling the perimeter of their base.

Lance kept switching back and forth between the three drones' video feeds until he found one showing his colleagues. He zoomed in closer. It had to be Sharon or Sarah. In their amplified suits, which Ewa had stolen from the *Spaceliner* supply ship, they would probably be hard to distinguish from their enemies. However, the suits fit tightly enough that it was easy to tell the difference between men and women. Now a man was approaching. That had to be Mike, and then another woman came into view. She was somewhat taller than the first figure, so it had to be Sharon. The three of them sat down on the Mars surface. Good. That way they would conserve their strength.

He switched over to the feed from another of the drones. It seemed to have locked in on the enemy's lead vehicle and was tracking it. From its perspective, the base looked very close.

"Mike, they're here," Lance warned the others.

He watched as his three colleagues got to their feet. The drone's video stream showed how the two rear vehicles were fanning out from the convoy.

"The column's separating," Lance said.

"How exactly?" Mike asked.

"Just a sec."

The two rovers in front were steering straight for the base, while the other rover and the tracked vehicle were now veering toward the left.

"Two are coming from the north, and the other two will reach the base from the northeast," he said.

"Thanks."

The three defenders conferred briefly, and then Mike set off for the northeast, while Sharon and Sarah head due north. In the meantime, Lance switched back and forth between the drones. He stopped in fear. The two rovers coming from the north must have separated. The video feed from the accompanying drone showed only one vehicle.

"Watch out! It looks now as if someone might be coming from the west," he warned his NASA teammates.

A female form darted through the picture. He couldn't tell who it was. Sarah and Sharon had probably separated, and one of them was going to tend to the vehicle from the west. The enemy knew that they had the NASA group outnumbered. It was a smart move to split up their limited force. If the enemy noticed that there were only three defenders out on the surface, the *Spaceliner* assault force would win.

Lance searched for a drone that had a view of the eastern area. He was right. The tracked vehicle and the rover had parted ways over there. The rover was now driving around the base to the south.

"People, I have bad news. They're also coming at us from the south," Lance said over the helmet radio.

"We'll handle it," Mike replied.

But how would that work? Lance considered simply leave Michael behind, crying. If he jumped into his spacesuit, he could be outside in five minutes. He gazed at his son, who stared back at him. They communicated without saying a word. *No, Michael, I won't leave you alone down here.*

"Watch out! Something's going on at the northern edge!" he called over the radio.

The drone's camera image showed three men on top of their rover's roof. They were climbing up on each other's shoulders. Suddenly, a man appeared above them. That had to be Mike. He shoved the person at the top of the tower, and the formation tumbled down.

"Sarah, Sharon, they're climbing up the wall where you are, too," Lance warned.

"I'm on it," Sarah replied.

Lance called up the feed from the drone to the east, and a woman with a long pole came into view. She looked like a modern knight, and she was in the process of knocking down another human tower.

"Bullseye," Lance said.

One of the attackers fell to the ground, about three meters straight down. However, this was less dangerous than it looked, thanks to Mars's low gravitational pull. The man stood up and dusted off his spacesuit, then climbed back up onto the roof of the tracked vehicle to join his colleagues. He took his time doing this. The attackers didn't seem to be in any great hurry. They probably knew that over the long run, they would have the upper hand. Or they knew that they were only facing three defenders. But that would mean that someone from the MfE had given them this information. Lance couldn't imagine that being true.

"Sharon, how are things where you are?" he asked.

"I just had a little altercation with someone," she replied, breathing heavily. "But the guy is now where he belongs."

"How are they equipped?"

"They seem to be unarmed," Sharon said. "Summers must really want us alive."

"That's comforting," Lance said.

"Most of them are wearing normal spacesuits, not the special models that Ewa brought us," Sharon said.

"Good," Lance said, "then this will level the playing field somewhat for you." Nonetheless, he had a nagging bad feeling. *The rover that headed to the south!* Unfortunately, they only had three drones.

A muffled pounding resonated through the base. Someone was banging forcefully against the outer door of the airlock. Michael woke up and wailed. Now they had roused his son! It was strange what got Lance the most riled up these days. It wasn't the fact that some strangers wanted to break into their base, but the fact that now they had disturbed Michael's sleep.

"This is the security team from Mars City," he heard announced. The attackers seemed to have some kind of megaphone. It had to be amazingly loud considering that he could hear it down here. "We have the right to access your base because you have harbored a criminal. Open your airlock immediately, or we will be forced to destroy it."

A shiver ran down Lance's spine. If they followed through on that threat and destroyed the airlock, the base's breathable air would be released. He could protect himself inside his spacesuit, but there would be no way to save Michael. The pigs were willing to kill his son! And the worst part was that the only way he could save Michael was by surrendering.

"Sarah, Sharon, Mike, can you hear me?" he spoke over the radio. "I have to open the airlock. They're threatening to cut off our air down here. I'm so sorry."

"Copy that," Mike replied. "It's clear you don't have a choice. We'll surrender up here as well."

Lance tightened his arm around his son, stood up, and walked over to the airlock. He opened the external hatch via the control panel. The enemy could now enter the base, though only one by one. He considered fleetingly if he shouldn't perhaps bash in the head of whoever opened the internal door. They deserved that. But they wouldn't be that stupid. If the first intruders stopped communicating, they would destroy the airlock anyway. Then Michael would suffocate in great pain. No, he couldn't do that.

He stepped back from the airlock and heard a rumbling in the lock chamber. Lance sat down at the table, his son still pressed against his chest. Michael was awake but silent. He must somehow sense how dangerous the situation was.

The light on the inside of the airlock door changed from red to green. The door opened with a hiss. A man in a special spacesuit stepped onto the bridge. He looked around, nodded, and removed his helmet.

"Hello, Mr. Leber. I'm Rick Summers, Administrator of Mars City. I'm glad you chose the sensible option and invited us in."

He should have bashed the man's head in. Lots of people would have been grateful to him if he had.

Michael started wailing again, as his father grimaced in despair.

EACH ARMED WITH A PISTOL, two intruders stood against the back wall of the bridge and observed the scene. Summers had asked—ordered, to be honest— the four NASA astronauts to take their seats around the table. Sarah was holding Michael. The administrator pulled a tablet out of his pocket.

"Just so you see that everything is in due order," he said, "I have here an arrest warrant for you. You are being charged with hindering the course of justice and with aiding and abetting several criminal acts." He swiped his finger through several documents. "Here is the search warrant. We don't want anyone to be in a position to accuse us of acting arbitrarily," Summers said, tapping his finger repeatedly on the screen.

"This matter seems to be quite important to you, if you came all the way out here yourself," Mike said.

"Indeed, it is. I think it is crucial for law and order to be upheld."

"I see," Sharon said.

"I also have the authority to rescind the arrest warrant, at least to a certain degree, if you support us in our search for the culprit."

"To a certain degree?"

"It's very simple," Summers declared. "Anyone who helps us will remain a free person. Just tell us what you know. My offer goes to the first person who comes clean."

"Divide and conquer," Lance quipped.

"I don't see it that way. It's an offer, a reward for cooperation. We will eventually find the culprit either way, but this would speed things along for us. We would save resources, and you would profit as a result."

"That is very generous, Ad-min-is-*tra-tor*." As he enunciated the title, he emphasized the last two syllables. Lance tried to pack into it every bit of disgust he felt at the sight of Summers. The man's face confirmed that he'd hit his mark.

"I advise you to not try our patience," Summers said bitingly.

"Ex-cuse me," Lance drawled.

"Mr. Summers, we would really like to help you," Mike interrupted sweetly, "but we have no idea where the person you're looking for is right now."

"We will turn over every stone here," Summers threatened.

"Do whatever you have to, Administrator," Mike replied. "But I need to be frank with you. You won't find Ms. Kowalska here. She up and vanished on us, just like that. She didn't say a word to any of us."

Summers didn't look convinced, but he also didn't send his two armed guards off to search the base. He seemed to be weighing his options, but then his face brightened. "Would you be so kind as to show me her quarters?" he asked amenably.

"Sure enough," Mike replied. "Lance, would you please accompany the administrator to Ewa's room. I'd hate for him to get lost."

He was now supposed to take this bastard on a tour of the base! What was Mike thinking? Or was this an order to break every last bone in the guy's body while they were in Ewa's room? Lance liked that idea even though he wasn't really a violent person. But how would the two guards react to that? He had to think about Michael.

Lance stood up. "Follow me."

There was no way he was going to be even a little friendly.

Rick Summers turned toward him and nodded with a smile. All that was lacking was him tucking his arm into Lance's! Before that idea might occur to Summers, Lance set off. Ewa's quarters were in the newest part of the base. It should still look just like it had when she left it.

Lance opened the door and led the way inside. It was slightly stuffy. It was evident that no air had moved inside here in the past two days. Ewa had made her bed neatly, and the room was orderly-looking.

Summers walked through the tight space. He pulled aside the curtain in front of the improvised closet. Several pieces of clothing were hanging along a bar. He went through each one of them. Was he hoping to find some of Ewa's underwear? The man probably had no idea how basic astronaut under-wear actually was.

Summers turned around and stepped toward Lance. Beside the bed, he knelt down suddenly and peered under the bed.

"Damn it, now you've found her," Lance said.

The administrator didn't react. He stood back up and dusted imaginary dirt from his knees. "Has she taken anything that didn't belong to her?" he asked.

Lance shook his head. Ewa's 'borrowing' of the enclosed rover was none of the other man's business.

"I'm simply asking because that would make you one of her victims. You could join the upcoming trial as a joint plaintiff."

"I thought she had already been sentenced."

"No, the trial is still in process."

"But you called her a culprit."

"Please excuse me, Mr. Leber. That wasn't correct. Of course, Ewa Kowalska is only an *alleged* culprit until the trial has been concluded. Everything proceeds by the books where we are concerned. We honor the state of law, and the judge is impartial and independent."

"Naturally," Lance said.

"Yes. That's why I can't simply rescind the arrest warrants, and leave you here in peace."

"Of course you couldn't do that."

"Unless you tell me more about Ewa. It's just the two of us here. Do you really want to stand by your claim that she simply marched off into the sunset with only her spacesuit?"

The man was trying to bribe him. Him, Lance Leber! "Yes, that seems to be her MO. I'm sure you've seen the logs from the *Spaceliner* from when she broke in there. She showed up in just a spacesuit there, too."

"That's... true," Summers agreed.

"See!"

"Mr. Leber, you have a young son. Do you want him to grow up without his father? Even if we wanted to, we couldn't take him along, or do you have a spacesuit for a baby? And I have to carry out the arrest warrants. I'm really sorry about that."

Lance stuck his hands inside his pockets to keep them from pounding the other man. Was the man actually threatening to leave Michael here all alone? That would be a death sentence.

"You're staring at me as if you think I would simply abandon your son here in this station. That isn't my intention. For humanitarian reasons, I've rescinded the arrest warrant for his mother. He will be cared for. What's his name?"

"Michael."

"Good. Michael will grow up here. At some point, he will be big enough to wear a spacesuit so he can visit you in the Mars City prison."

"You..." Lance bit his tongue.

"Unless you have something to tell me about Ewa that I don't already know."

Lance shook his head. He refused to be a traitor.

"Understood," Summers said. "You want it this way. I've tried my best."

Lance didn't reply.

THIRTY MINUTES LATER, they were saying goodbye. Summers was obviously in a great hurry to return to his settlement. *Maybe he's afraid there's been an uprising during his absence*, Lance thought. He still couldn't believe what was happening now. This administrator was making him leave his son whom he had only known for three days! He knew that Sarah would take good care of Michael, but now she and Sharon would be the only ones at the base, which would be several days away from all possible help. If anything happened, the two women would be on their own. And he probably wouldn't hear anything about it since he would be limited to whatever communication channels Summers made available to him.

"I'll be in touch as soon as possible," he said, wrapping his arms around Sarah who was carrying Michael.

"Have a safe trip, and don't do anything stupid," she urged.

They kissed.

Lance turned away so that nobody could see the tears in his eyes.

"Take care of yourself," Sharon said, suddenly materializing in front of him. She held out her hand. "You'll be back soon," she declared.

"We'll be back soon," Mike repeated.

The young commander hugged Sarah and Sharon, sealed his spacesuit, and stepped toward the airlock. One of the armed guards followed Mike through it, and then it was Lance's turn. As soon as he fastened his helmet and could no longer see any of his surroundings, he let the tears flow. At the airlock door, he looked back and waved. Michael waved back, or at least he imagined he did. He entered the airlock and shut the door behind him.

Sol 320, Mars Surface

EWA FELT GUILTY. She kept sitting down at the radio and thinking about whether or not she should contact the NASA base. Didn't Mike and the others have a right to know what had motivated her to flee? Because that was what she had done—flee secretly, in the breaking dawn after spending days loading the rover with the resources that would be the most critical for surviving out here for as long as possible.

If she pushed the transmit button and explained everything, she might feel better. Or not? Friday had advised her against it. In his opinion, she would just be burdening the NASA crew. If they didn't know anything about her departure, they also wouldn't be susceptible to blackmail. Ewa wasn't sure. She had grown fond of the four of them, and now there was the baby, too, who needed special protection. She had persuaded herself that Michael was the actual reason she had set off into the unknown. The administrator had to be stopped. But he was sitting so solidly in the saddle that this would only be possible through extraordinary measures.

She hoped that she could find these measures out here, but she hadn't gotten very far in the past two Mars days. She had only reached the mountain that had unexpectedly grown out of the desert several months ago and then had threatened their very existence. Her crazy plan was to somehow reactivate the mountain and to bring it under her control. *What could go wrong with that?* she asked herself. On her last visit, she had presumably destroyed the navigational computer, but there might be a backup system. Or perhaps Friday, the AI that someone had installed inside her brain without her permission, could find a way to command the giant machine.

Friday had tried to convince her otherwise. Unfortunately, he had handled his arguments clumsily and basically ended up confirming every one of her assumptions. Yes, in theory, the monster should be able to be steered externally. And no, something that had endured millions of years under ice and stone surely couldn't be entirely destroyed by an electrical short. His only real counterargument had been, 'We can't access it.'

The inside of the mountain, where the control system was located, had been buried under meters of rock ever since they had deactivated the machine. The mountain would have to re-emerge through the surface to let them inside, but that wouldn't happen until they restarted it. And, to do that, they needed access to the inside.

"Time will tell," Ewa had declared, pointing to the explosives that she had stolen from the storeroom at the NASA base.

For some reason, destruction seemed to be in her blood. She didn't really understand that herself. Was it some kind of Mephistophelian tendency? Was she driven to destroy things in order to create something new? Maybe this was just an excuse for her actual problem—her stupidity. If she were smarter, she probably wouldn't have to solve every problem with explosions and destruction.

Unfortunately, the clarity time had promised was taking its own sweet time. They had circled the perimeter of the mountain multiple times yesterday, a distance of about ten kilometers. They had initially driven the stretch with the rover, then Ewa had climbed out and gone on foot. It had been a nice hike, but except for awaking memories, the exercise was fruitless.

The recent past was brought back to life when she came across the remnants of the drill. They had needed most of the material for the reconstruction of the drill, but some pieces were simply lying around, like the hacksaw she had used to cut through the chain on which the drill head had been fastened. She'd briefly considered taking the saw with her, but then she had examined the blade more closely. It was utterly worn out. The saw was trash.

Now what? She repeated the question out loud in the hope that Friday would speak up. "Now what?"

He obliged. 'We're screwed,' he said through her mouth.

Ewa had to admit that she had missed these conversations. She had avoided them at the NASA base. It would've looked too odd if she had walked around talking to herself.

"You'd have to be a mole," she countered.

'What's a mole?'

"You don't know what a mole is?"

'The way you're using it I'd classify it as a member of the human race.'

"No, it's actually an animal that digs long tunnels. Its tunnel systems can stretch as far as three to five hundred meters long."

'That would be long enough,' Friday said with her voice. "We'd only need fifty meters to get inside.'

"The entry point we crawled through seemed longer."

'Yes, but that couldn't have been the only entrance.'

"Doesn't matter. We can't dig a fifty-meter long passage either way," Ewa said with a shrug.

'At the same time, the shell is made of nothing.'

"What are you talking about?" she asked.

'The distance between atoms is huge. Or at least between an atom's nucleus and its so-called shell. If you could increase a hydrogen atom's nucleus to the size of a pinhead, a ten-thousandth of a millimeter-sized electron could move up to a distance of fifty meters from your pinhead through empty space.'

"That's insane. The whole universe is made up of empty space."

Ewa felt like she had come across this comparison somewhere else. Unfortunately, the mountain's shell didn't feel as if it were composed of empty nothingness. Quite the contrary.

"This concept isn't helping any," she said. "In our world, what we have is a fairly solid obstacle."

'Maybe we could change our world,' Friday suggested.

"By losing weight, or how else am I supposed to fit through there?"

'No. Maybe we don't personally have to get inside the machine.'

"But rather?"

'I could communicate with the mountain's computer.'

"How would you do that?"

'We need to insert a very, very thin wire into the interior, into the spot where all the machine's computer systems are located.'

"You do remember how far we had to go to reach that spot, right?"

'Yes, Ewa. I even guided your body on our way back out, but that doesn't matter.'

"Doesn't matter?"

'Do you remember the chamber in which we found that strange computer?'

"Absolutely."

'What did we see up on the ceiling?'

"The outer world." Ewa now realized what Friday was getting at. "You think that, at that spot, we were quite close to the surface."

'I'm quite sure of that. The machine could make its external skin transparent to electromagnetic radiation. We were able to make radio contact with the NASA people. There are a lot of things I think the machine's creators were capable of, but there's no way they could have managed that through fifty meters of dirt and sand.'

"And if they did?" she asked. Ewa's mouth was dry. It had

been ages since she had talked so much without a break. She took a drink of water from her bottle.

'Then I'm quite mistaken, and we're back to square one,' Friday replied.

"In other words, we need to search for the spot underneath which the chamber is concealed."

'Exactly.'

"And how do you want to proceed, Friday?"

'I don't know yet. I am thinking we should use a very, very thin wire.'

"How could we produce that?"

'I suggest we solve one problem at a time. Let's first look for the entrance to the chamber.'

"Agreed," Ewa said. "If worse comes to worst, we can always blast a hole in the chamber." She laughed. No, it was Friday who was laughing. That was something new. The AI had never laughed through her before. It felt odd. Whenever Friday used her voice to speak, what she heard sounded like the words of a stranger. But when he laughed with her laugh, his emotion was... infectious. She had to be careful.

'A hole in the roof,' Friday said. 'You would like that.'

Ewa considered this. Yes, she would like that. It would be fun for her. She was probably not entirely mentally stable. Or was it normal to enjoy blowing things up?

"And when should we start hunting?" Ewa asked.

'The chamber should be situated close to the summit. We won't be able to reach it with the rover.'

"If I recall rightly, that's a pretty good climb," she said.

'We should plan everything out so we won't be returning in the dark. It would be unfortunate for me if you fell,' Friday said.

"For me, too."

'Which is why it would be better for us to set off early tomorrow morning. Then we'll have the whole day in front of us.'

"Sure. And now let me have a little time alone with my thoughts," Ewa said.

'Of course.'

Her mouth belonged to her once more. Ewa took another sip of water before standing up and starting to pace the cab. She really wanted to know how things were going for her friends at the NASA base. Should she risk calling them? But if the wrong people were listening in on the radio channel, she might give away her location. However, the radio range was limited. She now needed a little peace and quiet to figure out how to make the ancient device inside the mountain work.

Something banged against the cab window. Ewa glanced up and recognized a drone. It must have come from the NASA base. Maybe it had brought her a message. She pulled on her spacesuit. The rover didn't have an airlock, so Ewa released the breathable air and climbed outside through the hatch.

The drone was sitting beside one of the tires. It looked sad, like a bird that had broken one of its wings. She picked it up and carried it inside.

Sol 321, MfE Base

THE BASE HAD GROWN QUIET. Before the attack, life within the Mars for Everyone spaces had often seemed demanding to Rebecca. Six men and eight women sandwiched into about 120 square meters of living space, not including the storerooms and offices. Conflict had often been on the menu.

Now she missed that turmoil, because of how much she missed Theo. She had convinced herself that such daily altercations would have helped to keep her thoughts from constantly turning to him.

There were still nine of them here, eight women and one man.

The man, Walter Richardson, had been left behind at the last second by the administrator's henchmen. They had probably learned from his personnel files—they had seized everyone's—that Walter was suffering from a very slowly advancing form of cancer—and they didn't want to have sick people in Mars City. The 53-year-old American was a quiet man. He had previously worked in the oil industry and seemed to enjoy doing odd jobs. Rebecca couldn't recall exchanging a single personal word with him. Walter was just there when you needed him. She figured he had bought his passage on board *Spaceliner* with his considerable savings.

The new situation came with one advantage. Each of the

remaining crew members had more work to do, a reality that helped to distract Rebecca from her worries about Theo. She knew that he was strong, but that didn't help her. Instead, she was afraid that he would undertake something against the administrator and end up in trouble. Summers seemed to have no scruples whatsoever when it came to taking out his enemies. Theo, on the other hand... No, it was better if she focused on her work. Rebecca set aside the pickax before picking up the electric hammer drill again. She stepped across the thick power-supply line and pushed the point of the drill into the hard Mars surface. Then she flipped the start switch with her right thumb while keeping a firm grip on the handle, and the drill rattled alive.

The sound carried minimally, thanks to the thin atmosphere, but the vibrations grew unpleasant over time. Eventually she was unable to keep her teeth from chattering. That was her signal to set the drill aside and use the shovel and pickaxe to clear away the debris she'd created. She was digging a garden bed. Rebecca looked up. About 50 meters away, Marilou was standing over another drill. The new field would be about 100 meters long, 20 meters wide, and 1 meter deep. Once they had dug the beds, a transparent roof would be constructed over them, and ventilation and irrigation systems would be installed after that.

A different group was currently preparing the necessary topsoil. The administrator had ordered them to double their agricultural productivity within the next four weeks. If they hit that quota, they would be allowed to keep one-quarter of their production. *What a swell deal!* she thought with disgust. But they would hardly be in a position to fend off the harvest collectors when they drove up in their rover.

"Rebecca?"

"Yes, Marilou?" she asked over her helmet radio.

"I think it's time for lunch."

Rebecca glanced at the universal device on her left arm. It had just reached 11:30. She looked around. She had already done five meters, which meant she was making excellent progress. The ditch stretching behind her seemed unremarkable. On Earth, it would have only taken an hour of work with an ordinary shovel to get this far. However, the Mars surface was composed of compacted permafrost underneath a thin layer of dust. The hammer drill was the only way for them to make progress.

"Good idea," Rebecca said. "Let's take a break." She lowered the pickaxe and ambled over to the airlock.

Marilou caught up with her and placed a hand on her shoulder. They were passing a large, black spot that measured at least twenty meters in diameter. This was where the *Endeavour* had stood, the NASA ship that Ewa had stolen. Why hadn't they put a stop to her actions earlier? They should have collaborated with the NASA people from the very beginning. At least that would have made things more difficult for Summers.

Marilou held the heavy exterior airlock hatch open. Rebecca climbed in first. They filled the airlock with air, and Rebecca removed her helmet as soon as it was breathable. After the light switched to green, they opened the interior door and entered the base.

"Have you heard anything from the men?" Rebecca asked at lunch.

They were having cooked rice with beans from a can. Nancy had fixed the meal, which was heavily seasoned and tasted pretty good. Nonetheless, Rebecca wasn't hungry. They'd had rice and beans way too often. Hopefully, their field would soon deliver fresh food for them.

"Officially, there's been no contact," Ellen said.

"And unofficially?" Nancy asked. She was probably missing Guillermo with whom she had recently started spending more time.

"I'm sorry," Ellen replied, "I shouldn't have said, 'officially.' There haven't been any messages. They aren't responding to our requests. I suspect they haven't reached Mars City yet."

"If we aren't receiving any official information, then we have to find another way to communicate," Rebecca said, around her mouthful of food.

"I agree," Ellen said. "Any suggestions?"

Rebecca shook her head.

"Then come up with one!" Ellen urged.

"I studied telecommunications in college," Germaine interjected.

"And I spent time soldering together electrical systems in a factory," Marilou added.

"That's good," Rebecca said, "but I don't see how that can help us. Our men don't have anything that we could radio to from here. They even took away their spacesuits."

"We need some kind of messenger," Walter said. "Something that we can send into Mars City. I have an idea. Want to discuss this some more this evening in the commons?"

"I'll be there," Rebecca said.

'THE COMMONS' was what they'd named the large room that served as their lounge. However, it looked more like a storeroom than a lounge. It didn't have any real furniture, just heavy, brown cubes that were scattered all around. These served as supports for cushions they'd made and stuffed with straw. They had created the cubes by compressing and baking Mars dirt. On both the right and the left sides of the space, they had used two flat blocks of compacted dirt to build sofa-like seats, and at the center of the room, there was a seating area made up of chairs arranged in a circle. The seatbacks were made from perpendicular stone walls. Rebecca had made a few of these herself. She had no idea who had come up with the suggestion to use homemade adhesive instead of mortar. Regrettably, the sticky substance had stuck better to fingers and clothes than to the rocks. If you sat down in one of the seats, it was best if you didn't lean back too hard.

Walter and the others were already in the seating area, talking quietly. Gabriella, the doctor, was also there. As the last one to arrive, Rebecca was surprised that Gabriella was there, since she rarely had time when someone had a concern or request. Rebecca was suspicious that Gabriella had her sights set on Ellen's position as the unofficial leader of the Mars for Everyone project. In reality, there really wasn't any cause for envy. Ellen hadn't been elected to this post, but had simply been accepted as the one who got the final say on the basis of her competence. She received no advantages as a result.

Rebecca sat down in a free chair. Despite the cushions, the seats were somewhat hard.

"It's nice you could come," Walter said.

"Oh, thanks!" she said.

"It's nice that you could all be here, Germaine, Marilou, Gabriella."

The American suddenly seems quite chatty, Rebecca thought. "Your insinuations made me very curious," she said.

Walter blushed. He didn't seem accustomed to personal praise. "One of my hobbies is space history," he began. "Before we set off, I could've told you the biographies of any astronaut of your choosing."

"Not anymore?" Germaine asked.

"I think the radiation has softened my brain a little, but one important mission came to my mind yesterday." Walter hesitated, glancing around the group.

"We're all ears," Germaine said.

"Eleven years ago, the Japanese successfully landed their first mission to Mars—JAXA. Or was that twelve years ago already? I still don't really get the conversion between sols and Earth days. It was in late 2031, according to good old Earth chronology. This was an unmanned mission, and they chose not to deploy a rover. Instead, they had four robots on board that had each been equipped with enough AI capacity to independently explore Mars's surface. I can still remember that they all had common Japanese names, like Gray Rabbit and Nimble Mouse, but I can't recall the specifics anymore."

Rebecca smiled. Yes, the robots had been assigned amusing names. She'd been 14 or 15 at the time, and had even rechristened her stuffed bunnies after them, but she could no longer recall the details either.

"The robots had really caused a stir, because they made much faster progress than all the NASA rovers before them. They had simply rolled across the surface. One of them even managed to circumnavigate Mars."

"Way up at the North Pole," Gabriella said.

"Yes, it had searched out the shortest route, something that was later criticized," Walter continued. "And then there were the questions about what the four robots were actually capable of accomplishing. One of the Mars scientists even suggested that they were nothing more than mere toys that served no real purpose."

Models based on the robots had been sold in toy stores, and Rebecca's father had given her one in hopes of getting her interested in technology.

"But, of course, that wasn't true," Walter forged on. "The robots were equipped with all sorts of sensors, and they contributed significantly to our knowledge about the surface conditions on Mars, along with its water resources."

"Good old times," Gabriella cut in. "But could you please get to the point? I really have to..."

Rebecca sent her a blistering look. Walter looked unsettled, his eyes traveling from one to the other in the group. Rebecca nodded at him encouragingly.

"The main point," Walter resumed, "is that not all four robots set off. Only three did. One after the other, the three eventually stopped functioning. The fourth got snagged on the landing module after being unloaded."

"It was probably scared," Germaine declared.

"Whatever happened, it has to still be there. Its energy supply is presumably low, but I know that it was powered by solar cells and an isotope battery, which means it might still be functional even today."

"Despite the fact it wasn't operational back then?" Gabriella inquired.

"You would just need to disconnect it from the landing module. At the time, nobody was here to take care of that, but we could drive out there."

"Then what?" the doctor asked.

"Then we take it and program it to be a messenger that could take our messages to Mars City. The administrator doesn't know anything about the robot," Walter replied.

"Our men don't either," Gabriella said.

"The robot should be intelligent enough to only approach our people. It possesses a good optical system, and we could program it to recognize the faces of Theo, Ketut, and the others. As soon as it sees a stranger, it could hide."

"That sounds doable," Rebecca said.

"But we don't have the Japanese source codes. Andy could possibly locate them, but can we?"

Why is Gabriella being so negative today? Rebecca thought. "Nancy used to work as programmer," she said.

"I know my way around that world, too," Walter said.

"Well, that gives us a chance," Gabriella replied, though she didn't sound all that convinced.

"I'm all for us trying to retrieve that robot," Germaine chimed in. "Do you know where the module landed back then, Walter?"

"Fairly close to the middle of Syrtis Major."

"Isn't that a gulf in the Mediterranean?" Germaine asked.

"I don't know," Walter said. "I was never in Europe."

"I did a Mediterranean cruise once," Germaine explained.

"That means you know more than I do. The Japanese picked Syrtis Major on Mars because you can see it from Earth, even if all you have is a small telescope. It looks darker than its surroundings. Just like you've pointed out, someone could think it was a gulf and assume that there are seas on Mars. However, in reality, the feature is actually a volcanic plateau."

"Thanks, Walter," Rebecca said. "How far away is the site?"

"The landing area is somewhere in the northern zone of Syrtis Major. I would guess that it would take us two weeks to reach it in the rover."

Rebecca sighed. Since the visit from Summers' people, all they now had was the open rover. She remembered her last trip on it. She and Theo had gone out to search for water. It had been real torture. "Two weeks on the rover will be hard," she said.

"If you drive more than ten hours a day, it could be done in ten days," Walter declared.

"And if we drove straight through?" Rebecca asked.

"Then we'd need less than a week each way," Walter said. "But how do you think that would work? Wouldn't you need to sleep?"

"One person could drive while the other one sleeps," Rebecca explained.

"But it would be impossible to sleep while riding."

"No, it wouldn't. After a while, you can sleep anywhere, Walter. I know what I'm talking about. The passenger just has to strap in tightly, then it works."

"I still think it sounds crazy."

"All of us here are famous for being crazy. Would we have boarded the *Santa Maria* otherwise?" Germaine asked.

"That's true," Walter agreed.

"But there is one other problem we haven't thought about," Rebecca said. "Summers and his people will notice if our rover and two of us are gone for a long time. Our productivity would inevitably decline."

"Then the others would have to cover for the two who were gone," Marilou said.

"Hopefully, that would do the trick," Rebecca declared.

"One other detail," Walter interjected. "When would this happen and who would take the trip?"

"Tomorrow," Rebecca said, and everyone nodded. "I'll drive," she added, and everyone shook their heads.

"I'll go," Germaine volunteered.

"People would miss me the least," Marilou said.

"What makes you think that?" Rebecca asked.

"I... it's a good argument, isn't it?"

"But it won't be accepted," Rebecca said.

"Good, then we'll draw names," Germaine suggested. "Gabriella and Walter, do you want to be included, too?"

The two of them nodded.

"I'll write our five names on each of my fingers, and then Rebecca can select two fingers. Okay?"

"Good idea, Germaine," Rebecca answered.

The young woman turned around and extracted a pen from her pants pocket. She then wrote something down on her left hand before curling it into a fist. "Your turn, Rebecca."

Rebecca studied Germaine's fist. She had very slender, long fingers. Where might her own name be sitting? Of course, she didn't really want to go on this trip, but she had experience already. If she could choose, she would bring Germaine along. Hopefully, she wouldn't have to do the drive with Gabriella!

Rebecca tapped the pointer finger. Germaine extended it out from her fist. 'Marilou' was printed on it.

"Cool," Marilou said. "A trip!"

She won't stay excited for long, Rebecca thought. She then tapped Germaine's middle finger. The pointer and middle fingers created the victory sign. That worked. Germaine opened her fist. Her own name was written on her middle finger. She raised it triumphantly.

"It will be a marvelous adventure," she cried, hugging Marilou.

Rebecca had a bad feeling about this. Neither of them had

experience tackling this kind of trip. Did they really know how treacherous the Mars surface was? On the other hand, they had been trained just as rigorously for this mission as she had been. She shouldn't make any assumptions about Marilou and Germaine just because they were still so young. And how did one define *young* anyway? Germaine was only three years younger than herself, while Marilou was five. No, everything would work out. They just had to make sure that nobody missed them.

Sol 321, Mars Machine

'Could you please yank the external microphone out of your suit?' Friday asked.

"What?" Ewa's breathing was labored. The climb was strenuous. She was now paying for the fact that she hadn't been working out every day.

'We want to find the large window.'

"And you need the external mike for that?" The microphone was integrated into her suit's collar, which covered the helmet around her neck.

'Exactly,' Friday said. 'It will help me to locate the window. Just be sure not to cut off the electrical connection.'

"You need to explain that to me more specifically."

'You will hold the mike over the ground, and I will send sonic waves through the mike and measure the echo. The echo will change whenever the surface's composition changes.'

"I could just lie down on the ground. That way I wouldn't have to tear out the microphone," Ewa suggested.

'If you can lie down so that the mike is pressed against the surface, that would be alright.'

"I'll give it a try," she said. "Then we'll know if that approach might work."

She hoped that this method would work for Friday's idea.

She was very reluctant to deliberately damage the high-tech suit she had stolen from the *Spaceliner* ship. And so, she knelt down and searched for a position that would allow the mike to be pressed against the surface without having to forcibly jerk it out of her collar. She lowered her head close to the ground and turned her torso to the side. Her stance made her look like she was venerating some archaic god. Fortunately, nobody could see her, as this was the only way to make this work.

'Stay right there,' Friday said. 'Great position. Is that a yoga move?'

"Stop chatting and get on with it," Ewa said. "This isn't exactly comfortable."

'It wasn't my idea for you to get down on the ground,' Friday replied.

"Are you done yet?"

'Just about. I have to speak at a limited volume level, but things look good.'

"Have you found the window?"

'No, but you can get up again. I now have the first reference baseline. The window can't be anywhere around here.'

"Then why did I have to get down on the ground?"

'It was your idea, Ewa. But in this case, I need some comparative values in order to know how the echo from the substrate normally sounds.'

"Got it. Don't you have to keep saying the same thing, though?"

'No, this has to do with the volume level.'

"That makes me feel better then. I was worried that we'd have to repeat this pointless conversation a thousand times."

'No worries,' Friday said. 'After this, you may have other pointless conversations with me.'

"I'm relieved to hear that."

'I know. I'm stuck here inside you.'

"You know how I'm feeling, Friday?"

'Don't worry. I still can't read your thoughts, but I can tell from your movements if you're feeling panicky or calm.'

"Then you know more than I do."

'That's my firm assumption, Ewa. And now let's keep going up.'

EWA'S RIGHT KNEE HURT. That had to be a sign she was getting old. Who would have thought that? It hadn't been all that long ago she had stopped assuming she would grow old on this planet.

"How much longer?" she asked.

'I'm slowly zeroing in on it,' Friday replied.

They had already reached the mountain's summit and climbed back down the other side. Friday had supplied her with the approximate direction, which he had calculated from their recollection of the sun's position. In these mental images, the hall and its transparent roof seemed huge. But shouldn't they have come across it long before now? According to Friday, they hadn't had a point of comparison for the gigantic dimensions of the machine. Compared to the entire mountain, the window would be relatively small.

'Now, please,' he said.

Ewa carefully sat down on the ground to spare her knee joint the exertion. But she had to get her head all the way down to the ground. The collar with the microphone needed to rest directly on the surface. A small rock pressed itself into her forehead. Her breath blew away some of the dust that had worked its way into her nose.

"Achoo!"

'Crap! That was too short,' Friday said. 'You'll have to lean back down.'

Ewa sighed and followed his instructions.

'I'm going to tell you something now,' Friday said.

"What is that?"

'I'm still thinking. Maybe the story about the princess and...'

"And?"

'That's enough. You can stand up again.'

"But I want to hear the story."

'Are you a little girl or something?'

"Yes," Ewa said, laughing.

'You really need to check the nitrogen content in your bloodstream,' Friday said.

"Let me keep a little joy."

'But of course. I'll bring you an even greater joy.'

"You've found it?"

'Yes, I have.'

"That's fantastic!"

'But...'

Her joy slipped away. "Why the *but?*"

'I still don't know how we can reach the computers down there.'

"You'll think of something, Friday."

'That's true. Let's first check out the area.'

Ewa slowly stood up and turned around. The slope seemed to be composed of dark granite. The material was so dark that you would almost guess it was basalt. On Earth, in a highland area of volcanic origin, a hillside like this would hardly stand out. And yet, it had to be extraterrestrial in origin, just like the machine that was concealed within the mountain.

"Looks like stone," she said.

'Looks chemically produced,' Friday confirmed.

"And what's going on with the echo?"

'It indicates that the material is predominantly homogenous—up to the point that the sound meets a boundary layer.'

"How homogenous?"

'The large stone underneath you is a giant monocrystal. At least, that's how I'm interpreting the measurement results. The specific spatial directions in space within the stone are unusually asymmetrical.'

"Couldn't that be a coincidence?" As a teenager, Ewa had owned a chemistry set and had grown crystals with it. None had ever grown larger than a fingertip, at which point she'd lost her interest in them.

'With our technology, it would be impossible to grow such a crystal,' Friday said.

"How thick is it?"

'I would have to have more precise details about its characteristics in order to know that. You don't happen to have something with you that could measure its conductivity, do you?'

"Unfortunately, I don't."

'Then all I can do is guess. Four meters. It might be ten centimeters or twenty meters though, too.'

"You think that the hall, with the computers that could start this machine back up again, is sitting four meters below me?"

'Yes. We're tramping all over its roof as we speak.'

"So we could see ourselves if we were down there right now?"

'No. Or probably not. We saw the roof —at different times —as completely transparent or totally opaque. If we can't see down there right now, then nobody down there could see us either.'

"True. Now what?"

'Let's memorize the spot and come back tomorrow.'

"Too bad," Ewa said.

'Yes. But we need to give this some thought.'

"Well, I forgot to bring my explosives along anyway."

'Sorry about that!' Friday said.

THE AIR in the cab was frigid, but it was also gloriously refreshing. Ewa had spent the entire day in her suit and enjoyed relaxing in her underwear all the more because of it. She had the drone on her lap. A German lullaby was playing through her head. She had spent six months working as an au pair for a German family.

The song started with 'Kommt ein Vogel geflogen, setzt sich nieder auf mein' Fuss, hat ein Zettel im Schnabel...' Whoever had sent the drone might have had the same lullaby in mind, since she found a note had been inserted in one of its landing legs.

DEAR EWA,

As we feared, the base has been taken by Summers. We heard that the same thing has happened to your MfE crew. All the men have been taken to Mars City. Our communication is being watched. You should not contact us under any circumstances. Summers is searching for you. He wants to put you through a show trial, so stay away.

We have programmed this drone to search for the rover in ever-widening circles. Once you recharge it and push the yellow button, it will find its way back to us. Please write to let us know how you are doing. Summers has no idea where you are, and he won't learn anything from us. We hope that the situation will eventually change so that you can safely return.

Sarah and Sharon

EWA LEANED BACK. The situation wouldn't change, not on its own. She was probably the only person on the entire planet who could still oppose the administrator. But—a highly significant *but*—she couldn't take him on with empty hands. She needed something that would strike fear in Summers. A giant mountain that she could move at her command would be just the thing. Ewa imagined herself astride a saddle on top of the mountain, and jabbing her spurs against the extraterrestrial machine. *I must indeed be a little crazy*, she thought.

Sol 322, MfE Base

"Everyone, please come to the bridge." The order echoed through the base.

The command was repeated. Rebecca climbed down from the bike. She was sweating and really wanted to take a quick shower, but she hesitated, feeling uncertain. The order came over the speakers again. It wasn't an alarm-level signal, having been phrased as a request, but it wasn't a run-of-the-mill order either. Otherwise the computer wouldn't keep broadcasting it. She donned the jacket of her exercise suit over her sweaty t-shirt and left the workout room. She would obey Ellen's request.

Even so, she was the last one to arrive on the bridge. Again. The others had already gathered around the small screen. A man's voice now emerged from the loudspeaker. *Summers, the administrator,* she realized. Her stomach lurched. *What does he want now?*

"... back in Mars City," she heard. "I'm in the amiable company of Mike Benedetti and Lance Leber. The two former NASA astronauts have already declared themselves willing and able to support us in the creation of a new society here in Mars City. Please greet them warmly."

She could hear spotty applause. Apparently, Summers was speaking to a small number of people at his base. And this was what they absolutely had to be in attendance for? Rebecca walked over to Ellen and tapped her arm. Ellen glanced back at her.

"What's going on?" Rebecca whispered.

"Wait a moment," Ellen replied, holding a finger up to her lips.

All this secrecy! Rebecca inflated her cheeks and exhaled noisily. Summers kept going on and on about his heroic acts. Nobody cared about those!

Then, Ellen tapped her. "Now!"

Did Ellen already know what he was going to say? How?

"In addition, I am announcing, effective today, a new accountability regulation," the administrator declared. "All members of our satellite bases are henceforth required to personally check in with the on-duty security chief once a day. The only exceptions made will be for those whom a doctor or other medical personnel confirm as being sick."

Rebecca covered her mouth. *Damn it!* Departing secretly with the rover was now out of the question. Was it a coincidence that Summers was introducing this new policy now, of all times, or had someone informed him about their plans? Rebecca glanced at Ellen. How had she known about the administrator's announcement? She knew their plans! Then again, they all knew what Germaine and Marilou were going to undertake today.

Ellen tapped her once more.

"Furthermore, the use of the vehicles that remain at the satellite bases will be strictly supervised, effective immediately. The key is to be locked up in a room that will be under centralized video surveillance. We are all responsible for acting conservatively with our resources. Of course, this obligation rests especially heavily on those who sit in authority. I do not exclude myself from this purview, and vow to dedicate myself passionately to this task. At the satellite bases, the supervisors will be personally accountable to me. Thank you very much for your attention to this matter."

More scattered applause. The screen went dark.

"You have all heard what Summers had to say," Ellen said.

"Loud and clear," Rebecca replied. "But how did you know about it before us?"

Ellen stared angrily at her. "What are you trying to say?"

"You told me to pay attention just one second before Summers—"

"All he told me beforehand was that we should all listen closely to the conclusion of his speech. That's all I knew."

Rebecca massaged her hands. She was unconvinced. They had been lied to and betrayed before by someone they had all trusted. *Is Ellen now following in Ewa's footsteps? Or is all of this making me overly suspicious? Maybe. Innocent until proven guilty, right?*

"I see," Rebecca said in a conciliatory tone. "I didn't know that. I didn't mean to accuse you of anything."

"Good," Ellen said. "I understand. After what the five of you discussed yesterday, this reaction by the administrator seems very... timely."

"I don't mean to come to his defense, but perhaps this simply has to do with the fact that he has gotten back to his home base," Gabriella speculated.

"Yes, that could be. He has to show that he has everything under control," Ellen said.

"But what about our trip?" Germaine asked.

"I'm afraid that's now out of the question," Ellen replied. "No one can leave here without Summers knowing about it. And the rover has now been quasi confiscated. Marilou, could you please get the key? We have to hang it up somewhere where it can be filmed by a camera."

"Alright. Does anyone know where it is?"

Nobody spoke up.

"Then I'll look around in the workshop," Marilou said.

Rebecca glanced around. A depressed mood had settled over the bridge. Before the announcement, everyone had been chatting with one another, but now silence reigned. *The administrator's spirit is here*, she thought.

Wait—where is Walter? She hadn't seen the American today. She walked across the bridge. Maybe he was sitting somewhere that was hidden from her line of sight. But she couldn't find him anywhere.

"Did you notify Walter about our meeting?" Rebecca asked.

"The announcement went ship wide. You heard it," Ellen said.

"But Walter isn't here."

"What? Why?"

Ellen walked around the room as well, but she couldn't find Walter either. "Has anyone seen Walter?" she asked loudly.

No one spoke up. A chill ran through Rebecca. Walter was sick. Everyone knew that. But he should still have two or three years ahead of him.

"He must be in his room," Marilou said.

Ellen stopped dead in her tracks. "You think he's...," Ellen began, before realizing what she had to do. "Gabriella, quick. To Walter's room! He must need help."

Gabriella dashed off the bridge with Ellen at her heels.

Rebecca stopped the other women from following. "It won't help him if we're all underfoot," she said. She sat down but stood right back up. She couldn't sit right now. Hopefully, Walter was alright! Maybe he had just dozed off. She knew how naive that theory was, but at the moment, it made her feel better. She wished she could hold Theo's hand now, but he was far away.

Gabriella and Ellen reappeared. That had been fast! Their faces didn't look sad, they appeared to be bewildered.

"How's he doing?" Germaine asked.

"We don't know," Ellen replied.

"You don't know? Weren't you just with him?"

"Walter isn't in his room," Gabriella explained.

In the left wall, the door to the workshop opened with a squeak. Marilou entered. She came to a stop as she caught sight of the others' puzzled faces. "What's going on? Has the administrator come up with more ways to make our lives more difficult?" she asked.

"Did you find the rover key?" Ellen asked.

"I'm sorry. I searched through every drawer and box in there, but the key isn't anywhere in the workshop," Marilou replied.

"And Walter has disappeared," Ellen said.

Sol 322, Mars Machine

RICE AND BEANS. There was nothing else in the kitchenette. It would have been too noticeable if she had taken other food-stuffs from the storeroom. The rover possessed a microwave with which she could heat her food. Friday had let her sleep in today, so she was having a brunch this morning.

The microwave made its typical ping. She removed the plate and sat down on the folding seat beside the microwave. She scooped some rice from the plate with her spoon and tested its temperature. It was barely warm, but better that than too hot. Ewa hated burning her tongue. She filled her spoon, transferred the food to her mouth, chewed, and swallowed.

When would Friday check in? Her cohabitant was obviously taking his time. He was apparently having trouble cracking the puzzle of the machine. Ewa cleaned her plate in silence and then placed it on top of the microwave. It wasn't necessary to wash the dishes every day. That would just unnecessarily consume valuable water.

She sat down at the control panel. The rover was sitting at the foot of the mountain, with a view of the hole she had smashed into the mountainside with the drill tower. It was tiny compared to the gigantic dimensions of the machine.

Had she really believed she could crack open the mountain with the tower? Ewa looked over her shoulder. The sticks of dynamite were lying in the back. Since last night, her desire to use them had faded. Today she felt strangely peaceable. She felt like all she needed to do was ask nicely, and the mountain would open its gates to her. All she was missing was the *Open, Sesame*. Hopefully, Friday was getting along better than she was.

'How are you doing?' her own voice asked.

Ewa laughed. That had come as a surprise. She didn't know how, but before now, she had always sensed when Friday wanted to say something. Maybe their ongoing conversations were blurring the boundaries between them.

"I feel very relaxed right now," she replied.

'Is that a good thing? If so, I'm happy for you.'

"Yes, it's a good thing. Not being around other people takes the pressure off of me."

'I understand. I have been searching very hard, almost constantly, for an idea.'

"*Almost* constantly?"

'When I'm too active, my processors overheat.'

"And that's bad for you?"

'No, for you, Ewa. I'm embedded inside your brain. Your nerve cells would be damaged if I grew too hot.'

"You could roast me from the inside out?"

'No, but I do have to be a little careful.'

"Thanks, Friday. And what have you discovered?"

'I don't have a solution yet, just ideas.'

"*And?*"

'I asked myself why a crystal was used for the roof. It had to be quite expensive to produce such a giant crystal.'

"Maybe they enjoyed challenges."

'That's possible, but they might have depended on the special physical characteristics of crystals. I'm thinking about the electro-optical effect, also known as the Pockels effect.'

"How do you know everything?"

'I have to know how the world functions if I want to influence it. At any rate, with the help of this effect, they could alter the optical characteristics of their roof.'

"Electro-optical. In other words, they applied a voltage to it?"

'Correct. The voltage would change the light permeability of the crystal.'

"And now you want to try to induce this effect yourself."

'Exactly,' Friday said. 'It would be better than simply blasting the roof away, wouldn't it?'

"Yes, okay, I agree with you. However, I wonder how that'll help us. We'll be able to see into the hall, but then what?"

'The roof changes its permeability depending on the range of electromagnetic waves. Remember how you had radio contact with Mike while the roof was transparent?'

"You want to radio the Martians?"

'Something like that,' Friday said. 'Although they are long gone, guaranteed. They died out billions of years ago, I'm sure of that. But perhaps we can contact the machine itself. Considering this is the product of very advanced technology, it must have access to a well-developed AI program.'

"How can you be sure about that?"

'Think about it. Every civilization eventually reaches the point of developing artificial intelligence programs, and as soon as these move out of their infancies, it is inevitable that they take control.'

"I hope that isn't true," Ewa said.

'You don't know what I know.'

"What do you know?"

'That isn't relevant to this,' Friday replied evasively.

He had dropped hints like this one other time. She would have to eventually grill him about it, but not today. Rescuing her friends took precedence.

"What happens after you get in contact with this AI?" she asked.

'I'll ask it for help.'

"That seems easy enough."

'Yes, Ewa, but I'm afraid it won't be all that easy. It's possible that it functions in a way that will be totally alien to us.'

"To *us?*"

'You humans created us in your own image. I process ideas faster and more efficiently than you do, but I'm basically still the same as you. But who can say if what evolved on Mars was similar to what developed on Earth?'

"Isn't it physical environment that determines evolution? According to what we know, three billion years ago, it didn't look much different here than it did on Earth."

'I think, Ewa, that the devil is the details. You have ten fingers, which explains why the decimal system came into existence. But maybe the original Martians only had six fingers, or even three hundred seventy-six. And what if they didn't use acoustic speech, but communicated via finger taps. That is possible within the course of the evolutionary process. In the long term, it would lead to a completely different way of conceptualizing existence.'

"But under those circumstances, there wouldn't be any way to communicate with the AI," Ewa said.

'All I wanted to say was that we shouldn't celebrate our success too early.'

"Got it. Success is still a long way off."

'I didn't want to discourage you.'

"Don't worry. I still have my explosives."

'Yes, but let's try it first with the electrical voltage.'

THE AIR WAS UNUSUALLY clear today. Ewa turned around to study her surroundings. A mountain chain was running along the northern horizon. The sun had already passed its zenith. Ewa crossed her arms. If she waited long enough, she would feel the warmth from the sun. She wished she could take off her helmet. It was a tempting thought. She imagined what it would feel like for her hair to be blown back and forth, and for the wind to caress her face.

However, the air that cooled her cheeks, warmed from climbing the mountain, came from a canister. She would never be able to remove her helmet out here. The experience of the sun warming her head was a thing of the past. Ewa sighed. She would never again see a flock of birds cross the sky.

She laid the heavy backpack on the ground. She then knelt beside it and pulled out the battery and the drone. She turned the drone over and inserted the battery, being careful that her small letter remained attached. The yellow button was there too. She pressed it, just like Sarah and Sharon had instructed. Several lights started to flash, and the three large rotors slowly picked up speed.

Ewa flipped the drone back upright, stood up, and held it up high. The rotors were approaching maximum speed. Ewa released the drone. It dropped a short distance, then climbed back up to head height. It rotated to set its trajectory, then rose higher. At the last moment, it inclined its little camera-bearing head, nodded briefly in farewell, and flew off toward the west. Ewa waved after it until it vanished from her sight.

'READY TO START?'

"Of course, Friday. What should I do?"

'You could just let me take control so you won't have to keep asking me.'

"Thanks, but I would prefer to do this myself. It's enough already that you talk with my voice."

'As you like. We're still six hundred meters away from the crystal surface. Head slightly southeast.'

"Let's keep using the word *window*."

'That works.'

Southeast. That meant that she would have to scale the

mountainside. Ewa began sweating as she climbed, and she soon grew breathless. Like yesterday, she was annoyed at herself for not having trained more diligently. If only there weren't so many boulders lying around! She had to pay close attention as she went along because her heavy backpack was tugging her backwards, hard. It was a good thing she was wearing the enhanced suit, as otherwise there was no way she could have hauled the 150-kilogram battery from the rover up the mountain.

'I think we're there,' Friday said.

The dark, basalt-like surface spread out before her once more. "Now what?" she asked.

'We will need to run a few tests.'

"You have no idea what to do next, right?"

Friday shook her head. 'I'm sorry,' he said. 'That notion just came to me. No, how would I know how to control the window? Unfortunately, we don't have the instruction manual. I assume that we don't need to activate the entire crystal. A small section should suffice.'

"I hope so."

'If not, we'll grow old doing this, since our cable isn't all that long. Of course, we could tear the one out of the rover, but then we would be stuck here.'

"At least we still have the dynamite," Ewa declared.

'I won't let it get that far. Go ahead and unpack the battery.'

Ewa slipped the backpack off her shoulders and peeled the battery out of its package. It looked like a gray ashlar stone with several colorful jacks attached to one of its faces.

'Set it on its side,' Friday advised. 'It will have greater stability that way. Exposed like this, the cells are fairly sensitive.'

She carefully turned the battery on its side. As she did this, the two cables that she had taken from the tool compartment fell into her hands.

'You need the cables now anyway,' she heard her own

voice say. 'The red cable goes in the red jack, the black one in the black jack.'

She stuck the end of the first cable into the red jack, then did the same to the black one. On the other end of each of the cables she saw prongs that were almost as large as her bare hands.

"Is this in any way dangerous?" she asked.

'No, nothing will happen until you turn on the electricity.'

"That's very comforting."

'There's a chance that nothing will happen then, either.'

"That would be bad."

'You need to look for a heavy rock somewhere. Put it on top of the prongs on the end of the black cable, and push it against the dark stone.'

"Aye-aye, captain."

She got to her feet and went off in search of a boulder. The first one she found was much lighter than she expected. She still wasn't accustomed to the low gravitational force here. She kept looking for a more massive rock and eventually found one that looked half as big as the battery. On Earth, it would have easily weighed 80 kilograms, here on Mars more like 30. She picked it up, carried it over to the cable, and set it on top of the plug as she had been told. In a similar manner, she pressed the prongs on the red cable against the crystalline stone. The two contact points were about three meters apart. If they were lucky, they should be able to see into the chamber shortly.

'Now for the switch. You should stand back behind the battery.'

She followed Friday's advice and then flipped the switch. Nothing happened. The smell of burning rubber reached her nose. "It smells like something's burning," she said.

'That is impossible,' Friday said. 'The smell must have gotten inside your helmet somehow. Otherwise, you would be dead.'

"You can't smell it?"

'I smell something.'

Of course Friday was right. It couldn't be an external smell, so it didn't have anything to do with her little experiment. She checked her suit's status on her universal device, but no malfunctions or errors had been detected. She was obviously imagining things. However, the smell didn't go away. She exhaled forcefully through her nose, twice. It had to be her imagination.

'Ewa?'

She flinched. "Uh, yeah?"

'Nothing happened.'

Ewa examined the dust-free black surface. It looked the same as it had before. "Should I fetch the explosives?"

'Not so fast.'

"Man, Friday, that was just a joke. I'm sure you have other ideas."

'Absolutely. We could alter a few things. Let's reduce the distance between the contact points. We can also change the geometry and alter the voltage.'

"The geometry?"

'Crystals aren't symmetrical in all directions. There is always a preferred direction.'

"Like how customers always converge on the cashier with the shortest line?"

'Something like that. Maybe we need to send the charge either parallel or perpendicular to the dominant direction.'

"How do we figure that out?"

'Patience, Ewa. We will change one factor at a time and then check to see what happens.'

"That sounds tedious."

'It will be. If we limit ourselves to thirty directions with twenty different contact distances and a hundred voltage levels, that will come to sixty thousand attempts.'

"Are you serious? Even if each attempt only takes a minute, we'll be here for days."

'Forty-one days if we don't take any breaks," Friday said. "Fifty days would be more realistic.'

"Seven weeks. Great."

Those were the prospects. She had enough supplies on the rover to cover that amount of time, but the thought of spending day after day shoving the same prongs a few centimeters apart made her shudder.

'I could take control...'

"Forget it."

'It would feel like you had spent the time asleep.'

"No." In all honesty, this was a very attractive idea. If Friday asked one more time, she would give him permission. But he didn't ask.

'There is a chance that I have slightly exaggerated what we have to do,' he admitted instead.

"Really?"

'At least, I hope so. I don't think that we are talking about an all-or-nothing response in this case. As we run our tests, the window will gradually open. We will just need to keep adjusting the parameters of our test so that it keeps growing more transparent.'

"That seems doable," Ewa said. "Are you certain?"

'No,' Friday replied. 'It's just a theory.'

"Then let's test it."

'We are lacking one tool to do this. We need a gauge that will tell us if we are on the right track.'

"And where can we get that?"

'You will have to build it, Ewa. Let's hope we have the components for it in the rover.'

THEY REACHED the vehicle right at sundown. Ewa threw one last glance at the ground. All the small rocks around here were casting long shadows. *When the sun sits low upon the horizon, it doesn't take magic to conjure up a long shadow*, she thought. She should write a book of aphorisms. But she surely wasn't the first one to say something like this.

Should I ask Friday? No. She had already talked to him too much today. These ongoing monologues were draining. On her hike back to the rover, she had occasionally caught sight of someone next to or behind her—only out of the corner of her eye, and very quickly, but it had been convincing. She needed to take care of her mental health, which was why she kept Friday locked down for the rest of the day. She could assemble the gauge early tomorrow morning.

Sol 323, NASA Base

SARAH AND SHARON met in Ewa's former room. It was so new that no surveillance equipment had been installed yet. This was, in reality, a safety risk. Regardless of the issue of private space, Mars represented a danger for everyone if an undetected leak developed anywhere.

But now this oversight was a godsend, since it enabled them to talk without the administrator being able to listen in. The Mars City technicians had access to the station's entire technical system, but the only thing they could see from here was the increased oxygen usage in room 17.

Sharon pulled a piece of paper out of the pocket at the knee of her pants. "Here's Ewa's message," she said, handing it to Sarah, who was holding her son wrapped in a blanket.

"The drone?"

"I left it outside. No one will find it there."

"Good."

Sarah would have enjoyed going back up to the surface again, but for the time being, she didn't feel like she could leave Michael by himself below. Sharon had offered to watch him, but that wasn't the problem. Sarah was more frightened by the possibility of falling victim to a freak accident up on the surface. If that happened, Michael wouldn't have anyone! And every excursion out of the base brought with it a certain risk factor. Mars was an unforgiving planet. Or had she simply grown too fearful? Whatever the case, Michael shouldn't grow up an orphan. Once Lance was back again, everything would be all right. But until then, she would have to muddle through down here.

She wasn't bored by this. Michael made his demands known, but when they had been met, there was always enough to do in the garden. The two women divided up the household chores, but with just the two of them, there wasn't all that much to tend to.

Sarah unfolded the note. "Did you read it already?" she asked.

"Yes—I was too curious to wait," Sharon answered.

"That's okay."

Ewa had only written a few lines. She seemed concerned about her note falling into the wrong hands, so she hadn't revealed much about her plans. Or was it possible she distrusted them? Or, was it that Ewa wanted to protect them by not telling them much? At least they now knew she was doing well.

"Not very informative," Sarah declared.

"I thought so, too. The drone's battery wasn't empty, which means she sent it off today. She can't be far."

"At the mountain?"

"That occurred to me as well. There aren't all that many possible locations," Sharon replied.

"Hopefully, the administrator hasn't thought of this and sent people there, too."

"He shouldn't know anything about the machine since that all happened before his arrival."

"Do you really think that he hasn't coerced someone to tell him everything?"

"I don't know, Sarah. Mike and Lance have definitely not told him anything, but I don't know the MfE people well enough to say."

"That Guillermo shot at us for the sole reason that Ewa had ordered him to." The Mexican had apologized, but

Sarah still counted this against him. "We should warn Ewa, just in case it hasn't occurred to her that this might happen."

LANCE CALLED IN THAT EVENING. Sarah just happened to be on the bridge, showing her son all the instruments and explaining what each of them did. Michael was having fun, most likely because he liked to hear her voice. She had been talking to him since he was in utero.

"I have two minutes," Lance said.

Sarah held their son up to the camera. "We're doing alright. Don't worry. And you?"

"They're treating us okay. There's a lot to do, but the mood is very strange."

"Strange?"

Lance glanced around quickly. "I can't go into details. Not everyone likes the administrator, but he rules the roost. Everything feels a little unreal."

"When will you be back?"

"No clue. Maybe never. We're supposed to be given vacation time at some point—individually, of course. I'll believe that when I finally see it."

"Things won't always be like this, Lance."

"Just act reasonably and calmly, darling. You have to take care of Michael."

"Don't worry, I will."

"And please be careful who you trust. The administrator has more friends than you'd think. But I have to go now. I love you, Sarah."

"I love you, too." She lifted Michael's arm in a wave.

Lance laughed as the screen went dark.

Sol 323, Mars Machine

"You have to climb up the ladder."

Ewa groaned. It was tight here in the farthest back corner of the rover. Of all places, this was where the photocell that Friday wanted was attached to the wall. How could she fit the small stepladder in this space? She pushed several boxes together. It would have to work. She couldn't open up the ladder, but she could lean it against one of the steel shelving units riveted to the wall.

"I think I can get to it now," she said. She climbed two steps up and stretched out her arm. At that moment, the ladder slipped out from under her. She nailed her chin against the uppermost shelf, but managed to catch herself and avoid a fall.

"Shit," Ewa said. She set the ladder at a steeper angle and climbed back up it. With her right arm, she could just reach the circuit component. She shoved the blade of the screwdriver behind it and began to pry it free.

'Just tear it out,' Friday said. 'I need the cable to be free anyway.'

He had promised her that the rover could still be driven without it. The photo-sensor's function was to turn the interior light on when it grew dark. It was programmable for varying levels of sensitivity, and that was why Friday needed it.

She heard an unpleasant sound, a metallic tearing. Nonetheless, she yanked on the screwdriver one more time. The small box popped free from the wall. Ewa dropped the screwdriver in order to catch the sensor. The tool turned so that its blade pointed downwards just as it hit her bare foot. "Ow!" she cried.

'I told you to wear work shoes,' Friday said.

"Thanks for your compassion," she retorted. "At least there's no blood."

'Good. I should be thanking you. Now you just need to get the flashlight and mount it, along with the sensor, inside the box we constructed. We will then sync it with your universal device, and our gauge will be ready.'

The box that Friday was talking about had previously held cans of beans. She drilled two holes into the bottom of it and now mounted the flashlight at an oblique angle over one hole, and the sensor over the other. The sensor was composed of the photocell. Friday's idea was that the light from the flashlight would be reflected back from the window to the photocell, which would reveal to them any changes in the material's optical characteristics.

"DONE," Ewa said 30 minutes later.

She really felt done in, but—naturally—Friday wanted to test his invention. Ewa slipped acquiescently into her suit and released the air from the cab. With the gauge in her arms, she marched to the spot where the battery was still sitting.

'Put the box down right in the middle of the two electrical contact points,' Friday instructed.

She did as he directed.

'Now, please turn on the voltage.'

Ewa flipped the switch.

'Thanks.'

She switched the charge back off.

'Push the contacts a little farther apart and reactivate the electricity.'

Ewa did what Friday said.

'Thank you. I have good news. The gauge works. We won't have to keep working blindly, and now we can test every combination.'

"Is there any bad news?"

'We'll still need about a week to do it.'

"Damn it!" Ewa exclaimed. This stupid experiment would still take an entire week. She should have just stayed at the base. No, that wasn't fair. Friday was doing his best to help her and the other humans. It sometimes seemed to her that he was suffering from a guilty conscience, but it was probably just efficient for him to operate that way.

FRIDAY FINALLY RELEASED her about an hour before sundown. Ewa's back ached. If Friday were a person, he could at least give her a back rub. Unfortunately, he hadn't suggested even once taking over control for her. Of course, that wouldn't have protected her from the back and muscle aches, since he would have had to work using her body.

She didn't even have the energy to observe the sun's afterglow. When she reached the rover, she discovered the drone that she had sent off the day before. She carried it inside. Sarah and Sharon must have responded. It was nice to know that someone was thinking about her, mainly because those someones were people and not AIs. The two of them warned her about staying close to the machine mountain for too long. The administrator could presumably track her down there. And even though he wouldn't specifically be searching for the technology, he would try to use it for his own purposes.

Sharon and Sarah were probably right, but she first had to finish her work here. If it was risky, so be it. Nobody would benefit from her running away. Ewa responded immediately. Her meal would have to wait.

DEAR SARAH AND SHARON,

Thank you so much for thinking about me. I share your concerns, which is why tomorrow I will take the rover and move closer to the South Pole. Summers won't find me there. However, this means that you won't be able to reach me with the drone any longer. I wish you all the best, and hope that we will see each other again soon under better circumstances.

SHE READ through her reply once more and then signed it. It was better for Sharon and Sarah if they did not know where she was staying—at least better for them. They wouldn't have to lie for her. She tasted bitterness at the back of her throat. She would drop completely off the radar and be all on her own. Yes, that was the best for all of them. She would send the drone back to the NASA base with her message tomorrow.

Sol 324, Mars City

"Hey, Lance," somebody behind him whispered. Lance spun around, but no one was in sight. Now he was hearing voices! Being apart from Sarah and his son was driving him insane.

"Hey, Lance!"

He winced, but nobody was there.

"Look behind the box!" the voice ordered.

Someone was playing a trick on him. There was a gap of about four centimeters between the box and the storeroom wall. No one could be hiding there. He glanced around. He was probably being watched. He casually leaned his broom against the wall, strolled over to the box, and sat down on it as though taking a break.

"Good. Reach behind you."

Something would probably bite him on the finger, and several people would then break out laughing. *Whatever,* he thought. *I might as well play along.* He chose to lean back against the wall, turning slightly to the side and letting his hand fall into the crack. He patted around until he encountered a metallic object. He pulled it out, hoping he was keeping it hidden by his body. It was a small speaker that was apparently being controlled by radio.

"Slip me into your pocket and look for a quiet corner," the little cube urged.

Was this a trick? Was the administrator testing his loyalty? Lance reached up to his chest as though to scratch an itch, dropping the speaker into his shirt pocket. He looked around for a hiding place. He walked a short distance toward the restroom, but all it had was a plastic door. He didn't want anyone to see him, or be able to eavesdrop on him if he was inside there. He then remembered the new airlock. Its interior end was already finished, but it wasn't connected to the outside world yet. The airlock door was airtight and sound-proof, and it contained a small window.

Lance turned back to grab his broom and mop. The cleaning gear made excellent camouflage. He left the store-room, marched to the right, and made one more turn to the right. It was impressive how quickly Mars City was growing. The former *Spaceliner 1* passengers had quickly received their own rooms, and Administrator Summers was now managing the development of the community's infrastructure. Suppos-edly there would soon be a casino here! Most of the people that Lance had talked to sounded satisfied with their new lives on Mars.

The half-finished airlock was located at the end of a corridor that ran past a newly opened fitness room. Through the closed doors, Lance heard someone groan with effort.

The airlock door was standing open. A cordon ran across the doorway. He stepped over it, climbed into the airlock, and closed the door with the locking wheel. Nobody could listen in on him. He hoped the airlock wouldn't cut off the radio link that operated the portable speaker.

Lance hunkered down and held the small, round device up to his mouth like a microphone. "I've found a quiet corner," he said.

"Good," replied the voice he recognized from before. "I'm searching for like-minded people. Have I found that in you?"

"I don't know," he answered. "First, I need to know what you have in mind."

"You should be able to deduce that from the way in which

I've contacted you. But if not—I'm unhappy with how and by whom this city is being ruled."

"I might feel similarly," Lance said, "but how am I to know that you don't just want to test me? I haven't met a single person here who is unhappy with the administrator."

"That's perhaps due to the fact that it's inadvisable to express such an opinion in public. Even the walls here have ears."

"Maybe, but that doesn't convince me of anything."

"Then I can't help you, Lance. I understand your dilemma, but you also have to understand ours. We know that there are collaborators among the MfE people. This contact also represents a certain risk for us, too."

"Then we probably won't be able to work together," Lance said.

"I didn't expect that we'd become instant friends with this initial contact. You have two days to consider. You can meet me the day after tomorrow in the afternoon at the fitness room. I'll be there working with the free weights. The room will be secure."

"I understand."

"Please put the speaker back behind the box."

"Alright."

"Thanks, Lance."

Lance didn't reply. He slowly got to his feet. He checked through the window to see if anyone was in sight in the corridor before sticking the speaker into his pocket, opening the door, and leaving the airlock with his broom and mop. He definitely needed to discuss this offer with Mike and the MfE men. *What did the stranger say? Someone is spying for the administrator.* He found it hard to believe. No, he shouldn't let himself be swayed by vague innuendo.

Sol 324, Flammarion Crater

HE'D NEVER BEFORE HAD blisters on his backside. Walter sat in his tiny tent lit up by the flashlight he'd found in the rover and thought about the best way to disinfect the wounds on his skin and dry them so that he'd be able to sit in the rover again tomorrow.

He hadn't expected the drive across the Mars landscape to be so difficult. When Rebecca and Theo had given the reports about their trip, he had listened with one raised eyebrow. They'd sounded more like the kind of adventure stories you might tell around a campfire. It was clear to him now that the two of them had rather under-exaggerated it all.

Today, he had crossed the Flammarion Crater and set up camp near its far edge. Although the plain before him looked smooth, it wasn't. It was as if someone had sprinkled the entire planet with salt and pepper. The peppercorns were easy to avoid since they were easily noticeable. They were pointed rocks that he could steer around. For a while, it was even fun —at least, until his arm muscles started to ache from all the steering.

The 'salt' crystals were more menacing, as they were partly submerged in the ever-present layer of dust. It was as if they were baked in and anchored to the ground. The worst part was that they were hard to see, and whenever he hit one with the rover, it did a real number on his soft parts. And, unlike Theo, Walter was made up almost exclusively of soft parts, having never been particularly sporty. He had only embarked on this journey because he was nearing the end of his life. He had wanted to do something sensible with all the money he had made from a lifelong career—and colonizing Mars sounded very enticing. Then, unexpectedly, someone had offered him a place on the *Santa Maria*, presumably thinking that was what he had wanted when he'd donated his millions to the cause.

It had been his chance. His cancer, unbeknownst to anyone but himself, was already far advanced. Before leaving on this journey, his doctor had told him what signs to look for in order to gauge on his own how his cancer was progressing. He had only another three to four months left. The doctor who had been along for the ambush at the MfE base had picked up on the severity of his condition, and that was why he alone had been excluded from the men's roundup. And, to his surprise, the doctor had honored his request not to tell anyone else just how bad off he really was.

This final trip was a way for him to kill three birds with one stone. He would find the peace and privacy he longed for in which to meet his death, his actions would present a deliberate snub to the administrator, and he had spared the MfE women from having to put themselves in danger by making this trip. As his last good deed, he would activate the Japanese robot and send it to the MfE base so that they could use it as a secret messenger and, he hoped, eventually play a role in bringing down the administrator. It would be the final piece of the puzzle, and he would have made some difference with his life.

But first, he needed to reach the Japanese probe. Its name, which had finally popped into his head after all, was *Nozomi 2* and meant something close to 'Second Hope.' Its predecessor had been damaged during a solar storm on its way to Mars and had been orbiting the sun ever since as an artificial asteroid. Walter had found *Nozomi 2*'s landing position written down in his own records. He had never expected this information to be of any use to him.

He pulled off his underpants and lay down on his stomach. It was the only way to bear the pain. However he wasn't going to be able to drive the rover lying down tomorrow. He took a dry towel from his bag and pressed it lightly against his lower back and buttocks. It was worse than he had thought. His skin was one big open wound. He carefully laid the thin towel over it. It provided momentary relief, but how would things look tomorrow? If he lay like this for long, scabs would start to form that would almost certainly rip open when he stood up again. He pressed the towel a little firmer. Perhaps it would keep his skin more supple. There wasn't anything else he could do for the time being.

And what about tomorrow? Walter couldn't imagine sitting on his wounds for twelve hours. He had intended to make the journey in ten days, and the robot would need even more time to return to the base. Perhaps... could he drive the rover while lying on his stomach? It was certainly worth trying. He could take the board from the tent base and fasten it over the seat. He would probably need to shorten the back end of it, which would also make the tent shorter, but that didn't matter.

Would he be able to secure the board at the right angle so that he could still steer the rover with his arms? He wouldn't dare make any crazy turns or he might be thrown off by the inertia. Fortunately, he was alone, and there was enough room in the rover. However, if he'd had a passenger with him, that person could have strapped him to the board, which would have made his idea much less risky.

But he had no passenger with him, and didn't want one either. He was having enough trouble with just himself. It was becoming more and more difficult to endure his current state. If he wasn't on his own, he would have to take the other person's feelings into consideration. He would have to radiate confidence despite knowing that this was the end, feigning interest for the other person though he had barely any interest in himself. He just wanted it all to happen as painlessly and as peacefully as possible.

Walter laughed. In this respect, his plan was a flop. He had never before had to endure such pain as he was coping with on this journey.

"If nothing else, it proves you're still alive," one of those rarely-welcome eternal optimists might have quipped.

What bullshit! Walter thought. He had absolutely no use for the pain at the moment. If this was his end, then so be it. Although, it would be nice to be able to accomplish this one last thing beforehand.

Sol 325, Mars Machine

'A LITTLE MORE,' said Friday.

"I'm on it." She pushed the contacts in a little harder. Her back was hurting like crazy. She sneaked a glance at the time so Friday wouldn't notice. Wasn't it noon yet? She felt a flash of annoyance. She didn't owe Friday anything! If she felt like it, or if her energy flagged, she was going to take a break, whether it was noon or not.

'Just... no, wait.'

"What's wrong?" she asked while still desperately holding on to the contacts.

"I thought...," said Friday.

"Well, that's a new one."

'I thought I had something. And look... the values are now better. The surface is becoming transparent!'

"That would be wonderful!"

'Yes, I will play around some more with the current. You don't have to press on the contacts anymore. I have recorded the coordinates.'

"Good." She let go, and her muscles were immediately grateful.

'Do you see that?'

Friday was right. The formerly black surface was becoming more dimensional. It looked like a large lake you could peer into. Not to the bottom, but if fish had been swimming near the surface, they would have been clearly visible.

"Amazing," she said. "It really worked."

'And it wasn't wizardry,' Friday answered. 'Just physics.'

Ewa took a step forward. She now stood at the edge of an increasingly transparent structure. Something was happening below. It looked like whirlwinds were rising from within it, as though the source of the deep lake was at its bottom. Of course, it was only an optical illusion. Its transparency was not yet complete. Friday was apparently still working on that.

And then, quite abruptly, she was hovering over a cavern. The material had become invisible. The black boulder had made space for atomic nothingness. The transparent effect was absolutely perfect. Ewa knelt down and ran her hand over the surface to convince herself that it was still there. Humans were not yet able to produce such impressive effects.

Below her lay the great hall she remembered. She had already spent time in there with Friday trying to put the machine out of commission. But this time, she and Friday needed to do the opposite. She wanted to use the ancient technology to solve an immediate and urgent problem. She needed to free her friends from the administrator's tyranny, and to do that, she required a convincing argument. An enormous mountain that she could drive to Mars City, that would indeed be a compelling argument. But there was a long way to go yet. They hadn't done more than see the command center of the machine. They still had to somehow make contact with it.

"And now?" asked Ewa.

'Do you want to relax in the rover for a little bit while I think of a solution?'

"I don't need a break at the moment, but thanks," she replied. "Or would it help you if I go hang out in the rover?"

'No, not at all, I can't stay here on my own anyway. If you don't need a break, we can keep going. I don't need one.'

"Then let's go!"

'My plan is to communicate with the computer's

internal system via all the possible transmittable means. Electromagnetic impulses can easily penetrate the window below us.'

"And what do you expect to happen then?"

'Some kind of reaction. I'll see it when it happens. I will just need to have you work the radio transmitter. But first, we have to make a technical change.'

"What do I need to do exactly?"

'I'm referring to the sensors that record your biodata.'

"What about them?"

'In your helmet is a device for measuring your brain activity. It lets others know from far away whether you are conscious or not.'

"But only someone who is inside my signal area."

'I need to ask you to reroute this sensor, so it is no longer connected with the biodata collector, but with the transmitter.'

"What's that supposed to mean, Friday? You want me to transmit my brain impulses out into the world?"

'No, not yours, but mine. It won't be enough to just say something in English into the transmitter's receiver. The Martians have probably never heard this language before.'

"There are no Martians."

'You're right. I mean the machines that they have apparently left behind.'

"And how will you give them commands?"

'I will go through all the established coding languages. I can go through them one after another at lightning speed, until I hit one that causes them to react.'

"And then?"

'Then I will give the commands.'

Aha. Friday intended to take control of a giant machine that was constructed ages ago by the former inhabitants of Mars. Was this really a good idea? Had this been his plan the entire time? Ewa couldn't really imagine it. There was so much that had gone wrong that no one could have foreseen. Thus, a tiny bit of uncertainty remained.

'Was that not your objective?' asked Friday, who had noticed her reservation.

"Yes, but I'm wondering whether all this was a good idea. I haven't been very successful in the recent past with my ideas, even though each one seemed extremely clever at the time."

'Then your misgivings are a welcome change.'

"You're right. Okay, I'll agree to it."

'That's not enough, you have to reroute your biosensor.'

"And how do I do that?" asked Ewa.

'Just a moment, I'll explain it to you,' Friday replied.

CONVERTING her biodata system took about half an hour. Afterward, her universal device beeped continuously. It was sending out the alarm announcing that she was apparently brain dead and in need of medical assistance. The system was not programmed to recognize the contradictory input from her ongoing heartbeat, even though it was still being recorded.

"That beeping is annoying," Ewa said.

'I know, but I can't change it. We would need to deactivate the circuit, but then you would no longer receive any signals from your biosensor.'

Beep—beep—beep—beep—beep... she couldn't *not* hear the device. The sound would drive her mad, sooner or later, but for now, there was no other option.

"Then hurry, please," she said.

According to the scale on the transmitter, she saw that Friday was already at work. The system's control functions were now reacting to certain action potentials from his own artificial consciousness. Ewa imagined an electric current from Friday's thoughts fluttering over the sensitive devices down below.

She was watching one of the devices when it suddenly leapt at her, landing on her face and sticking to her skin. That was impossible. The meters-thick ceiling separated them, even if it was transparent. The strange apparatus was wise and pulled itself back. Ewa stumbled a little and decided it was better to kneel down.

"What was that?" she asked.

'What was what? I didn't notice anything,' answered Friday.

"Nothing? I must have imagined it." But it wasn't her imagination. The thing had clung to her face and reduced her air supply. It seemed as though it had wanted to go right inside her head. She observed the large box down below. Friday was right. Nothing from down there could have jumped on her. Perhaps the incessant beeping had driven her insane quicker than expected, and she really was bonkers.

Bonkers. That's a funny word. She repeated it a few times in her head. Each time it sounded even stranger. Then it transformed itself into a worm. The worm crawled over her face. She had only just managed to grab hold of its tail as it tried to slip inside her ear. It hissed slightly as she gripped it. She held it up close to her face in order to understand what it wanted.

To go into your brain, is what it sounded like. She shook her head. That wasn't happening. Her consciousness belonged to her and her alone. But the worm wriggled, and its skin became hot. She couldn't hold it any longer without burning herself, so she let it go.

Dumb bug, she thought, just as the worm made a great leap and buried itself inside her right nostril—except that its tail was still hanging out. She grabbed for it but wasn't quick enough this time. The worm ate its way to her brain. She reached for her temples with both hands but only hit against her helmet. How could the worm have gotten through her helmet's visor?

Impos...

She didn't get to finish her thought. Her vision went black, and she crumpled to the ground.

SHE OPENED her eyes to a dazzling light. This must be the afterlife, just as she had imagined it as a child. God would appear momentarily, a man with a beard, and would take her by the hand and lead her to a beautiful place. She had arrived in paradise. That was good news, considering all the things she had done wrong.

But the bearded man never came. Ewa had to pick herself up, which she did with no trouble. Her body felt like new.

"Friday?"

There was no answer. Friday didn't seem to be here. Hopefully he hadn't been destroyed. Had they possibly mixed up the connectors on the biosensor? Ewa did a few deep knee bends. Then it hit her that she wasn't wearing a spacesuit. After the initial shock, she calmed down. If there weren't any breathable air here, she would be long dead by now.

Then it occurred to her to look around. She was in the great hall she had just been observing from above. Did the Martians possess some kind of beaming technology that had just deposited her here? She'd always thought that beaming a living being was impossible due to the uncertainty principle.

To her right she saw a set of the cubes that they had identified previously as the computer. It seemed intact. Ewa hadn't needed to feel bad about it after all. She walked over to it to take a closer look. As she did, she reached out her hand to touch the material—and her hand went right through with no resistance, which meant she hadn't been beamed anywhere. Rather, this was more of a projection, even though everything felt very real.

Ewa shaded her eyes with her hand against her forehead and glanced up. Up above her, she saw something about two meters long and somewhat less than a meter wide. It was a human in a spacesuit. It was her body, lying up there. Ewa tried to steady herself on the computer, but again her hand went right through it.

"Friday?"

She tried again, but her live-in companion didn't seem to have been duplicated. She was alone, and it was getting dark.

Ewa took a deep breath. None of this was real. Friday had hacked her biosensor early that afternoon. It couldn't be getting dark already, but what she saw was obvious. Night was falling. The sky was black. The roof was so clear that she could even make out some stars.

However, the night only lasted for two minutes, then the sun came up again. The sky was brighter than yesterday, with less dust in the air. *None of this is real*, she told herself. If an entire day had passed, she would feel ravenous, and her bladder would be full. But then the new day also quickly ended. The sun was already hanging low on the horizon. But something wasn't right.

Then she remembered. The sun was setting in the east. She needed a few minutes to draw the right conclusions. In the meantime, the day turned to night and back to day again three more times. And the sun kept moving from west to east. What she saw was not reality, that was crystal clear. But it was also not a projection of the present. Someone was replaying the past. Time was moving backward. Whoever was showing this film was speeding up the reel. Day and night were no longer alternating every few minutes, but now by seconds, until finally the sky turned to a reddish-gray—the mean chromatic mix of day and night.

The images changed so rapidly that no distinguishable structure could be seen. Only the ceiling window, the hall, and she herself were constant fixtures. And the roughly 200-by-80-centimeter-long body lying at the edge of that window. It comforted Ewa immensely. She knew without anyone needing to tell her that she could go back at any time. She didn't know exactly how, but it would surely reveal itself to her if she only wanted it badly enough, of that much she was certain.

How far along was the film now? The speed at which it was being rewound was impossible to judge. Beyond a rate of about 20 images, or days, per second, the human eye couldn't register the flickering. All the same, she didn't think this was a timeframe of years or centuries. If this had any purpose, the projection could only have one goal, and that was to show her the past of billions of years ago, as the early inhabitants must have fought a losing battle for their homeland. The computers in the great hall must have recognized that communication was futile, that they wouldn't be able to find a common language.

Ewa stared in anticipation at the ceiling. The back of her neck should have been screaming in pain, but that was one of the advantages of not having a real body. She turned her head to the side just to see how far she could look over her right shoulder. *Just a little bit more*, she thought. She expected some resistance, but there wasn't any. Now she could see what was behind her. Ewa laughed out loud. For the first time in her life, she could see behind her own back! Slowly, she turned her head further until she could see her left shoulder. This was crazy. And now she could see forward again. She had just succeeded in turning her head a full 360 degrees! If nothing else, this experiment was worth it purely for that.

A stroboscopic flashing began. She looked at the ceiling again. The days and nights were changing more slowly. One instantly recognizable difference was that the days were much brighter than in the present. The sky was sometimes gray, sometimes blue. Then Ewa noticed that the gray color was coming from the clouds as they passed over the blue sky. It was not the same blue as on Earth—it was much paler—but it was also not the same yellowish gray-brown of the Martian sky. How far into the past had she been taken? Human scientists estimated that there had been water, as well as a dense atmosphere, on Mars about three and a half to four billion years ago. Evolution hadn't had much time to fill this world with life.

She heard a rustling noise. It was coming from all around her. Ewa looked to her feet. Coming out of invisible jets in the floor she saw clear water. She was standing up to her ankles in it. The cold water was probably around ten degrees Celsius, but it wasn't unpleasant, and her feet weren't getting wet. The water ran at a downward slope. It was now clear to her why the computer was set into a recess. The depression was a basin. She was inside a giant swimming pool. All that was missing was the smell of chlorine. And she wasn't alone. In the pool were large animals that resembled manatees, up to two meters in length.

No, she corrected herself, they weren't animals. Some of the creatures were focusing intensely on the computers in the middle of the basin. They had flipped out levers from the machines, which looked something like the manual buttons on an organ. They manipulated these with their front extremities. Ewa also observed the opening and closing of round orifices on one part of their bodies, presumably the head. They were probably communicating with one another. She couldn't hear anything, so it must have been through infrasound or ultrasound, which her human ear couldn't detect.

Ewa felt drawn to the creatures. She would have liked to touch or hug them. On Earth, she had once seen a manatee stranded on the beach. There, it had been clumsy and slow. But here, these creatures glided elegantly through the water. One of them came up to her, raised its right extremity as if in greeting and then turned away again.

Another one pulled itself onto the dry floor a little way away from her. It lay on its back and pulled what looked like a miniature version of itself out of its stomach pouch. Ewa took it to be its baby. It held its wriggling offspring up to its face so that their mouths touched. Then it looked the baby deep in the eyes before shooting something out of its mouth and into the baby's. Food—what else?

But Ewa needed to be careful. It was much too easy to interpret something falsely. These creatures were not manatees. They had a completely different backstory. Their stomachs could have been located in their heads, and their brains might have spread out over their bodies like skin. The notion that evolution had coincidentally taken the same course here as on Earth was implausible, unless these beings had somehow influenced development on Earth. But that was probably beyond their abilities. They obviously hadn't managed to save their own planet either.

And how could they have influenced evolution on Earth? During the Archean Age, approximately 3.5 billion years ago, Earth's surface had still been barren. All the life that existed was exclusively in the oceans. The atmosphere contained barely any oxygen. Not until a billion years later, once Mars was already dry and dead, did the great oxidation event of the Proterozoic Age lead to the formation of ideal conditions to support modern life. At the same time, most of the organisms that had developed prior to that point went extinct.

Another of the manatees approached her. The creature, like the one before it, raised its right extremity and made a waving motion. It had four fingers that were connected by a sort of webbed skin at their base. Ewa waited, and the creature continued to wave. Was that really meant for her? She turned her head to look behind her, but there was no one else around. So she interpreted the gesture as an invitation. The creature splashed its rear legs on the water's surface, turned around, and moved along the edge of the basin through the hall.

She followed it. The water here reached her hips. The other creatures seemed to not see her. They were busy with the devices they were working on, which Ewa assumed were computers. They all seemed to have screens. Ewa thought she recognized a map of Mars on one of them. Numerous bodies of water, especially in the southern hemisphere, were highlighted on it. Now and again, her guide turned around to check that she was still there. Then it continued on its way.

They reached the end of the hall where the basin also ended. Her leader briefly disappeared under the water but reappeared a minute later, this time wearing a mask on its head and a sort of case on its back. The case was made of a soft material. It had two hoses extending from it that were attached to a helmet that the creature was also wearing.

Through the transparent visor, Ewa could see that water was flowing through the hoses and it kept the lower part of the creature's head wet. She presumed it was breathing by filtering its respiratory gas out of the water. It was hard to guess whether the gas was oxygen or something else. And the fact that she was able to breathe here also provided no information, since she was a mere projection of herself.

The creature climbed out of the basin. Its movements on the dry ground were awkward, but also very efficient. They came to a circular structure containing a likewise-circular door that seemed to have been opened by some unknown hand. The creature hobbled through the opening. Ewa had to crouch down since the chamber inside was so low. Her gut told her that they were going to move upwards. They quickly reached their destination, and the door before them opened as well. The creature crawled out first, and Ewa followed. They found themselves on the mountain.

But it was not the mountain she knew. She was standing on the roof of an enormous, intimidating construction made of pitch-black material that extended far across the area. To the south, she could see a broad river flowing. The water reflected the sun, now at its zenith. A few small gray clouds floated by.

The slopes of the shores looked as though they were very recently dug out. The machine was standing at precisely the spot where the river ended. That couldn't be a coincidence. They had falsely interpreted the machine's function! Yes, it did turn over Mars's surface in its path, but it wasn't intended to release carbon dioxide. That was simply a byproduct of the present day, because there was by now a large amount of carbon dioxide in the soil. In reality, the machine's true purpose must have been to increase the living space for Mars's inhabitants by creating a landscape of canals across their home planet.

However, even from the beginning, Mars had possessed fewer water resources than Earth. A greater surface-mass of water meant more living area for the Mars inhabitants, who had seemingly adapted to the shallow bodies of water. This process must have also increased the rate of evaporation. As increasing amounts of water were absorbed into the atmosphere, it was an easy target for the solar wind due to the lack of a magnetic field.

The manatee-like creatures had apparently accelerated Mars's evolution into a hostile desert through their own actions. Could they have already been aware of this at the time? Ewa observed the giant machine. Whoever controlled such technology must certainly have foreseen what was in store for the planet. But that didn't seem to have prevented each subsequent generation from striving for a better life for themselves.

Ewa sighed. Why was this all so familiar to her? The creature that had led her up here was quietly observing the landscape. It was just as much a part of the simulation as she was. She couldn't ask it anything since she wasn't even able to hear the sounds it made. Ewa took a few steps. The dark material gave slightly underneath her as she walked, or was that just her imagination? Something lay at the edge of the platform. She immediately recognized its shape. It was the thing that connected her to reality. She still had a problem to solve. Exploring the secrets of a long-extinct culture was definitely exciting, but it would not help her friends. Her disappointment manifested itself through a tightening in her chest.

It was time to head back. The manatee that had led her here now ignored her. Perhaps the communication between her and the AI that would be protecting this machine for all eternity only went this far and no farther. It had given her, its visitor, a glimpse into the past. That was what visitors from the future were interested in. It couldn't have had any knowledge of Ewa's current problems, and Ewa also couldn't think of any way to have explained anything to it.

How would she return to her body? She looked around, but there was no one there who could help her. She approached the manatee with the breathing apparatus. The creature was holding what looked like a ball in its hand, its outer surface glowing like a computer screen. With its delicate fingers, it touched the display, and the perspective changed each time it did so. What she saw was a miniature version of Mars. The oceans disappeared and were replaced by thin lines that ran outward from the South Pole. Lines of communications, or even streets?

The image transformed into green and red surfaces. Ewa could not interpret what they meant. The northern hemisphere was more red than green, and in the southern hemisphere, it was just the opposite. Ewa tried to take the sphere from the creature. Perhaps something would happen then, but her hand reached right through the manatee. Nothing here was real.

What could help her? Maybe she could return to her body if she went outside the projector's range and thus became invisible. It was worth a try at least, and nothing would happen anyway as she was merely a projection—and a projection couldn't die. She stepped closer to the edge of the roof. It was a deep drop, more than a hundred meters down.

She was scared, but she jumped anyway.

Sol 325, NASA Base

"I just can't believe it," said Sharon. "She can't have been that crazy."

Sarah shook her head. "You know her. When she gets an idea in her head..."

Sharon smoothed out the paper with the message. "Which is why tomorrow I will take the rover and move closer to the South Pole," she read aloud from Ewa's note.

"That was yesterday," said Sarah. "She's long gone."

"Perhaps it was just a ploy," said Sharon. "She doesn't want the administrator to find her."

"But her message came to us."

"Maybe she thinks that one of us is working for the administrator," said Sharon.

Sarah could only laugh. It was a relaxed laugh. Sharon had to be joking. No one was so cowardly as to join forces with the administrator.

"Do you think we should see how she's doing?" asked Sharon. "Maybe she was hoping one of us will beg her to come back."

"Ewa doesn't think like that."

"I wouldn't put it past her," said Sharon.

"Good, then I know your thinking, for future reference."

"You mean, you don't think we should check on her?"

"No I don't. Let's leave her in peace," said Sarah.

Sharon sighed.

Sol 326, Mars City

Lance entered the fitness room and flipped his towel over the handlebar of the bike. He was here just to work out, nothing more. He needed to be sure that anyone watching would think that as well. It wasn't going to be easy for him. He had never been a fan of secrecy, lying, or deception.

He got on the bike and started pedaling. It was set to a high gear, but he left it there. He wanted to get his heart rate up and break a sweat. In the left corner, a guy was lifting weights. The man was about 1.9 meters tall and had the stature of a boxer. He looked like someone you wouldn't want to cross, but he had a friendly face and smiled at Lance.

The door to the fitness room squeaked shut from the outside. Lance gave a start. Was this a trap?

"Relax. I told you it would be okay," the other guy said.

"Was that a friend?"

"Yeah, there's someone outside keeping watch so we can be undisturbed. The lock on the door needs to be fixed."

"How practical," said Lance.

"I'm Terran, Terran Carter."

"Pleased to meet you, Terran."

The would-be boxer put down the free weights and came over to him. They shook hands while Lance remained on the bike. "I'm sorry for what Summers did to all of you," said Terran.

"How do you know about that?"

"Things like that get around. Not everyone who was part of the expedition agrees with what he did."

"I'm glad to hear it. Does that mean you have formed a sort of secret alliance?"

"If you want to call it that. Actually, it's only a few of us who discuss how we can eventually replace him with a new administrator."

"Are there any concrete ideas yet?"

"You have probably already noticed, Lance, but there are a number of people here who are totally content with the status quo. Everything is advancing, and for them, that's all that matters. They'd do themselves a disservice by going against the administrator."

"That's how people are."

"You, too? I would understand it if you were. If you don't want to be involved, you'll never hear from us again. None of us will blame you or say anything. If the administrator finds out that you aren't on his side, and he's quite good at that, it'll be the end of your career."

"Career. That's a good one! We're only here for him to use us as pawns against each other."

"That's exactly what I thought," said Terran. "That's also why we approached you guys first."

"Mike and me, you mean? Our MfE friends also have a bone to pick with Summers."

"Are you in touch with them?"

"I discussed it with everyone before meeting you here today."

Terran fell silent and scratched his chin. "That... that wasn't quite our plan."

"Then you'll need to alter your plan."

"The problem is that Summers has a spy working for him among the MfE folks. We know that for sure."

"Who is it?"

"*That* we don't know."

Now Lance was silent. Five of the men from *Mars for Everyone* were here, Theo, Andy, Ketut, Shashwat, and Guillermo. He wouldn't have thought any of them would spy for the administrator. But there was no way to be sure, either.

"Maybe it's one of the women," Lance said finally.

"Maybe. We urgently need to test that."

"Test it?"

"We've been spreading various versions of false information and checking which version is passed on to the administrator."

"Have you done that before?"

"Yes, on board the *Spaceliner*. And it worked."

"I see."

"But for it to work again, now, you can't say anything. Can I trust you?"

"Promise," said Lance. "But who are you? If I'm to support you, I need to know who all is in your group."

"I understand. I will discuss that with the others and introduce you to them at our next meeting."

"We'll be seeing each other again?"

"I sure hope so, Lance. I'll send you a message with the time and place."

Sol 327, Mars Machine

EWA DIDN'T DIE. She woke up on the roof of the machine with her joints stiff and aching. Before sitting up, she glanced to the right and the left. Nothing around her had changed.

"Friday?"

'You're back! Oh, Ewa, I'm so glad!'

"Why? I was only gone for a little while."

'Look up.'

The sun had not quite reached its highest point yet, which meant that her body had been lying here for almost one whole day, unconscious the entire time. No wonder her joints hurt. Her mouth was dry, so she sipped on her straw.

"I didn't notice that almost a whole day had passed."

'Two days,' Friday corrected her.

"What? That's impossible!"

'But true. I was really worried about you. I was very close to disabling your biosensor and manually cutting the connection. But I was afraid you might not find your way back if I did.'

"Thank goodness you didn't interfere."

Ewa sat up. *Shit!* Her body must have relieved itself instinctively during her absence. And she wasn't wearing a diaper! By now she should know to expect the unexpected.

125

She had a real mess on her hands. Ewa groaned just thinking about it.

'Problems?' asked Friday.

"Yes, but nothing that concerns you."

'Were you successful at least?'

"Unfortunately not. We aren't even slightly further along."

'What happened?'

"I was given a tour through the history of the planet. We misjudged the machine's function."

'Slow down. It would be better to tell me everything in detail. Perhaps the solution is hidden in there somewhere. The thought pattern of the Mars inhabitants might have been so completely different that you may have sped right over the pivotal information.'

"Okay. But, in the rover. I need to clean up and find something good to eat."

'Of course.'

EWA SAT on the bed in her underwear and ate a dry cracker. It was delicious. She had found the package on the shelf under the bed. With every bite, she felt more and more like a person again. In her head, she filed through the images the machine had displayed for her over her biosensor. They were still unbelievably vivid. It was almost as though someone had taken a magical paintbrush and painted the innermost layers of her consciousness with it.

She swallowed her last bite.

'Could we do it now?' asked Friday.

"Did you listen in again?"

'I couldn't help it.'

"It was also just a joke."

'You seem to be in good spirits, Ewa.'

Friday was right. She really was in a good mood. And she hadn't even been able to solve their main problem. The things she had learned were of no use to anyone. At the moment, it also looked as though she wasn't going to be able to tell anyone about them.

"Yes, I feel good," Ewa said. "Very fresh and renewed, as if my mind has gone through a complete overhaul."

'Who knows, perhaps the outside influence,' said Friday.

"You mean, someone might have manipulated me?"

'It isn't impossible, though highly unlikely. Now, please fill me in on everything you experienced as you were lying there unconscious.'

Ewa told Friday what she had seen. The memories streamed back in perfect order, and she was easily able to put them into words, something that Ewa couldn't remember ever experiencing before. It was as if she had been highly alert at every moment during that time. Was her brain really capable of such an achievement?

Friday simply let her talk. Ewa even had enough mental capacity to be aware herself as she gave her report. Fortunately, Friday didn't interrupt her. He seemed to know that there was no need for any questions. The images in her head were of such perfect quality that they couldn't have been natural. Then again, they also didn't stem from a natural source.

Her report ended with her jump from the machine's roof.

'That was irresponsible,' said Friday.

"It worked."

'You were just lucky.'

"No, I was pretty sure that it would work."

'Fine, Ewa. Now to our problem.'

"Have you thought of something?"

'The solution is definitely not hidden in the history that was presented to you. Humans already know enough stories like that.'

"They certainly would have died out at some point."

'For sure. They had no other alternative. The Earth wasn't quite so far away at that time. It wouldn't have been any more livable than Mars is for us today.'

"But we are still attempting to survive here."

'Yes, Ewa, and there you can see how much more advanced the Mars inhabitants were versus modern humans.'

"You old skeptic."

'I am a realist, Ewa. But that's not what matters here. Even if you haven't seen a solution for our problem, in my opinion, we have some important clues.'

"And they would be?"

Ewa felt cold. She considered whether she should turn up the heat or put on something warm to wear. Spotting her comforter, she lay down on her cot and covered up.

'You looked at screens several times, and then the last thing was that sphere with the map of Mars. There is a common thread.'

That was correct. The maps had all looked very different from one another, but one specific area had always stuck out.

"The South Pole," she said.

'Exactly,' Friday answered. 'The South Pole is now covered by an ice cap many kilometers thick. But underneath it, there are supposed to be lakes with liquid water.'

"You mean, the Mars inhabitants have survived there?"

'I don't consider that possible. They would have left their traces everywhere. No, they died out a long time ago, but they must have migrated there during their last few centuries. You are looking for a miracle. Maybe we'll find something among the things they left behind that we can use against the administrator.'

"So, we should head to the South Pole?"

'That's what I would do, Ewa.'

"Then we should set off today—now."

'Don't you want to rest first?'

"No, Friday. I'll put the rover on autopilot, so we can set off immediately."

Sol 328, NASA Base

SARAH HEARD A METALLIC DRONING. Its tone was so deep that she couldn't tell where it was coming from. Or had she dreamt it? The sound returned. Sarah looked at the clock. She was now on duty since Sharon had ended her shift a short time ago. She sighed, got up, and wrapped her jacket loosely around her shoulders. Michael was sound asleep in his bed. The noise, however, didn't seem like it was going to go away on its own.

In the corridor, Sarah noticed that the sound could only be coming from the airlock. Someone was trying to get in. Since no one was answering through the radio transmitter, it must be uninvited guests. Or was it Ewa, perhaps, in some kind of need? Sarah reached the inner chamber. In its current mode, the airlock could only be opened from the inside. Sarah quickly released the outer chamber. The noise stopped. The indicator light on the control panel showed that the chamber was filling with breathable gas. A few moments later, the inner chamber opened.

Sarah took a step back. She recognized a *Spaceliner* suit, like the one Ewa wore, but it didn't contain a woman. It was a man with a noticeable paunch. He was followed by another man who was about ten centimeters shorter. Sarah waited for the men to take off their helmets. She felt a hand on her shoulder and flicked a startled glance over her shoulder. Their visitors had obviously awakened Sharon, who was now standing beside her.

"Please excuse the intrusion," the portly man declared.

"You don't have to apologize," the shorter man corrected him.

Sarah looked for name badges on their suits, but didn't find any.

"I was raised to be polite," the first replied.

"If you're too friendly, they will be disrespectful," the shorter man replied, casually pulling a weapon from the tool bag attached to his suit.

"I don't think so. You two ladies are sensible, now, aren't you?" the stout man said, glancing first at Sarah, then at Sharon. He'd initially seemed more likeable to Sarah than his partner, but closer scrutiny of his eyes revealed an almost palpable arrogance.

"That depends on what you want," said Sharon.

"We don't want anything at all from you," he replied.

"That's not true," corrected the shorter man, once again. "We're here for information."

"About what?" asked Sarah.

"That's better," said the large man. "The sooner we get what we need, the sooner we can get out of here."

"That is, unless you'd like us to stay," said the shorter man. "You've had to go a long time without your men, so there must be something that needs fixing, or maybe you have other preferences."

Sarah struggled to keep from bursting out in laughter. From which zombie cemetery had the administrator dug up these two guys? The scene reminded her of an old film—a low-budget one.

Sharon was apparently able to control herself a little better. "Well, what do you want to know?" she asked.

"We heard there was supposedly some sort of interesting machine in the area," said the fat man, inflating his cheeks and puffing as he exhaled.

"What kind of machine?" asked Sharon.

"Let's not beat around the bush," he replied. "Our sources are trustworthy. Don't try to fool us."

"If you know everything already, why are you asking us?" retorted Sharon.

"We don't know its exact location."

"I really don't know what you're talking about," said Sharon. "What is this machine supposed to do?"

"We think that it takes carbon dioxide from the ground..." The shorter man shut his mouth after the fat man elbowed him.

"Ah. Well, like I said, we've never seen it," Sharon said, turning around, about to walk away.

"Don't move when we're talking to you," said the shorter man, grabbing her hair and yanking her back.

"Let go!" Sharon screamed. She looked about ready to attack him.

"Stop it," said Sarah. "She didn't deserve that."

Sharon leaned against the wall and tried to catch her breath. Sarah was glad that it hadn't escalated into a brawl. There was no playing games when a weapon was involved, even if Sharon was a qualified martial arts instructor.

"You seem to be the more reasonable one here," said the fat man to Sarah. "It looks like you seem to get that we have the power to determine whether your child grows up to see its father or not."

You pig, Sarah thought, keeping silent.

"What's with the machine then? All I need is a general direction."

"North," said Sarah without thinking. She couldn't bring herself to give the man the correct answer.

The fat man nodded his head. "Ok, fine," he said, "we'll see about that. And it had better be the truth, or else." His radio buzzed, and he took the call. He listened for a moment, then smiled sheepishly.

"Müller?" the shorter man asked.

"Yeah, Müller."

"North, you said?" the fat man said to Sarah.

"Yes, north," she confirmed.

"Except that our colleagues have found vehicle tracks going in a completely different direction, leading out into the desert."

"We've also driven in the other directions, of course."

"But to the north, the terrain is as smooth and clean as a baby's butt," said the fat man.

"We purposely covered those tracks."

"You're lucky that I don't hold a grudge," said the fat man. "Come on, Tanner, we're going."

"It was nice chatting with you," the shorter man said as he entered the airlock.

The fat man followed him without another word. Neither of them had put their helmets on yet. Sarah briefly considered bypassing the airlock controls and letting the two of them suffocate. But that would be murder and, almost worse, she would be lowering herself to their level.

"Hopefully, Ewa has already left," said Sharon.

Sarah faced her colleague and hugged her. She just now realized how much strength this visit had cost her. She was glad that she at least had Sharon here with her.

Sol 328, Mars City

IT WAS time for the next meeting in the fitness room. Again, the door seemed to be locked from the outside as if by magic. A man and a woman were standing at the weights. Lance didn't know either of them, but the woman looked slightly familiar. He must have seen her once at NASA.

She approached him. "I'm going to make this short and sweet. I'm Jean Warren."

Of course! She had made a name for herself at NASA for having manually coupled a passenger capsule with the space station after a complete failure of the electrical system at the station.

"I know you," said Lance.

"I was the captain of the *Spaceliner*," she said.

"That too, but I mean from your days at NASA."

"Oh, that." She laughed.

Now the man also approached. He looked slightly younger than Jean and introduced himself as Isaac McQuillen. "I'm a biologist," he said.

"Still?" asked Lance.

The man regarded him quizzically.

"Well, as an enemy of the administrator..." Lance said, the question evident in his inflection.

"Oh, Summers hasn't picked up on that so far," said Jean. "Isaac is our connection to the scientists."

"That's good," said Lance. "Where's Terran?"

"He couldn't come today. It wouldn't look right if he were to meet with you over and over again. And you should meet the rest of us anyway."

"I am glad to," said Lance. "Actually, I'm thrilled. You guys are giving me a bit of hope that we will solve this problem."

"It won't be that fast," said Isaac.

"One step at a time," said Jean. "Today, we are going to start with a different problem."

"The informant," said Lance.

"Exactly," said Jean. "We have prepared a little something. Your job would be to speak to each of the MfE guys and give them a piece of information."

"About what?"

"One of the storage rooms contains secret files on the conspirators."

"But how am I supposed to know that?"

"As a cleaner, you have access to everywhere. You will just tell them that you inadvertently found something that seemed strange to you. That should be enough."

"And what's supposed to happen then, Jean?"

"Of course, you will tell each of them a different storage room. We will observe the rooms. When that specific room gets inspected, we'll have our informant."

"I don't know," said Lance, "it feels... awkward. As if I were an informant too."

"I know what you mean," replied Isaac. "It's called a guilty conscience. The administrator is making us all do things we would otherwise never do. Just for that, he deserves to be removed."

"I hope this bit helps," said Lance.

"It will certainly bring us a step further. We need to know who we can trust."

"Man, I would put it all on the line for Andy and Theo."

"I'm sure I would feel the same," said Jean, "but you can't see inside their heads."

"No, I sure can't," said Lance. "When should I begin?"

"As soon as possible," answered the former captain. "We'll have our eyes on all five storage rooms starting immediately."

Sol 329, NASA Base

SARAH WAS SWEATING. It had been a long time since she'd last undertaken such a strenuous journey. She not only needed to cover the trek to the machine, but to do it in such a way that the artificial mountain shielded her from any possible Mars City spies. Sarah set off before sunrise after the two women had tossed a coin. Sharon would stay back and watch Michael, feeding him during the day with pumped breast-milk. Actually, Sarah hadn't wanted to take any risk that something might happen to her outside, which would result in Michael growing up without either of his parents, but today the prospect of getting out of the confining underground rooms and finally seeing the horizon again was simply too enticing.

The Mars landscape never bored her, despite its limited diversity. The light always changed in a peculiar and, for the human eye, unique way, which left her feeling like she was walking through a fairy-tale landscape she had never seen before. She would climb a dune to get a better view, or shimmy her way along the steep walls of a crater, and suddenly descend into the dark, icy-cold underworld of Hades. The pure black shadows thrown by the sun on the floor of the crater almost looked like the mirror image of an endlessly deep sea.

Sarah looked at her universal device. She was making good progress. Her day-after-day workouts at the base had obviously done some good, since she wasn't tired. On the small, central mountain of one of the craters, she paused and examined the mountain before her. She couldn't see anybody else's tracks climbing up it. She seemed safe from being discovered and quickly continued her journey.

THIRTY MINUTES LATER, she reached the foot of the artificial mountain. From here, it was a steep climb to the summit, and the mountain's slope made it immediately apparent that the mountain was not natural in origin. Or did she think this because she already knew its origin and wasn't just an unwitting observer? Cautiously, she walked to the left. She now needed to be very careful since there was a good chance she might run into the Mars City team. The fact that the thin atmosphere didn't carry much sound was both an advantage and a disadvantage. No one would hear her, but she also wouldn't have any audible warning of anyone else's presence.

In fact, it was almost too late when she spotted the first person. A man was climbing the mountain approximately 50 meters above her. Fortunately, he didn't look back, but kept moving forward. Sarah pressed herself against the rock to stay out of his field of vision. But where there was one, another person could very well be nearby. With each step she took, she scanned all around her to make sure no one could see her. Luckily, the next section was where the machine had churned up the ground. Large boulders covered the area. If she crouched down, she could easily hide behind them. She made it as far as their rover without being seen.

For a brief moment, she was tempted to steal the vehicle, but that wouldn't help anyone. She was only here to collect information, nothing more. Up ahead, at the foot of the mountain, where Ewa had bored that hole, she could make out four figures. She thought she recognized the fat guy and his shorter companion, but she didn't know the other two. The four had gathered inside the hole in the mountain, and were apparently discussing what the hole meant and what its purpose might have been. Unfortunately, Sarah couldn't hear what they were saying—until she remembered the frequency Ewa's helmet had always transmitted from. She was wearing one of the *Spaceliner* suits from Ewa. Perhaps she would be able to listen in on that frequency.

She programmed her universal device to the frequency and suddenly heard the men's voices as clearly as if they were standing right next to her.

"... a highly unique material," one of the men lectured. "It has a maximum reflection of 0.001 percent."

He must be a scientist, Sarah thought. *They were the only ones who would feel compelled to give such exact data. Instead of saying, 'a maximum of 0.001 percent,' a normal person would just say, 'it doesn't reflect at all.'*

"And what does that mean?" asked someone else. That must have been the fat man. Yes, she recognized his voice.

"I don't know yet. A material like this would be great to make an energy collector out of. Every beam of light that hit it would be stored. The tip-off about this mountain was a jackpot."

"But we'll need to mine the material. It seems pretty hard to me," the fat man replied.

"That's not my expertise," said the scientist.

"I don't completely agree. You were responsible for getting us here, Dr. Cline. Those were the administrator's orders, and there will be no shortcuts while I'm in charge."

"Pawlidis, don't intimidate the scientist. These people are very sensitive."

That was the voice of the shorter man. The fat one, who now also had a name, had called him Tanner before. The last of the foursome must have been Müller.

Pawlidis, Cline, Tanner, and Müller. Sarah tried to commit them to memory.

"Where did the tip about this machine come from," asked Müller.

"That's an open secret," said Tanner. "From that Italian lady."

"Tanner, shut up! That's a security department matter. Müller, go get the drill," the fat man ordered.

Ah, Pawlidis, Sarah added in her mind. *Sounds like a Greek name.* She had always imagined Greeks differently. Then she realized what Tanner had just revealed. An Italian woman had supposedly told the administrator about the machine? That could only have been Gabriella. The doctor! Sarah was dumbfounded. She needed to warn the others!

A tall, slender figure started to move toward the rover. She had to hide, but had no idea in which of the rover's compartments the drill was stowed. If Müller had to go around to the other side of the rover and she didn't change her position, he would discover her. But if she moved, the others would notice her. Sarah glanced around. About ten meters away, behind the rover, lay another large boulder. She checked to see whether her trajectory from here to there could be seen from the front. It couldn't. The boulder was her rescue. She ducked down, ran to it, and hid behind it.

"Phew." She inadvertently let out a sigh of relief once she was safely hidden.

"Is someone else here?" asked Müller. He moved toward her but then stopped.

"What's wrong, Müller?" asked the fat man.

"Didn't you hear that? I heard someone exhale loudly."

"I'm not sure," said Tanner.

"I am sure," said Müller. "Someone has linked into our channel, someone who is watching us out here. I think we need to activate the encryption. We should have done that right off the bat."

"There's no one else out here," said Tanner. "Who'd want to eavesdrop on us?"

"Müller's right," said Pawlidis, who was obviously the man in charge. "I don't really think anyone would be sitting here in the dust and watching our exciting probe, but better safe than sorry. Start the encryption."

The others obviously followed the fat man's instructions since Sarah could no longer hear their conversation. That was too bad. Now she couldn't find out what they were planning. Müller approached the rover. What if he searched the area? This would have been a good time for her to retreat, but Sarah stayed put.

Sarah burrowed a little deeper into the dirt, and she didn't care about getting dirty. Her main concern was keeping out of their sight, because she was sure that these guys would kill her without blinking an eye if they thought it justified.

She waited for five minutes. Müller must have reached the rover. She cautiously peered over the boulder that was providing her cover. Müller had his back to her. He opened a large compartment door and removed a device painted camouflage green. Without turning around, he carried it back to the others. In his wake, she moved back to the concealed side of the rover for a better look.

The four men took almost half an hour to set up the drill. Dr. Cline, the scientist, jumped wildly back and forth between the others, gesturing constantly, presumably because he thought the rest of them didn't know what they were doing. Finally, they succeeded in getting it set up. They gathered around the drilling spot and seemed to be waiting to see what would happen. Sarah already had an idea of what was coming. If what Ewa had said was true, the drill had no chance.

Sure enough, Tanner suddenly tipped backwards like a felled pine tree. The rest of the group were instantly kneeling beside him, apparently trying to help. It seemed that a piece of the drill had broken off and injured him. That meant that they would need to take him away.

It also meant that it was high time for her to disappear, which she did while the other three were focused on Tanner. Sarah calmly strolled to the mountain's edge and headed down the slope. She needed to speak with Sharon as soon as possible about how to inform their two fellow NASA officers in Mars City about the potential double agent.

Sol 329, Mars City

LANCE WAS NERVOUS. He had passed on the information yesterday as they had discussed. His cleaning schedule for today had coincidentally placed him near storage room 7, which was the number he had told Guillermo. Lance believed that he and Shashwat were the most likely to become spies for the administrator. After all, they were also the ones who had carried out Ewa's orders to use force if necessary to seize the Insight probe. The plan hadn't succeeded, but that was mainly due to Sarah's quick reaction. Anyone willing to aim a weapon at another astronaut might shoot with words as well.

Lance looked around and acted like he was looking for any dirty spots. Of course, everything was sparkling clean. He actually cleaned far too much, but the administrator had no other job for him. Plus, this would give him the opportunity to witness in person when...

The sound of boots on the floor came from behind him. Two men he didn't know were carrying a heavy motor. Lance held the door open for them, and they thanked him. Shortly after that, they left the storage room again. They really had been here just to drop off the motor. Then it was quiet again, except for the noise of the life support system.

He checked on storerooms 3 and 17. The objects that he had deposited there in seemingly random order were all still

143

in place. No one had been here to hunt for anything, not even to pick up a cleaning rag or shift a foot mat.

THE RESULTS that evening were clear. None of the five men passed on any information. It was also possible that they had seen through the plan, but Lance preferred to stick to the belief he had maintained the entire time. None of them was the spy for the administrator.

Sol 330, Syrtis Major

FOR THE PAST TWO DAYS, the journey had been a constant upward climb. That was good news. He was getting closer to his destination, which was located on the high plateau that stretched out before him. But the rover couldn't go as fast uphill. It looked as though this torture would be extended for one more day. Another problem was the increasingly deeper layer of dust, which, at especially steep spots, caused the rover's wheels to spin freely.

Much to his surprise, the idea of steering the vehicle while lying on his stomach had worked out very well. The cramp in his neck was much more bearable than the pain if he had sat on the open wounds on his backside. In the meantime, though, the skin on the front of his body was now also getting sore. If he could have been granted a wish, he would have chosen an immediate arrival.

Despite his pain, Walter's mood was overwhelmingly positive. He finally had the feeling that he was doing something useful, something that only he was able to do. Now that he had made it this far, he would be able to manage the remaining two or three days.

He double-checked the route on the navigational computer. The rover was recording a continuous file of their progress. Walter planned to transfer the route data to the autonomous robot. It was a sure shot, though occasionally there were sections that might have had more optimal alternatives. The satellite data, of which the rover also kept a record, were relatively less accurate because of the altitude. In these cases, Walter manually corrected the stored data so that the robot would be able to advance more easily. It drew its power from the sun, and for that reason, it was essential to use it efficiently.

Another blow to the stomach, right in his gut. Walter looked behind him. He had just missed spotting a chunk of rock the size of a soccer ball that protruded only about a quarter of the way out of the dust. Actually, it was about time to eat something. Due to the painkillers he had to take to keep his cancer symptoms under control, he had no appetite these days. And now that the end was in sight, it was difficult for him to find the motivation to sustain his body with energy intake, but it was necessary for a little while longer.

Luckily, he used to be huskier and, for that reason, he was still a long way off from looking like a skeleton. The remaining 72 hours without nourishment wouldn't do him any harm, but it would likely mean that he would quickly run out of strength. Reaching his destination but not being able to repair the robot was not an ideal situation. Walter used his lips to feel for the straw inside his helmet through which he could drink his food. Once he found it, he sucked on it a little at a time. The stuff was slimy and tasted somewhat bland, and in recent days he had developed an almost unbearable feeling of nausea. He was thankful he still had a supply of dry crackers for his evening and morning snacks.

THE TASTE of the liquid nutrients still lingered on his tongue as he watched the sun slowly sink toward the horizon. The sky was filled with dust again today. Walter could barely remember the last time he had seen a clear view of the sun. Perhaps it was because a stable western wind blew the dust from the plateau ahead of him down into the plain. In the west, the sky had already assumed its typical blue color. It wasn't the same blue as Earth's sky. It was much dirtier, and the sun was whiter than the yellowy-looking sun at home. Still, it reminded him much more of his home planet than the constant reddish-brown sky did. Walter followed the sun with his eyes. His body once more did what it wanted. A tear trickled down his cheek, even though he wasn't aware of feeling even slightly melancholy.

The sunset didn't linger as long here as it did on Earth. He would continue driving for another hour in the dark and then set up camp for the night.

Sol 330, Mars City

"Give Michael a great big kiss from his daddy."

Sarah held their son up close to the camera, and Lance blew him a kiss.

"Thank you," he said to Sarah, "and kudos for everything you do."

"By the way, I found a worm in a can of noodles yesterday," said Sarah.

"Aha," was all he could say before the time ran out and the screen went blank.

Lance immediately started thinking. Why had Sarah wasted their precious time together with such trivial news? Or was this piece of information simply more important to her than it was to him? Sarah was much more of a foodie than he was. Perhaps having a worm in the can was such a shock to her that she felt the need to tell him. He simply couldn't imagine it. And how could a worm even get into a sealed can of food? If it had gotten in there during production, it would have certainly gotten cooked and no longer be recognizable as a worm. And if it had gotten in there at any other time, that would mean that the can had a hole in it and its contents were no longer edible—whether it was one worm or multiple would make no difference.

He sighed. He urgently needed to check in with Mike

about this. His colleague from NASA and now close friend was the only person he could trust here. The members of the resistance group were still a mystery to him. Did they really mean it? Or were they just bored here on Mars and looking for some way to entertain themselves? He had met plenty of such people on Earth.

Lance left the communication room. The technician on duty wished him a good evening.

HE FOUND Mike in the bar located on the docked spaceship, which was now accessible by a subterranean tunnel. This meant you didn't need a spacesuit to get to it. The bar was open to everyone, and the prices were extremely affordable, at least for the half chemically, half biologically produced alcohol they made themselves. The administrator seemed to assume that drunken subjects were less likely to do dumb things. Lance had once asked the bartender how the alcohol was produced, but he had said that it was better not to know. Since bartenders usually had lots of life experience, Lance had decided to take his advice.

He ordered a double and clinked glasses with Mike. The bar was reasonably full, the noise from the others masking their conversation and eliminating the risk of eavesdroppers. It was hard enough to understand what the person speaking directly to you said amid the noise. How would anyone else secretly listen in? Any spy would need to be practically sitting on his lap.

They talked to each other in a normal fashion at first. Mike told him how much he missed Ellen. Even before all this, the two had rarely seen each other since Ellen had been hundreds of kilometers away, building up the MfE base. But now, this forced separation was proving very difficult for him. Lance then turned to Sarah's final words.

Mike sat up straight, cocked his head to the side, and

scratched his forehead. He looked so funny that Lance smacked him on the shoulder.

"Stop it! I'm trying to think," said Mike.

Lance left him alone like he asked, picked up his schnapps glass, and stared at the floor. He slowly rotated the glass in his hand and enjoyed the bright colors as it bent the light.

"Well, if you ask me...," said Mike, and then he stopped.

"Yes, I am asking you."

"... then I would say, the statement was a hint at something. There never was an actual worm."

"I had already gotten that far myself," said Lance. That wasn't quite true, but he had at least considered the possibility.

"A worm is something that disrupts something else," said Mike.

"Or something disgusting," added Lance.

"Yeah, and it can be found just about anywhere. There's the proverbial can of worms."

"Something that's gone wrong."

"Everything here has gone wrong," said Mike, "but Sarah doesn't mean that. We can all see it ourselves."

"You don't usually see the worm before opening the can," Lance suggested.

Mike rubbed his chin. "Yeah, something unknown hiding inside it. It must mean something that we don't see yet, but probably need to."

"Was she trying to warn us about an informant?" asked Lance.

"That might be. But why use this as the code word?"

"So that no one else will know what it might mean?"

"No, I think it was more of an encryption. She's trying to tell us who the worm is."

"From the way you say that, have you got a suspicion, Mike?"

"I'd start with the type of food she mentioned. It isn't just a can of noodles."

"You're right. A worm inside a can doesn't make any sense," said Lance.

"Exactly. And where do people like to eat noodles? In Italy," said Mike.

"So, Gabriella?"

"I'd guess that's who she means."

"Buddy, do you know what people in Bali or Cameroon or in the Philippines eat? Noodles, too! I was on vacation in Bali and had fried noodles there."

"Still, Italy is world-famous for its noodles," said Mike.

"Umm, don't you also have an Italian mother?"

Mike laughed and slapped him on the shoulder. "Nice play, but I am not spy material."

"Of course, that could be exactly your strong point. No one would ever think it was you."

"You don't really believe that do you, Lance?" Mike looked at him, his eyes narrowed.

"No. It was just a joke, don't worry. I just think we need to be careful not to make any snap judgements."

"And of Gabriella," said Mike.

"If she has switched sides, we will need to warn the other women at the MfE base."

"Right, Lance. We need to discuss it with the MfE men here."

Sol 332, Hellas Basin

THEY SPENT a long time debating whether or not they should cut across the Hellas Basin. Friday was against it for safety reasons. The name of the region conjured up false expectations. It was an impact crater, the second largest in the solar system. Thus the ground was fairly level. The walls of the crater reached nine kilometers at spots. In addition, the impact from approximately 3.7 billion years ago had created a two-meter tall ring of loose material surrounding the crater.

The alternative, namely driving around the basin, would have cost them too many days. But Ewa had to admit that this wasn't the main reason to insist on taking the direct route. The drive through the homogenous Mars landscape was incredibly dull, and the prospect of a view from inside the basin seemed to her like a nice change of pace.

The descent wasn't all that treacherous. Ewa had informed Friday at the outset about the crater's dimensions. A depth of nine kilometers sounded challenging, but these were spread out over a more horizontal incline of many kilometers. An uncharted mini crater of ten meters could pose a greater risk to the rover's computer than the consistent downward movement here.

In the meantime, they crossed the plain, which couldn't have been any less accurate of a description. The further south they traveled, the colder it became. That morning, the hills were covered with glittery carbon-dioxide snow caps, which remained intact for the rest of the day. Ewa was intrigued. Closer to the South Pole, there were supposedly areas where meters-thick layers of snow dominated the landscape.

The rover drove down a dune. Ewa had expected the wheels to sink, but the material was solid. In the distance, she saw a small hill lit orange by the sun. The horizon was flat, and the opposing cliffs were still very far away. Ewa deactivated the autopilot mode.

'Do you really have to do that?' asked Friday. He already knew the answer, but that still didn't keep him from asking the question over and over again.

She sometimes felt like Friday was the husband she had never had, who only wanted the best for her but who had no idea what she thought and felt. In this case, she wanted to floor it and tear down the dune, steering the rover with perfect precision around the sloping curves and holes of the crater which no human had ever touched before.

Sol 332, Syrtis Major

HE WAS ONLY two or three hours away from his destination, but Walter decided to set up camp one more time anyway. The necessary steps were so routine that his hands almost moved automatically. He ran his glove over the tent's thin fabric. Less than one millimeter of manmade material became the dividing line between life and death.

This was the last time he would use the tent. Since reaching the plain yesterday, he had made much better progress. The dark, basalt surface was almost dust-free. Any obstacles were easily seen from far off, and the rover's wheels gripped the ground much better. He patted the wheel housing. The vehicle would be making its way back without him. He had considered whether he should continue the last few kilometers to the Japanese probe today, but then decided against it. He wouldn't be able to carry out the necessary repairs in the dark anyway.

WALTER GROANED as he peeled his LCVG off his chafed body. It wasn't worth it to treat his wounds anymore, and he had already gotten used to the unpleasant smell after only three days. Today, he was going to treat himself to a feast. He had brought along a can of sour cherries from their food stocks, which he now opened cautiously with his pocket knife. He sniffed the open can. The contents were still good even though the cherries had been harvested over two years ago.

As he had read the words on the label, he simply couldn't resist taking them. His grandmother used to have a cherry tree in their garden behind the barn, a Morello cherry tree. His sister had spent practically her entire summer vacation up in the cherry tree next to the asparagus beds, but he never had any interest in it. Just the name alone! *Morello...* it had such a mysterious ring to it. And its fruit, which none of his friends ever wanted to eat raw, were all destined for him alone.

He drank some of the juice from the can, the acidity burning his throat, and then he fished out a cherry. The fruits were pitted and not as fresh as straight off the tree, but the taste was the same. Walter closed his eyes and returned to the shade of the barn, 40 years ago. Despite the noise from his suit's life support system, he could imagine the crickets chirping and the sparrows chattering as they tried to steal the cherries from the tree he heroically defended. They were the best cherries he had ever eaten, and they would also be his last.

All of a sudden, the small wooden door in the back wall of the barn opened, and his grandmother stepped out. She was wearing wooden shoes and a brightly colored apron. With one hand, she motioned him over to her. He stood next to her and leaned his head against her apron bow. He was a little boy. His grandmother stroked his head, and Walter wept.

Sol 332, MfE Base

THEO WROTE HER A MESSAGE.

Don't worry. They are taking good care of us here. There is so much to do that I hardly have any time to think. The city is growing by leaps and bounds! But sometimes, before I go to bed in the evenings, I think about our time together. Then I look at our pictures, like the one I have attached for you. It was in one of the subfolders on my universal device, and I am so happy I found it.

Rebecca opened the attached file on the screen. It was a group photo of the MfE crew. She was on the far left-hand of the picture. Theo was missing. He must have been the one who'd taken the picture. Marilou had a paper crown on her head. Rebecca remembered now. The photo must have been from her birthday party. They had at some point decided to convert their Earth birthdays to sols.

She examined her own face. From close up, she thought it almost looked like she was cross-eyed. And there was a sparkle in the corner of her right eye—a tear. Rebecca remembered more details. She had been thinking of all the birthday parties on Earth.

She moved on to the person standing next to her. It was Ellen, looking cool as always, with one arm around Rebecca's shoulders and the other one slung around Andy's. Andy was gazing at Ellen, not at the camera, as though he was in love with her. Except that they all knew that Ellen was seeing Mike, NASA Mike, the one who was with Theo, her Theo, forced to live in Mars City. Rebecca wiped a real tear from the corner of her eye. She didn't want to get sentimental right now.

Who else was in the picture? In the front row, she recognized Germaine, Marge, and Sophie, the French woman. Ketut, Guillermo, and Walter made up the row behind them. Shashwat stood alone in the third row. He looked distracted, and his eyes were focused past Ketut and Guillermo, beyond the camera's location. Why was he standing alone, way in the back? He was relatively tall, but would have fit in with the other three men in front of him. And where was Gabriella? She was also rather tall. Perhaps she had been standing next to Shashwat and had left the room briefly? But then why wouldn't Theo have waited with the photo? That was strange!

Rebecca looked through her own photo files. She had arranged everything chronologically. When was that party? She flipped back, sol before sol. From one day to the next, all the men had disappeared from her photos. There, it was Marilou's birthday. The paper crown on her head was proof. She had a number of pictures from the party. Gabriella also appeared in some, which meant that she hadn't been sick or anything.

Rebecca tried to see if she could find a picture taken from a similar perspective. She found a two-person portrait of Marge and Sophie where they were standing in front of the same wall. Marge's smile was a little forced. Sophie was holding her hand as though they were a couple. Why had she only just now noticed that? Maybe they really were a couple. Rebecca shook her head. If they wanted to keep it to themselves, that was their business.

The wall in front of which Sophie and Marge were standing was completely bare. Rebecca only recognized it from the boxes that were stacked there. She compared it to Theo's photo. Just then she realized that in the space between Guillermo's head on the left and Walter's on the right was a picture. It was a framed portrait of the administrator. That was impossible. The party took place long before the raid. Even today, no photo of the administrator hung there.

Theo must have implanted the portrait into the picture. But why? What was he trying to convey by doing that? It must have something to do with the person missing—Gabriella. Rebecca wiped the sweat from her forehead. Was Theo trying to tell her that Gabriella was secretly working with the administrator? What had Summers promised the doctor for that? At what price was she selling out her friends?

She had to calm down. Perhaps there was another interpretation for this photo montage. It was evident that a hidden message was embedded. She needed to talk with Ellen about it. Or was it better not to? Only a few days ago, she had questioned Ellen's loyalty for apparently possessing some background knowledge. What if Ellen really was a spy? It could be that Theo really was warning her about Gabriella, but that didn't automatically mean that Ellen was also trustworthy. The administrator could very well have two spies in place. He was more than capable of that. It would enable him to more efficiently keep track of what his spies were doing. All he would have needed to do was tell them that there was another spy among the ranks.

Rebecca closed all the image files and folders, and stood up. She first needed to think about all this. It was hard enough to accept that one of them had switched sides. She never would have guessed that any of them would've done that. They had such a long history together, so full of perils and challenges. That should have made their bond unbreakable. Rebecca would have trusted any of them with her life without a second thought. And that was something crucially important, since life on Mars was certainly no walk in the park. She had to be in a position where she could trust her friends.

She simply couldn't take Theo's message at face value. She needed to find out what it was behind it.

Sol 333, Syrtis Major

Sol 333. Sounds like a good day to die, Walter thought. At the same time, he also noticed something foreign in the plateau's crater-pocked landscape, something illuminated by the red sky. It must have been *Nozomi 2*. The chances that a second probe would have landed right around here were very low. Walter accelerated the rover. The entire trip was based on the fundamentally crazy idea that the last of the four autonomous robots remained tangled on the landing module, but was still fully functional.

The strange object gradually took shape. The landing module resembled a metal spider. It stood on six legs, and some sort of spike had been drilled into the ground beneath it. In fact, this had been an experiment to analyze the composition of the upper layers of the surface. Walter remembered this detail because JAXA had made history with it. Never before, and never since, had anyone penetrated any farther than 15 meters into the Mars surface.

As he got closer, the spider illusion faded away. Walter parked the rover a few steps away from it. From this perspective, the four-leaf-clover-like solar collectors were more noticeable and looked like insect wings on the clunky frame. He slipped up to the probe as quietly as he could so that he didn't scare it, feeling as if it might fly away. However, the probe didn't react. Not even when he touched one of its solar panels. Still, Walter stayed alert, so the exotic animal wouldn't fly off at any second.

He walked around the probe. On the back of it was an IDA, an Instrument Deployment Arm. Attached to its two front joints was an IDC, an Instrument Deployment Camera. It had taken the very famous photo which showed the last of the four robots, the one that had gotten hooked on one of the spider legs. And Walter saw his sacrificial journey had not been in vain. He put his hand to his heart. The robot was still at the same spot. He only needed to free it and set it into motion.

Walter took a deep breath. It was his last mission. There was nothing else for him to do, not in this world, nor in the one to come. He ran to the rover and pulled out the toolbox and diagnostic equipment before carrying them back to his patient. He still couldn't recall the robot's name.

He inspected its structure. The robot looked like someone had stuck several bicycle rims together concentrically but at all different angles. The result was a sphere without any defined sides. The spokes throughout the inside gave it stability. The outer material of the rims was springy—if the orb fell down a cliff, it would bounce. But because the shell of the sphere was partially open, it allowed the robot to also roll over uneven ground.

At its core was a motor with two axles, not especially robust, but durable. It was purely electrically powered. Highly efficient photoelectric cells on the exterior of the rims collected solar energy. The robot could roll through the nights and recharge itself during the days.

Walter immediately realized what the problem was with this one, which he christened 'Silver Rabbit.' One of the probe's six feet had a feeler on its front, some sort of measuring device, which had jammed itself inside the robot, preventing it from moving back and forth. The foot had blocked the robot from maneuvering itself out sideways.

If the probe could have simply retracted its foot, there

wouldn't have been any problems. It had five other legs to support it and wouldn't have tipped over. But the engineers hadn't foreseen this problem, and the extender mechanism only functioned in one direction. This and other similar issues were the final straws that tipped the scales toward sending humans to Mars.

For Walter, it was a win-win. He only needed to lift up *Nozomi 2*, and the robot would be able to free itself. But first, he would need to give it a good brain-scrubbing. If left to itself, Silver Rabbit would probably still follow its original research program instructions and explore Mars on its own. But that wasn't what Walter wanted it to do.

He set down his tool bag and searched for the programming and data bus. In wise foresight, the space agencies of the 2020s had begun establishing international interface standards. He found the port in the motor housing, pulled the connection cable from his diagnostic device, and attached it to the robot. Now, all he needed was a little patience. The robot's internal batteries were completely drained after such a long time—of course. The diagnostic device was providing some initial energy. That would enable Silver Rabbit's operational controls to boot up.

Walter counted to 60 in his head. Then he started over again from zero. He reached 40 when the one definitive light on the diagnostic device started to blink yellow.

Yes! It's working! thought Walter.

The robot's electrical circuits were still alive! Another two minutes, and the color of the LED switched from yellow to green. The robot's internal software's initial boot-up messages appeared on the display.

It turned out that its program memory was empty. The robot was as intelligent as a newborn baby, albeit one that could already walk, since its rolling action was stored in a nonerasable data unit. *Very good*, thought Walter. And, in an unimaginably lucky break for him, the robot had also forgotten that it was supposed to ask him for an access password. Obviously, no one could have foreseen that the robot would ever find itself in such a situation on Mars.

Walter didn't set any new password himself, either, because he wanted his friends at the base to have easy access to the robot. He copied the rover's control program over onto the robot as the language was independent of any specific hardware. Its memory had to be quite generous in size considering that it was meant to hold a large amount of data. Walter only needed to set the destination and the robot would be on its way.

He hesitated. As soon as he pushed the green button, his work would be finished—and his life with it. Walter didn't regret his decision. It had been right to give his ailing body one last, important task. He'd never wanted to watch himself miserably and painfully wasting away. It was too late to save him. His cancer was incurable. Perhaps he would have had a few more months ahead of him, but the drive into the wild Mars landscape alone was a generous tradeoff for the time he might have had left, disregarding this trip's difficulties and pain. 'Adventures are more important than hours.' That had always been his motto, even before the cancer.

Walter pushed the button. Two LEDs started blinking, and the robot gave a quick jerk. Walter laid the diagnostic device on the ground and lifted the probe up enough so that Silver Rabbit could free himself. As if the robot had been waiting for precisely this moment, it rolled far enough to the side to clear the entangling spike. Walter set *Nozomi 2* back down. He groaned as he did so, because even under Mars's gravitational pull, the probe was still quite heavy.

Silver Rabbit hesitated and Walter wondered what was making him hesitate. The robot rolled a little farther to the east and stopped again. What was wrong with him? Walter sighed as he picked up the diagnostic device and followed the robot. He hooked it up. Of course! The battery was still nearly empty. Before he was completely drained, the robot had decided to replenish its battery with solar energy. Very wise. He ought to have thought of that.

But what did it mean for him? Could he now resign? He observed Silver Rabbit. Everything seemed to function, but he could only be certain of that once he saw the machine roll away. It meant he had to stay alive for one more day. Walter caressed the robot. Then he turned around, walked back to the rover, and unpacked the tent.

Sol 334, Mars City

THEO ENTERED THE FITNESS ROOM. Who would he encounter here today? The network of people unhappy with the work of the administrator seemed incredibly large. Chad, whose last name he didn't know, seemed to actually have access to the bridge. Also, there appeared to be open resistance among the researchers. Their biggest grievance was that the administrator was hell-bent on pushing through his ludicrous notion of causing one of Mars's moons to crash into one of the planet's poles, which would release the carbon dioxide stored there into the atmosphere with that one single blow. As though that would bring them even one significant step further!

"Come in," Jean called.

The former commander stood next to the free weights, working her upper arms. She was obviously over 40 and didn't have a single ounce of excess fat on her. Theo admired the poise with which she served out her punishment. It didn't seem to bother her that she had been reduced to carrying out menial jobs. Maybe that was also normal for a person who had spent most of her life at the top. On the other hand, she must have had her reasons for devoting herself to this covert undertaking against the administrator.

Theo greeted her. "Are we alone?" he asked.

BRANDON Q. MORRIS

Jean nodded. "It's less conspicuous. I'm happy you're here."

Over the past few days, they had met in varying groups, usually of threes.

Theo went over and sat on the stationary bike and began to pedal. "Is anyone watching the door?" he asked.

"Not today, but there is an infrared sensor on the wall in the corridor that will warn us if someone's coming. It's nice to have access to the science lab."

Theo nodded. He needed to be careful not to bang his knees against the handlebars. The bike wasn't exactly the right size for his long legs.

"Any news from your guys' side?" asked Jean.

"I sent the photo. The idea with the portrait of the administrator was good."

"It wasn't mine," said Jean. "And how do you know that it worked?"

"Rebecca emailed me a picture, a selfie with Ellen. But Ellen definitely had Gabriella's features. They did a good job with that."

"Clever. I just hope they can do something with the information."

"It won't be easy," said Theo. "They can't let on that they know anything."

"I have an exciting new development to report from the bridge," said Jean.

"Oh, yeah?"

"The Chinese. You knew about the Chinese spaceship that was on its way here, right?"

Theo remembered. The ship had been christened *Long Journey 2*. It made contact around Sol 99, with six people on board. Since then, they had been silent. Everyone had assumed that something had happened to the ship.

"That was more than 200 Sols ago," he said. "Have they made contact again?"

"They haven't contacted us, but one of the survey telescopes on the Mars satellite discovered it."

168

"Is it confirmed as *Long Journey 2*?"

"From its course, it's unmistakable," Jean explained. "It is using a Hohmann transfer orbit from the direction of the Earth and heading directly for Mars. The ship weighs the same as *Long Journey 1*, and its hull is also made of metal, so what else could it be?"

"Understood. That really is a surprise. But, could a death ship be headed our way?"

"Death ship? Well... Since it was intended to stay on Mars for a few months, they would have more than enough resources on board to survive the long flight. Perhaps they've run out of fuel, or one of their engines has failed. At any rate, they were certainly traveling slower than they should've been."

"We'll soon find out if it's the engines."

"You mean because then they'll fly past Mars?"

"Yes, Jean."

"In that case, there certainly are alternatives. They could attempt to use the atmosphere to slow themselves down. But I also don't know what their ship can accommodate."

"That's true. The Chinese don't like to give out much information, do they?"

"That's how it is," said Jean. "We only know that the ship is an enhanced version of *Long Journey 1* and was supposed to land here shortly after NASA did."

Long Journey 1 was the Mars spaceship with which China had intended to win the race to Mars. However, the ship had broken apart as it left the Earth's atmosphere. At the time, the Chinese had claimed sabotage, but the rest of the world viewed that as a mere excuse.

Theo thought about what had happened to the *Santa Maria* around that time as well. Had they also been sabotaged? Was everything somehow connected? Perhaps the rest of the world should have believed the Chinese instead and aided them in investigating the cause. Except that the other nations were somewhat relieved that China had suffered a setback. For many of them, the Asian superpower had already become something of an overly domineering presence. Everyone was relieved to see NASA succeed instead.

"Has anyone tried to contact the ship?" asked Theo.

"According to our information, multiple times. Unsuccessfully."

"So, they're all dead?"

"Hard to say, Theo. Their communications system may have failed, or they might need to conserve energy. We will only know whether anyone's still alive once they attempt to enter into orbit and land."

"But that could also be done by the autopilot," said Theo.

"You're correct, but as long as they're not communicating with us, we'll have to wait and see once the hatch opens on their landing capsule and someone comes out—or not."

"I imagine the administrator will be very interested in the newcomers," said Theo.

"No doubt about that. He will do everything he can to be the first person there when they land," Jean declared.

"Then one of us needs to definitely be there as part of the welcoming committee."

"We will be."

Sol 334, Syrtis Major

THE SUN WARMED his wrist where it was touching the tent's outermost layer. Walter opened his eyes. The position of the sun told him it must be late. He felt very well rested, better than he had for a long time. Even his pain seemed to have subsided, but he wasn't going to give in to any illusions. There were no miracles.

Walter peeled himself out of his sleeping bag, peed into a urine bottle, and then ate some crackers for breakfast. Why hadn't he brought along two cans of cherries? He then pulled on his LCVG and his spacesuit on top of it. His skin hurt all over. He didn't count all the places where the scabs had ripped open. Or should he just put a quick end to it? All he would need to do was open the tent, and the suffering would be over shortly.

No, there was still some work waiting for him. He sealed his spacesuit, attached his helmet, and left the tent. After he stepped outside, he noticed the steam clouds that had formed outside the entrance. The breathable air inside the tent was obviously more humid. He walked to the east, where he had last seen the robot the day before, but it wasn't there anymore. Walter was disappointed, although he should have been happy. The robot had simply rolled away without saying goodbye. He was being foolish. Of course, it was good that Silver Rabbit was now on his way to the MfE base.

The rover was still where he had left it. He wouldn't be needing it anymore either. He stood next to the control panel and switched on the autonomous mode. Its destination was the MfE base. The rover could travel almost around the clock in autonomous mode and would reach the base by Sol 339. All he needed to do was press the start button—but Walter hesitated. Shouldn't he first pack up the tent and stow it in the storage compartment? And what about his suit? Couldn't his colleagues still use it after he died? He could strap himself into the rover and then open his helmet.

But what would he be doing to his friends with that? He should keep the suit. And he wouldn't send the tent back either. He rummaged through the rover's storage compartments and took out all the foodstuffs he thought he could carry along with the tent. He decided to slightly change his plans. There would be plenty of time to die later. He pressed the start button, and the rover set off on its trip back to the MfE base. Walter watched as it pulled farther and farther away. The vehicle quickly disappeared. It didn't leave so much as a cloud of dust behind it on the high plain.

Now he really was alone. It felt good. Would the mood last? And how would he feel when he ran out of air? Walter checked his universal device. Without the rover's fuel cells, which continuously produced oxygen, he was left to his suit's reserves. And that would last for approximately the next 48 hours.

He was going to make the best of them, he decided. He had no more goals he needed to achieve. Instead, he would casually stroll through the magnificent Mars landscape and take a break whenever he wanted. He would still have one, maybe two more nights inside his tent. Perhaps he could return to the garden in his dreams, to the Morello cherry tree behind the barn.

Walter bent over and packed up the tent before attaching it to his backpack, then he swung it all onto his back. The

MfE base lay to the east. He had headed west long enough. He now set off to the south, toward the equator. It supposedly got up to 20 degrees there during the day. As long as he held his breath, he could take his suit off. It would be the last time he felt the warm sun on his face and naked body, and then he would die.

Sol 334, Hellas Chaos

A VALLEY SPANNING east to west stretched out before them.
Ewa stopped the rover at the edge of the cliff. It was an image
of otherworldliness. The valley below her seemed to have
been sliced by a powerful water current. She could even make
out the river's arms. In the middle were a few smaller islands,
which may have been made of some harder material resistant
to the water's erosion. What was most fascinating, though,
was the fog rising above it. The sun was just beginning to
shine in the valley. Its warm rays melted the carbon dioxide
snow, which in turn caused the mist. It looked like something
straight out of a fairy tale.

THE SHOW WAS over 15 minutes later. Ewa flew down the cliff
in the rover while Friday protested. They reached the river
valley. Ewa was tempted to drive a few kilometers inside it.
She was having fun imagining she was on a ship. Then they
came to one of the islands they had seen from above. It was
not made of solid rock, but rather a pile of smaller rocks.
Perhaps a group of giants once took a vacation here and
made these little rock towers for fun.

Ewa laughed. The towers were proof that first impressions of Mars were often misleading. The valley had obviously been formed over many millions of years by the wind, not by running water. That was the only way those rock towers could have survived.

CLOUDS ROLLED IN LATER that afternoon. They were not the sort of mountainous clouds Ewa knew from Earth, but somewhat flatter, gray entities of lighter and darker gray stripes. Actually, she wasn't anywhere near the southern polar region, where such weather was to be expected, but the Hellas Basin was so deep that an area of low pressure always hung above it. Ewa leaned forward and put her forehead against the windshield to get a better view of the sky.

IT BEGAN to snow about two hours after sunset. Ewa barely noticed it at first, but then, in the beam of the rover's headlights, she saw a strange, thin mist slowly moving toward the ground. The flakes were tiny, and they didn't leave behind any wet marks on the glass. It was the same as when a snowflake landed on a hot stove. The crystals made of frozen carbon dioxide immediately transformed into their invisible gaseous state.

The snowfall increased. Ewa could see it, especially in the higher reflectivity of the headlights on the ground. She stopped the rover. She had to experience it for herself! She pulled on her spacesuit and skipped the usual quick round of aerobics before exiting, because she was afraid the snow might stop falling before she got outside. She discharged the air from the airlock and went through the hatch.

The short ladder on the outside of the rover was covered by a very thin layer of snow, but it wasn't slippery, which was the reason why crystallized carbon dioxide was also called dry snow. Ewa checked the temperature with her universal device.

It was an icy, minus 125 degrees. She had never experienced such a cold night on Mars before. How much colder would it be once she reached the South Pole?

Ewa stepped down onto the Mars surface. The snow crunched under the soles of her boots. She couldn't hear the sound transmitting through her external microphone. It was carried through the suit as impact sound. Ewa was taken aback. She wasn't afraid of the darkness, although she was far away from any other living soul. In the dark, Mars lost its character. Around her she could only see 10 or 15 meters of the desert. The sky was black, not one star could be seen. She could just as easily have been on Earth.

Slowly, she took a few steps into the desert, moving over a thin layer of fresh snow. She had expected it to crunch when she stepped on it, but it made no sound. The carbon dioxide sublimated instantaneously and left no trace. She looked around. Her boots had left clear footprints. If she used her flashlight much longer, the crystals would disappear, and the dark brown nighttime dust would be revealed. She looked at the display on her universal device. Minus 126. And winter was just beginning.

Sol 336, Utopia Planitia

SILVER RABBIT WAS able to orient himself from all sides simultaneously. He didn't know his own name, didn't call himself anything, and couldn't have shared it with anyone if he had. When he reached his destination, someone would give him a new name, but that didn't make any difference. He was a robot that was taking on its mission to explore the planet, many years behind schedule. Even now, he wasn't out and about as a free explorer as his AI had intended, but rather as a sort of messenger.

But none of that mattered to him. The robot had no emotional connection to his task. He felt neither joy nor excitement, just curiosity. He wanted to collect data; he was hungry for information. Maybe his programmers had wanted it like that. Or he'd been automatically 'born' that way. Humans and animals were born to live, and they fought for survival to the death. Silver Rabbit had been created to collect information, and that was his primary motivation.

The pattern of the terrain before him felt familiar. His pattern recognition had compared it with his master data and came to a strange result. *Honeycomb.* In front of him lay an area consisting of hexagonal craters, but instead of wax, his laser scanner revealed, they were filled with a mixture of dust and dry ice. If bees indeed lived inside, they would have to be many meters in length. Silver Rabbit simulated the flight of such bees in his processors. It was impossible. To take flight in the thin atmosphere here, one of these meters-large bees would have to have wings that were very light and as large as a hectare. Or the entire bee itself would need to exist of an altogether-unknown, incredibly lightweight material.

Silver Rabbit knew from the outset that musings of this kind were senseless. But since his reserves had the capacity for it, he could afford to devote some of them to such far-fetched notions. His programmers probably would have agreed that it wouldn't hurt anything, and sometimes even the most far-fetched of ideas resulted in practical solutions.

No, the honeycomb structures in front of him couldn't have been created by Martian bees. The planet's thin atmosphere had formed them. Scientists called it 'polygonal patterned ground,' and it resulted when dry ice and dust settled together and the dry ice then sublimated into its gaseous form during the summer. Occasionally, water ice could also be found in the mixture.

Silver Rabbit knew all this. If he wanted to successfully traverse Mars, he needed to know every possible structure he might run into. In this case, he also knew that the honey-combs didn't pose a threat to him. Their surfaces were sunken, as though the honey that used to be there had dried up. He rolled over the edge of one of the cells and let gravity pull him down, his own momentum swinging him partway up the other side. When he slowed, he had to engage his motor to reach the rim between this cell and the next one.

Once he was out of the cell, Silver Rabbit reoriented himself. The sun had fallen below the horizon, but his star finder enabled him to quickly find both Mars moons. He was on a good trajectory. The data he possessed wasn't the most current anymore—it was based on the time period when he was initially supposed to have fulfilled his mission on Mars, but he had used it to calculate a forecast for the coming days. The accuracy of these prognoses was typically close to 100 percent. He estimated that he would just barely miss his destination, and would have to cover the last part through visual analysis. That meant, as soon as he got close to his destination, he would have to switch from nighttime travel to day mode. Otherwise, he would just roll right past his destination during the hours of darkness.

Silver Rabbit used the planet's gravitational pull to help. It was a constant give and take. Once he was on the floor of the honeycomb cell, the rolling robot had reached maximum momentum which he then quickly traded with the planet for potential energy. Then he needed a little chemical energy from his battery cells to pool all his potential energy into motion at the highest point. He found the planet a trustworthy partner. It didn't mislead him with lateral winds, and although it put stones in his way, which he could roll around, it didn't set any traps for him.

The robot thought about its siblings, at least that's how it seemed, because even though he knew that their time had already long passed, he kept trying to coordinate with them through his radio transmitter. He called them, over and over again, because he'd been programmed to do that. His programmers couldn't have known that Silver Rabbit would enter his mission much later and utterly alone. These continuous and fruitless connection attempts used energy—energy that the program hadn't initially allowed for because, under normal circumstances, the other three robots would have answered him immediately. It wasn't much energy, but enough that the gap between his consumption and his reserves was gradually increasing.

The moment came, and that was now, when Silver Rabbit noticed that he couldn't reach his destination under these circumstances. He calculated whether it was better to stop. No, that wouldn't help him either. He needed to keep rolling while he searched for a solution.

Sol 337, Holmes Crater

THE ROVER WRESTLED with the edge of the crater. With its 120-kilometer diameter, the Holmes Crater belonged to the smaller of the topographical formations. The navigational computer had informed Ewa that she would make better progress if she took the easterly route around it. A section of the terrain was, however, especially rough. At about 10 kilometers, the rover needed to cross along a narrow ridge, because there was a smaller, but even deeper, unnamed crater directly adjacent to the east.

Since this morning, she had been able to see her destination on the horizon. It was a mountain unlike anything Ewa had ever seen before. The South Pole ice mass stuck to the planet like a monster-sized blob of bubble gum that had been stepped on by a giant. The horizon looked misshapen, and Ewa automatically tried rubbing her eyes to remove the obstacle.

Over billions of years, the ice and snow found at the Martian South Pole had grown into a mountain range resembling the shape of partially flattened bread dough, although towering many kilometers high. And somewhere in between, Friday presumed they might find the vestiges of its former inhabitants. If he was correct, how probable was it that they would be able to use the things left behind? Years ago, two old cars had been parked behind Ewa's family home. As a child, they had seemed to her like remnants from a different industrial age because of their old-fashioned look, when in reality they were only 30 years old. Still, they had been thoroughly rusted. What would three billion years have done to the technology of the planet's former inhabitants, no matter how advanced it was?

The rover gave her another good shaking. Ewa held on tightly to the armrests and admired the scenery. From the look of the crater to her left, it was undoubtedly the result of a meteorite collision and seemed relatively new. The typical protrusion in the center was still clearly recognizable. The rock that caused it must have fallen from directly above, since the crater was a perfect circle as best she could see. Its floor was covered with snow. The farther south she traveled, the more often she encountered snow-covered areas that survived the day's warmth if they were protected by the shade of the crater's walls. She assumed she would soon be driving over ice instead of the usual dust. Ewa needed to take into consideration that this would slow her down.

She looked to her right side through the hatch window. The Holmes Crater was so massive that it looked more like a valley. It also seemed quite old. The crater floor was at a noticeably higher altitude than that of the smaller crater to the left. It also had a structural pattern within it that resembled a network of ancient canals.

Ewa imagined how the manatee-like creatures inhabiting Mars had once farmed this area. Perhaps they'd used these canals as streets? Of course, she assumed, the creatures at the time lived primarily in the water, but at the same time they must have made productive use of the land. *Humans also make fish farms*, Ewa considered. *Made*, she immediately corrected herself.

Sol 337, Mars City

THIS TIME, Theo had a bad feeling. He wasn't a natural pessimist by any means, but everything was going too smoothly. They were never interrupted during their meetings in the fitness room. How did the little resistance group around ex-captain Jean Warren always manage to keep the coast clear? Were they getting a little help from above?

Naturally, there were two other fitness rooms on board the two *Spaceliner* ships. Out here, the desolate rooms below the Mars surface were the home of only those people with menial jobs. But even among this group, there were still plenty of people who supported the administrator. Theo had experienced it already in several conversations.

Summers was a master of the horse and carrot concept. He had even erected a small casino where the workers could rack up impressive winnings. Of course, there was nowhere for anyone to spend these winnings, but the administrator promised that would change. And the majority of them believed him, because their lives had improved remarkably since they landed.

Theo opened the door, took a step into the room, and looked around. Jean was standing on the treadmill. He was glad to see her because he liked her a lot. She hadn't let herself be corrupted. And, although she was only carrying out manual labor and was bored to death, she didn't seem bitter.

"Ah, it's you," he said.

"Sounds like you mean 'it's you again,'" she answered, smiling.

"I didn't mean it like that. But won't Summers get suspicious of us meeting so often?"

"He'll just assume we're having an affair."

Theo turned red. "Ah, yeah, right," he stammered.

"Would that be such a strange thing?" asked Jean.

"No, of course not." He forced himself to look her in the face and hold her gaze.

"Sorry, I didn't mean to embarrass you," said Jean. She started the treadmill.

Theo got on one of the stationary bikes and started to pedal. "Anything new?" he asked.

"Just a moment." Jean stopped the treadmill, got off, and strode over to the wall where her jacket hung on one of the hooks. She took something that looked like a tablet from an inside pocket. She brought the device over to Theo. "Look," she said, "this is camera footage from the bridge this morning."

Jean tapped on the screen, and Theo recognized the room full of monitors that was being filmed from an overhead angle. Three astronauts in *Spaceliner* uniforms were sitting at three separate, staggered tables.

"What have you got for me?" It was the administrator's voice. He was not in the camera frame.

"Summers," said Jean.

Theo nodded.

"Radar images from the probe," explained a female astronaut at the frontmost table.

"That's Maggie," Jean stated. "She's one of us."

Theo tried to see what the radar images showed, but the contents of the small screen were too hard to make out on Jean's even smaller tablet. Luckily, Maggie explained to the administrator what was there.

"*Long Journey* 2 looks to be in good shape externally. The ship is positioned counter to its direction of movement," she said while concentrating on her screen. "Oh," she exclaimed suddenly.

"What is it?" asked Summers.

"They activated the engines. That means the ship is decelerating."

"So, the Chinese are still alive?" asked the administrator.

"We are still not receiving any signs of life from them. The braking maneuver could have been programmed," Maggie explained.

Jean took her tablet out of Theo's hand. "Let me just fast forward a little," she said. She tapped on the screen and gave him the device back. On the central display on Maggie's table, a red circle moved from left to right.

"1,900 degrees," the astronaut commented.

"2,020 degrees."

"2,100 degrees."

"What can the ship withstand?" asked Summers.

"We don't know yet," Maggie answered. "If it's a normal design and aerobraking was included as part of the original concept, maybe 2,500."

"They are braking using the atmosphere," Theo commented as he watched the recording.

"Yes, and it must have been goddamn hot inside their ship," answered Jean.

"2,220 degrees," Maggie said in the video.

"2,350 degrees."

"2,470 degrees."

"If they don't abort soon, the atmosphere will fry them," Summers commented.

Was that schadenfreude he'd just heard in the administrator's voice? Theo scratched his chin.

"2,550 degrees," said Maggie, seemingly unaffected. "They can't abort. The maneuver has to finish as planned."

"And the end result is a Chinese stir fry, or what?" asked Summers.

"We don't know what the cabin can withstand," Maggie replied calmly. "But the braking maneuver is working. When this ordeal is finished, they'll enter orbit."

"Then we'll be getting a visit?" asked the administrator.

"We don't know," said Maggie. Theo admired her patience. "A Mars orbit is not the same as a landing. But—theoretically speaking—they could be here as soon as tomorrow."

Jean gently took the tablet from him. "That was the gist of it," she said. "The administrator is preparing an expedition to the landing site."

"But they don't even know yet when and where..." Theo's voice trailed off.

"Of course not. But for us, it's important that we know they will be needing two good rover drivers. One of their top two is—unfortunately—currently suffering from an acute upset stomach. It seems it was something he ate."

"Already? Isn't that a little too early?"

"Let's just say, he will be out for a while. We're keeping an eye on him. It means that you will be recruited as a replacement, Theo. The administrator has already been informed of your extensive rover expedition to the ice crater. He needs people like you."

"That's incredible news," said Theo. "I can finally get out of here for a little while!"

Sol 338, Flammarion Crater

HE WOULD FAIL to reach his destination by exactly 1.2 kilometers. His energy consumption was still too high, but he simply couldn't stop trying to contact his brothers. This routine was buried deep inside the layers of his operating system and was something his highly sophisticated operational processor could not access. He was aware of what he was doing wrong, but had no way to control it.

It was frustrating. Silver Rabbit was programmed to reach his destination. Coming an entire 1.2 kilometers short of that didn't meet the goal. He simply wasn't able to absorb enough energy from the sun during the day to make up for what he needed at night.

But the problem must be solvable. Silver Rabbit went through his defined conditions. The most crucial factor was the amount of time he spent in the daylight. Ahead of him lay the high wall of the Flammarion Crater. If there were anywhere he could find maximal sunlight, it was there. He decided to change his course. He had access to this data. He might reach his destination late, but he wasn't going to allow himself to fall more than a kilometer short.

Just before daybreak, he reached an optimal position at the edge of the crater. Silver Rabbit went to sleep.

Sol 340, MfE Base

THE WORLD JUMPED BACK and forth.

That was because the light on her helmet was bouncing in rhythm with her steps, and the small cutout view of the world she saw shifted in the same rhythm. In the surrounding area where the beam of her light didn't fall, it was dark. Whatever was there could just as easily not exist. There was no way for her to know, was there? Which of the old philosophers had said that?

Rebecca enjoyed these solitary walks. She deliberately set out long before sunrise. It was as dark as ever just before the sun started to ascend above the horizon. A dense layer of dust over her head filtered the light of the stars, as though their dim shine needed to be dimmed even more. She stopped and bent her head all the way back. The light on her helmet illuminated the cloud of dust. It seemed to be only three or four meters above her and was slowly falling, enveloping her, and burying her under zillions of dust particles.

Rebecca was not afraid of it. It was only an illusion that made her shiver in horror-show fashion. She would have enjoyed talking to Theo about it. He would have liked her idea, expanded on it, and added a few more horrors to it. They shared a similar sense of humor.

But he wasn't here.

She looked at her universal device. The screen's backlight wasn't working. She tapped on it a few times until it turned on. These old MfE suits were annoying. If only she had one of the modern *Spaceliner* models, too! The status display told her she had covered six kilometers and that the sun would be appearing in a few minutes. *For that, the sky is still pretty damn dark*, she thought. Rebecca turned around. The layer of dust must have been the reason there was no sign of the sunrise in the east.

She switched over to the map. At 150 meters to the west sat a small hill, maybe around 50 meters high. She turned and headed in that direction. The incline was surprisingly steep. *That's not fifty meters, it feels more like eighty*, she thought before she reached the top. By now, something was happening on the eastern horizon. The layer of dust was taking on a milky tinge. She felt as though she were standing at the bottom of a milk bottle, but, by some miracle, its contents were suspended just above her head, keeping her from drowning in it.

Something moved on the horizon. It was tiny and quick, and it was jumping. She thought of a gazelle chasing through the wilderness. A rover couldn't move that fast. Wasn't that the direction they assumed the Japanese probe to be, the one that Walter had wanted to find? Yes.

The perspective was deceptive. The moving object was closer than she had thought. It had to be about the size of a bicycle wheel, maybe a little bigger. Walter must have found the probe! It wouldn't be long now before he returned to the base himself. He would have sent the robot ahead.

Rebecca took a deep breath and ran down the hill, the beam on her headlamp dancing wildly. She estimated how fast the robot was moving. It rolled straight towards the MfE camp. Walter would have reprogrammed it, ordering it to go there. Rebecca picked which direction she should go to intersect its path.

However, she must have miscalculated. No, she realized, the robot was slowing down. She adjusted her angle, but the robot came to a halt one meter before the point she'd estimated their paths would cross. She walked up to it slowly, as though it were a wild animal that needed to be calmed.

"What are you doing out here all by yourself?" she asked.

Of course she got no answer, but the robot jerked slightly as if it were giving her a signal. She knelt down in front of it. It was a simple but intelligent construction with limited battery space. That must be the problem. When the sky was clouded by dust, like it was today, its photocells couldn't absorb enough energy, and its reserves wouldn't suffice. She tested her theory on the control module at the center of the sphere where a couple of lights and buttons were located. The lights were off, and none of the buttons reacted.

Rebecca stood up again. Out of curiosity, she tried to lift the robot by one of its feet. Thanks to the low gravitational pull on Mars, the robot wasn't heavy, but its spherical shape made it difficult to carry. Rebecca held it in front of her stomach and started walking. She needed a break every 200 meters or so. After the first kilometer, she tried to strap it to her back, but it was too bulky, and she didn't have any bungee cords along to help her. She sighed and continued as before. *Only 5 kilometers left to go.*

IT TOOK her an hour and a half to reach the base. Ellen had radioed her 30 minutes ago, concerned because Rebecca had said she was just going out for a short walk. So, everyone knew what she was bringing with her.

Ellen came out to meet her, and they carried the robot the last 500 meters together. That made it much easier. They set it down outside the airlock. It wasn't hard to get the robot into the chamber, and Ellen crawled in after it and sat down, rolling it onto her lap. This way, it would only take two steps

BRANDON Q. MORRIS

for them to enter the base with the robot. Everyone was waiting for them.

Rebecca was showered with questions but wasn't able to answer any of them. It had been pure chance that she'd found the robot.

"And what would have happened if you hadn't found it?" asked Marilou.

"Then it would have arrived tomorrow," said Rebecca.

Someone eventually found a connection cable and plugged the robot into the grid. The small light on its front panel began to blink. It took a little while for the robot's system to boot up.

"Wait. I'll try to connect it remotely to our network," said Ellen. She disappeared onto the bridge. The little lights soon stopped blinking frantically and began to blink in a steady rhythm. Ellen seemed to be having some success. She came back with a tablet, a diagnostic program already up on its screen.

"Did Walter leave us a message?" asked Rebecca.

Ellen tapped on the program's interface. She was so fast, it was obvious she knew how to use it. Nonetheless, it took a while and then she shook her head.

"No. It looks like the memory has been wiped clean. It only contains the route from Syrtis Major to us, nothing more. Sorry."

"How did Walter program the route?" asked Marilou.

"He would have simply transferred his log over to the robot," Ellen replied. "And then the robot rolled back the same way."

"Perhaps he'll be able to explain it to us himself soon," said Rebecca. "How long did it take him to get out there? You must be able to see that in the log."

Ellen tapped through a few menus. "Eleven sols," she said. "He reached the farthest distance from us on Sol 333."

"Then he ought to be here by Sol 344," Rebecca calculated. "In four days."

194

"We'll give him a proper welcome," Ellen promised.

"But what should we do with the robot?" Marilou asked.

"We could send it to our men as a secret messenger," Germaine suggested.

Rebecca chewed on her lower lip. Maybe she should have spoken to Ellen when they were alone. Gabriella was here. If she really was a spy for the administrator, there was no need for a secret messenger. But how was she supposed to explain that to the others without Gabriella getting wind of it? She looked at Ellen, who seemed to be waiting to make eye contact with her.

Ellen nodded subtly.

Good. Ellen seemed to have understood that she had a concern that had nothing to do with the others.

"Yes, that's a good idea," said Rebecca.

"Let's all take till tomorrow to think of something we could have the robot carry with it," said Ellen. "Then we can decide on what sounds like the best option. Gabriella, do you think you could put some medical supplies together?"

The doctor nodded.

"What's its carrying capacity?" asked Rebecca.

"Good question," Ellen replied. "We don't have a manual for it. We'll have to experiment. I would say no more than a kilogram."

Sweat ran down Rebecca's back. She'd already gotten enough exercise for the day, but she was bored. Not knowing what else to do, she'd gone back to the stationary bike and was pedaling as hard as she could.

"Everyone to the bridge, please," came over the loud-speaker.

What is it now? She wiped a few beads of sweat from her forehead. Maybe she had misheard it, or whatever it was would be over quickly.

"Everyone to the bridge."

It was the voice of the system's computer and was therefore to be taken seriously. Rebecca got off the bike. There was no time to shower, so she dried herself with a towel. As she left the fitness room, she threw the towel in the laundry basket.

The bridge was full. The room wasn't very large. Ellen stood at the central computer with her back to it. Two women were struggling to get their suits on. Rebecca couldn't tell who they were from behind. "What's going on?" she asked. Ellen turned and pushed her chair to the side so that Rebecca could look at the monitor. A set of headlights showed on the screen. "What is that?" she asked.

"Look more closely," said Ellen.

Rebecca stepped closer and wiped her eyes. It could have been a vehicle. Their rover? But that was impossible. Walter wasn't supposed to arrive for four days.

"Looks like a rover," said Rebecca.

"It is," confirmed Ellen. "It's our rover."

"But Walter can't be back already?"

"That's correct. Germaine and Nancy are getting themselves suited up to go out and have a look."

Have a look? Why was that even necessary? Shouldn't Walter already be in the airlock by now? He could tell them everything himself.

"Walter?" asked Rebecca.

"We don't know. The rover's empty. And it has no cabin. Walter must have tucked himself in one of the side compartments, but why would he do that? Germaine and Nancy will go out and look anyway."

"What does the rover's computer say?"

"The rover set off from Syrtis Major on Sol 334. It was able to drive during the nights, but not as fast as during daylight, for safety reasons," explained Ellen.

"No human passenger could ever withstand that."

"No, Rebecca."

"Maybe Walter fell out somewhere along the way?"

"According to the rover's computer, it didn't start for home with a passenger on board."

Rebecca swallowed hard. "Walter's not coming back," she declared.

"No," said Ellen. "It doesn't look like he is."

THEY WATCHED Germaine and Nancy in their old-fashioned MfE spacesuits as the two inspected the returned rover. The two of them opened each and every compartment, and even unscrewed the panels that covered the motors and generators. They wanted to be 100 percent sure they hadn't missed anything. But there was no sign of Walter. It was as though the rover had found its way back all by itself. The things the two women did find Ellen compared against the inventory list. They couldn't have known what Walter had secretly taken with him, but a few things were missing from their standard rover inventory. The most important object was certainly the tent, along with some of the technology that eased their survival on Mars.

"He kept the tent," said Ellen.

No one made any comment about it. It seemed like good news, but only at first. The tent wasn't sufficient for surviving out there. It didn't have a real life support system, and it was nowhere near as good at recycling air as the rover's closed cabin. It needed a fresh supply of oxygen regularly.

"How much O_2 did he have?" Rebecca asked.

Ellen tapped the screen again. "When the rover left for home, Walter had enough breathable air for three sols," she then said.

That means he must have died on Sol 337, Rebecca thought. She wiped a tear from the corner of her eye. She wasn't the only one.

"Germaine, Nancy, would you please come back in? You've done a good job," Ellen radioed to them.

On the screen, Rebecca watched the two of them finish

up and turn away from their task, their arms now hanging slack at their sides.

"Tomorrow at nine o'clock we will have a memorial for Walter," Ellen said, including Nancy and Germaine by radio.

A murmuring spread throughout the bridge, and they all retired to their rooms.

Sol 341, Mars City

It was wonderful to be outside again. Theo hadn't realized how much he had missed these vast spaces. Despite his height, the suit they had given him fit perfectly. It was expensive *Spaceliner* technology. He could yank up trees or pile rocks into mountains with it.

Theo was sitting in the driver's seat of the open rover. The navigational system was intuitive. The first thing he had done was to deactivate the autopilot. He didn't want to feel like a mere passenger. Behind him sat an armed man he didn't know, one of the security people. They were waiting as the Chinese spaceship finished its landing procedure. Everyone had calculated on a long drive out to the landing site, but *Long Journey 2*'s current trajectory revealed that it was going to come down near Mars City.

He hoped they would know soon precisely where that would be. Theo was itching to go. He loved the feeling of the vast Mars desert, of being far away from all civilization. He had already thought about giving the security guy at his back the slip. The guard was acting too self-confident for Theo's liking. He could steer the rover like a stubborn donkey, and the man would end up crashing quick as lightning to the ground.

However, the pleasure would only last a short time, even if

the man believed that what happened had been an accident. No, it would be better to keep his actual role in this game a secret. The fact that the Chinese ship's landing site was so close to Mars City strengthened the assumption that someone on board was still alive. After all, the Chinese crew couldn't have known the ultimate location of Mars City at the time of their launch from Earth, and Mars was too large for coincidences.

The crew had yet to make radio contact, but they must have realized that they could get the most assistance from the *Spaceliner* settlement. It was very likely that they needed help, that more than just their communications system was failing. Relatively little time had passed since entering orbit and the start of the landing procedure.

"Bridge to field team, can you hear me?"

It was time. Theo slid a little closer to the steering bar. "Rover 2 is ready to start," he said.

"We have calculated the landing site. It is located approximately fifteen kilometers to the east. We are sending the complete coordinates to your navigational system."

"Thank you, bridge. We are departing."

Theo glanced over his shoulder and nodded at the security guard, who nodded back before reaching for the armrest, a finger-thick rod that ran along the right side. Theo pulled up the coordinates on his screen. The computer offered him route guidance, but he declined it. With that, he turned the steering rod to the right and pressed the accelerator. He wanted to reach the landing site as quickly as possible. The second rover, the enclosed model, would be slower.

They tore off through the desert, leaving behind a trail of dust. The speedometer hovered around 22 km/h. Theo didn't pay any attention to the smaller rocks, though he dodged the larger ones. He didn't need to spare the tires since the rover would definitely hold together through the 45 minutes it would take them to reach the landing site. He careened down a crater wall as fast as he could. A small rise at the center of the crater caused the rover to sway briefly, but then they tore up the other wall back onto the surface.

The sun suddenly emerged. It had been concealed behind haze until now. It was a glorious sight. Maybe it was curious? After all, Mars was about to receive a few new residents who would soon be gazing at it year after year. *If I were the sun*, Theo thought, *I would want to know who was now landing within my kingdom*. Or would it not matter to him if the people watched him from a spaceship or from the planet's surface?

"BRIDGE TO FIELD TEAM, LANDING CONFIRMED."

"Rover 2, copy that," Theo replied. "The coordinates?"

"No new data," the voice from the bridge said. "They landed exactly where we calculated that they would."

"Thank you." Theo studied his monitor. "We will be there in ten minutes."

"Confirmed. Rover 1 will probably need an additional ten minutes."

Theo didn't reply. He made the snap decision to cover the distance in eight minutes instead of ten. The others could eat his dust. It had been ages since he'd had as much fun as he was having today.

A LOW, black object that didn't belong in the Mars landscape appeared on the horizon. Theo slowed down.

"Field Team Rover 2 to bridge, we have located the landed ship," he reported by radio.

"Approach cautiously to make a visual inspection."

"Gladly," Theo said.

He nodded at the guard, who understood the gesture and grabbed the armrest tightly once more.

Wise man, Theo thought. But he didn't resume maximum speed. Something was holding him back. He was reluctant to call it a premonition. That wouldn't have suited him. Facts counted, not feelings.

THIN WISPS of steam curled around the landed spaceship. It was an odd sight. *The ice or dry ice on the Mars surface was probably quickly recondensing after having been evaporated by the ship's high temperatures*, Theo thought. The ship itself resembled the NASA spaceship. It was less elegant than *Spaceliner* and considerably smaller. Several oval modules had been stacked one on top of the other. He could see that corridors ran between them, looking for all the world like the banding on a bee.

The entire structure was externally reinforced with metal struts, and it sat upright on a three-legged landing framework. The bottom module contained an airlock door at a height of about two meters. That was where the visitors should be coming out, any minute now.

Theo parked the rover, but nothing happened. Were they waiting for a little while, until the landing site cooled down? Or had the heat of the deceleration phase ultimately cost them their lives? That would be tragic irony—to have survived for so many months just to be killed during the orbit entry. He decided it was best not to speculate. The actual events would soon be known.

"Rover 2 to bridge, no one has exited yet. Should I knock on the airlock?"

"Negative, Rover 2. The specialists on Rover 1 will undertake a closer investigation. You will stay in reserve as the support team."

"Understood."

He turned the steering bar to the left. If he wasn't being allowed to check out the spaceship more closely, at least he could drive around it. It didn't look like it was completely symmetrical. The one side was almost black, and there was a metallic shine to the other side. On which of the two sides was the brake shield located?

"Rover 1 to Rover 2, can you see us?"

Theo looked over his shoulder. Yep, the enclosed rover was heading their way. "Confirmed," he said. "Should we do anything?"

"Thanks, boys, but we'll be fine. Just keep an eye out."

For what? Theo wondered. He kept this thought to himself. *What could happen?* But then he recalled his premonition. "Just my imagination," he muttered.

"What is?" the guard asked.

"Nothing."

Theo parked the rover in a location from which he had a good view of the ship. *It doesn't even really look like a ship,* he thought. Who had come up with the word *spaceship* after all? He strongly preferred *rocket,* but *Spaceliner* was the only one that could be described as such. The structure in front of them reminded him more of a primitive canoe. You could cross seas with it, but you couldn't be particularly proud of it.

The other rover approached *Long Journey 2.* What were they planning? "Rover 2 to Rover 1, please come in," Theo said.

"Yes, Rover 2?"

"If we should be watching things, wouldn't it make sense to include us in your radio communication?"

The voice on the other end didn't answer immediately. The man probably needed to consult with the person running the com system. "Sure," he said. "Good suggestion."

"... still no response."

Oh, they were already online. Theo's spirits lifted. At least things wouldn't be quite so boring now that he was in the loop. But, the Chinese crew seemed to still be incommunicado.

"You have authorization to implement the recovery according to Plan C."

What was Plan C? Plan A and Plan B seemed to have failed already. The enclosed rover came to a stop about two meters from the spaceship. A man in a spacesuit climbed out of it, carrying some kind of extension cord. He connected one end of it to the rover and the other to the ship. Obviously there was some kind of port on the lower part of the airlock. Cheers to international standards!

"Electrical connection now live," Rover 1 announced. "The voltage level is normal. Data transfer in progress. Starting diagnostics."

"No errors detected. Continue with Plan C," a voice replied.

One minute later, a full-height tube extended from Rover 1 and headed straight for the airlock. Aha, they assumed that someone on board was still alive, but unable to move. At least, they didn't want to run the risk of releasing the air on the ship if there was any chance someone on board was alive.

"Connector tube in place. Stable pressure established and checked."

"Thank you. Begin recovery operation."

Shit, now he wouldn't be able to see what was going on. Should he ask for access to the camera footage?

"Airlock opening. We are in the chamber."

"How is the air?" the bridge asked.

"Slightly dry, but breathable. The oxygen is at eighteen percent, the carbon dioxide is negligible."

That was strange. Either the Chinese had an especially efficient recycling system, or the air on board hadn't been breathed in a long time. That would mean that everyone was dead.

"Everything alright, bridge?"

The recovery team was apparently waiting on a green light. The bridge didn't reply.

"Sorry, boys. We had to discuss something briefly. What is

happening isn't one hundred percent in line with Plan C. This has made us suspicious."

"Abort?"

"No. We still don't see any danger. Just because something isn't the way we expected doesn't mean that we have to abort the mission immediately."

"Understood. We agree with that."

"So, proceed and open the inner airlock door."

Theo heard several squeaking sounds over the radio. The inner airlock door was apparently being opened with some force.

"We are inside. It's dark."

"Rover 1, can you turn on the light inside the ship?" the voice from the bridge asked.

"One moment, we'll have to check."

"Our team says thanks. That was fast!"

"Rover to recovery team, is the light on?"

"Yes, thank you!"

"We didn't do it."

"That's fine, too. We seem to be on their bridge. There's all sorts of computers in here and seats for three people, but nobody's here."

"Bridge to recovery team, there are three levels."

"Understood. We'll head upstairs."

"Good luck! We're watching via your helmet cameras."

The ship had landed without anyone sitting in the captain's chair? Theo shook his head slowly. Of course, the computer could handle the navigation, but it would be doubtful that none of the crew would want to watch! Or were the Chinese crew members simply hiding in one of the other modules? There had been instances of temporary space insanity on long voyages before.

"Okay. There should be some kind of workshop on the second floor, as well as a kitchen. It smells like something burned up here, but everything is clean."

"Then all that's left is the upper module."

"Yes, bridge. We're standing at the ladder already."

Silence fell for a moment, followed by a loud, metallic clang.

"Sorry, the hatch swung down our way, but everything's fine."

"Alright, recovery team. Proceed."

"We... shit. We've found them. They're all dead. Six people in four beds. It looks like four men and two women, although they all look very similar."

What did the man mean by similar? Did all Asians look alike to him?

"We can see it from the camera footage," the voice from the bridge said. "The crew is extremely dehydrated, completely desiccated."

"This is... awful," the man from the recovery team said. "Sorry, Nigel had to go back. He was about to be sick. There's only the two of us here now."

"We don't detect an imminent threat. At least, the six crew members don't represent one, so keep going. However, we need to make one request of you."

"I can already guess what that is."

"Yes, you have to bring one of the corpses with you. We need to run an autopsy on them. Or wait, it will be enough if you transport one into the rover. We'll send a forensics team out to you. Until we know more about what happened, we shouldn't bring the bodies into the base."

"Got it. What a disaster. I'm under quarantine now, too, right? My wife's birthday is the day after tomorrow."

"Yes, Sam, sorry about that. But as long as the cause of death is uncertain, you will have to stay outside the base. Don't worry, though, the life support system probably failed, and they all simply suffocated. From the video footage, it doesn't look like there are any signs of sickness."

"That's comforting."

"I'm sorry about that, but Mars City's safety comes first. Could you now take one of the corpses over to the rover?"

"Sure... We'll get on that now. Any preference? Man or woman?"

"Doesn't matter. Whatever looks the easiest for you."

"José thinks he could carry all six of them since they're so light. The dehydration combined with Mars's gravity—"

"No, one will suffice."

"Copy that, bridge. José is carrying one of the women. We're now leaving this 'hospitable' place."

Theo visualized the six bodies. They were probably wearing thin uniforms. But why were there six people in four beds? That wasn't how things had been at the time of launch. What tragedy had occurred?

"Recovery team to bridge. We have reached the rover and are now disconnecting the airlock tube."

"Proceed, Rover 1."

Theo watched as the airlock tube twitched. It looked funny, as if someone had stuck their finger onto an ice-cold spot and couldn't pull it free. *What's going on?*

"Um, Rover 1 to bridge, the tube doesn't want to cooperate."

"Doesn't *want to?*"

"The computer isn't responding. It simply won't detach. It's almost as if the ship doesn't want to give it back."

"Stay calm. Have you tried from the other side?"

"But then we'd lose the tube."

"Nonsense. It would just remain attached. Rover 2 could recover it."

"Of course. Sorry. We'll manually disconnect it from inside. Do we need our suits for that?"

"No, you can operate the clamps mechanically from inside. It would be unfortunate if you first had to exit the rover to do that."

"Sorry, I should have thought of that."

"No problem, Sam. You've just discovered six corpses. That would rattle anyone."

The tube slid down the outer wall of the enclosed rover and landed on the ground. Theo drove closer and waved at the security guard. They would load the tube onto their vehicle. At least some good would come from him being there.

"Rover 1 to bridge, we have a small problem."

Theo heard someone coughing in the background.

"What's wrong, Rover 1?"

"The oxygen level in the cabin is sinking rapidly. There must be a leak somewhere."

"Immediately into your suits!"

"I... we... Nigel is completely undressed. He's vomited everywhere and is very woozy. He... It all went too fast for him."

"Sam, leave Nigel. You have to seal your own suit. That is the most important thing. Bridge to Rover 2, can you help them?"

Theo leapt out of his seat and ran over to the other rover, the guard at his heels. But the cabin was sealed. They couldn't access it from the outside since there was no airlock. If they opened the hatch, all the air would rush out of the rover.

"Rover 2 to bridge, there's nothing we can do," Theo shouted into his radio. The guard placed a hand on his shoulder.

"Sam," a voice cried from the bridge. "What's going on? How are you doing?"

"I... made it. I'm wearing my suit, but Nigel didn't make it. I tried to do CPR with his mask but he didn't show any response."

"And José?"

"José? I don't know. He's leaning against the wall. José? José? Say something, please!"

"His suit isn't showing any values. Is he wearing it?"

"Yes, he has it on."

"Then he's dead."

"Shit! What did this?"

"We don't know, Sam, but we will find out."

The enclosed rover slowly started moving. The electrical cord that connected it to the Chinese ship popped out of the connector box. The rover dragged the plug behind it.

"Rover 2 to bridge, do you see that? Rover 1 is departing. It is heading toward Mars City. Did you do that?"

"No, we had nothing to do with it. Sam, did you start up the rover? We understand that you want to get home, but we can't let you inside with the body on board, at least not until the cause of death has been determined."

"No, bridge. I didn't do it. The rover is moving entirely on its own."

Sol 341, Promethei Planum

THE ROVER'S ENGINE SCREECHED. It sounded like a howl of pain. Ewa stopped the vehicle instantly. Friday was right. Just this morning, he had advised attaching the snow chains to the tires. This would slow their rate of progress, but it would certainly beat getting stuck in the ice.

The plateau across which they were driving reminded Ewa of an ice desert, but it had nothing in common with the snowy world of the Arctic on Earth. Underneath the rover, the ice wasn't anything like the water ice they knew, instead it was dry ice. The layer was three to four meters thick, according to the radar. Ewa was glad that it wasn't thicker, as must be the case in deep winter. Their drive at this point was not as dangerous. On Earth, cracks in the ice presented the most significant risk, but here the rover itself could prove to be a problem, primarily whenever the outside temperatures wavered around the point when the dry ice might suddenly vaporize, sublimate.

The major danger was tied to the energy given off by the rover, which could cause the solid ice layer underneath them to disappear. Worst case scenario, they would sink to the actual surface level in a matter of mere minutes. It wouldn't be impossible for them to get out of the ice hole, but the length of time this would require would depend on the depth of their fall. The ice layer wasn't universally treacherous since in spots it was stabilized by impurities formed by dust and much more stable water ice, which first melted around zero degrees. But they would eventually reach a point after which it would be best for them not to stop until they reached their destination.

Ewa closed her eyes and listened. Was the rover already sliding downward, slipping into a hole? Nothing happened. The vehicle seemed to be sitting on a safe spot. She got ready to leave the rover.

THE SNOW CHAINS were stored in a compartment below the toolbox. NASA had apparently thought of everything. Or had they made an expedition to one of the poles as part of their research program? How would Mike respond if she asked about that? The Age of Innocence, during which the four NASA astronauts had viewed themselves as temporary visitors on a new world, was long over. Ewa unscrewed the storage compartment cover. It was secured at several spots. Exactly two chains were lying in the compartment. They looked just like the ones made to put on car tires, only much larger to fit the significantly bigger tires on the rover. They were intended for use on just the front tires. Enclosed in plastic, the mounting instructions were fastened to the side wall of the compartment. Ewa studied them. The mounting really was similar to the procedure for cars. She recalled a drive she had once taken from San Francisco, over the mountains. She had been by herself in a self-driving car when the computer's voice had asked for her assistance. She had hesitated at first because she was too lightly clothed for the outside chill. But if she hadn't agreed, the car would have been forced to turn around. So she had agreed to the request, while the computer had explained what to do through the open passenger window.

Ewa first stretched the chains out in front of the vehicle.

This surface, on which no human had ever walked, felt strange. She stepped down firmly with her boot. The material felt brittle, though also porous. It called to mind a sponge. She then drove the rover over the chains, to the middle of their length, and fastened the chains around the top of the tires.

A few tiny clumps of snow were stuck to the wheel. They seemed to have been pressed together by the tire tread. Ewa shined her flashlight on them. The clumps dissolved into the air as if they had never been there. It was crazy. Things here were never as they seemed. She needed to stay alert. The higher she went, the more surprises the terrain would have for her.

Sol 341, Mars City

"Bridge to Rover 2, you have to stop your colleagues."

"Understood," Theo replied.

"Hold on tight, buddy," he said into his helmet radio. He should have asked the guard's name a long time ago. In emergencies, it was always good to be able to communicate quickly.

The distance between them and the enclosed rover was about a hundred meters. He could easily overtake them. But after that?

Thanks to its construction, the other vehicle was at least three times as heavy. His open rover was comprised almost exclusively of its chassis, while the other one was hauling an entire life support system around with it. What happened in those old action flicks? Did the motorcycles ever manage to stop the semis? Their roles were reversed! He should be the one running away from the other rover.

Theo sped up and quickly caught up to the other vehicle. Should he try to ram their opponent? Obviously, the collision would end badly for his rover. He shouldn't jump the gun on this. There was enough time.

"Bridge to Rover 2, do not get too close to Mars City. We can't run the risk of contaminating the settlement."

The people at the base were getting on his nerves. They

should tell him how he could get the heavy rover to come to a stop! Why should he risk his life for this? The vehicle couldn't present that much of a danger. Horror films were the only places in which infections killed off people lightning fast and then lurked in wait for new victims. Maybe he should just act as if he were earnestly trying to do what they were asking. He could graze Rover 1 over and over again at a flat angle. His vehicle would definitely be able to handle that.

"Bridge to Rover 2, if your vehicles cross the city's protection boundary, we will deploy antitank missiles."

They had brought military-grade weapons to Mars? That couldn't be true! Transporting them up into space alone was a violation of the UN Convention. Or was this a bluff? Theo knew the impact of missiles like that. He instantly let up on the gas. He would have to create enough distance between them and the other rover if he wanted to survive this.

"Bridge to Rover 2, I was speaking in the plural. If you don't fulfill your task, you will also become a target."

The guard in the back seat tightened his grip on Theo's shoulder.

"Yeah, buddy, I understood," Theo said. "They're serious about this. Do you want to get out?"

"My name's Pierre," the man said with a slight accent.

"Canadian?"

"Yes, exactly. If I get out now, that would be the end for me, so keep trying to run the other rover down."

"All right, Pierre. I'll think of something, and we'll both come through this."

"Thanks. My wife would appreciate it."

So would Rebecca, Theo thought. He accelerated until he again drew even with the other vehicle. How could you stop something that was significantly heavier than you yourself were? Could a horse make an elephant tip over? He studied the other vehicle. It was staying close to the ground. While his own vehicle seemed to get airborne with every little bump in the ground, their opponent seemed to be stuck to the surface.

But the other rover also appeared to have a weakness—its

weight distribution. Most of its mass was concentrated in the cab which was situated about three meters above the chassis. Of course, the enclosed rover had short legs, but it still might be possible to destabilize it. All Theo needed was for its center of gravity to lift off the surface.

He thought through the conditions. He didn't know the precise weight distribution situation, but he did know where the heavy life support tanks were sitting and where the batteries and fuel cells were mounted. The chassis and cab were replaceable, so all the heavy components were located at least one and a half meters above the surface. If he could manage to get the enclosed rover into a 30-degree slope, he might succeed in his effort. But what would happen to Sam, who was probably the only survivor from the recovery team?

"Rover 2 to bridge, what is going on with Sam on Rover 1? Can he do anything?"

"Sam is no longer responding. There seems to be some problem with the com system. You are the only ones who can rescue him at this point."

Thanks a lot, Theo thought. If he could knock the rover over, its only living occupant would be put in danger. He was supposed to put three human lives at risk just because some idiot on the bridge was having a panic attack over a couple of dead bodies? Theo shook his head. If he refused to do this, he would place those three lives—his own included—in even greater danger.

He glanced over at the navigational monitor and pulled up the map. A relatively fresh crater, no more than a few thousand years old, was located about a kilometer away. Its walls weren't eroded yet. It wasn't located directly on the route to Mars City, but perhaps he could force the other rover to make a little detour. Who was sitting at the steering wheel at this point? If it was Sam, he would probably figure out his intentions and swerve to the other side. It didn't matter though. He would have to try.

"Hold tight, Pierre," he said. He then wrenched the steering bar hard. The curve was so tight that the one side of the rover momentarily left the ground. Nonetheless, he managed to cut right in front of the other rover, causing it to steer off to the left—toward the crater. Theo then dropped back a short distance from his opponent to check out their new course. Ha! It had worked. The heavy rover wasn't trying to return to the old route, but was heading straight toward Mars City from its new position. As a result, Theo now had a chance to implement his plan.

He repeated the maneuver. Success again! Then once more. The crater was practically located in their path now. Why hadn't the driver in the enclosed rover noticed what he was doing? Was Sam not acquainted with the vehicle's schematics, or had he simply overlooked the crater? He hoped this would continue. Theo checked the map. There were only two other craters along the route to Mars City, but both of them seemed too large for his plan. He needed steep crater walls that hadn't yet been seriously chewed on by the teeth of time.

"Hold on tight, Pierre," he again warned the guard. It was time for his last maneuver. He floored it, passed the other rover, and cut it off with an audacious jerk of the steering handle. Shit. The nose of Rover 1 nailed their vehicle in the side.

Pierre screamed.

Theo didn't turn around. The other rover must have shattered Pierre's leg, but he couldn't focus on that right now. The heavy rover shoved them through the Mars dust, churning up a lot of dirt in the process. The visibility dropped rapidly. He had to get their vehicle safely out of the way! He attempted to do this with a couple of sharp turns of the handle. Whenever he wrenched it to the right, the man behind him groaned over the helmet radio. *I'm sorry, Pierre, but otherwise you'll die*, Theo thought. He yanked the handle to the left, pressed the accelerator, and they were finally free. *That was damned close!* he thought.

"I... need a doctor," Pierre groaned.

"I know, but I have to save our lives first," Theo said.

He wiped the dust from his visor, then roughly cleaned the screen. The crater was right in front of them. The maneuver had probably cost Pierre his leg, but the maneuver hadn't been in vain. The heavy rover was still heading straight toward Mars City—but it would now have to cross the crater to do that. This was their chance. Theo drove his vehicle along the edge of the crater. The distance might be greater along here, but he was still faster.

The critical moment was now upon them. Would the enclosed rover choose to make a detour in order to avoid crossing the crater? No, and from a navigational perspective, this would be a logical decision, since the rover's chassis could easily handle the slope. On the other hand, they would have to hurry if they wanted to chase down their opponent. Theo ducked. It was an instinctive movement, though he wouldn't reduce the wind resistance by doing that. They absolutely had to be the first ones to reach the crater's exit point.

"Heads up!" he warned Pierre.

The heavy rover was completely inside the crater. He couldn't see it at the moment, but a flashing light on the monitor indicated its location. Theo steered right for the spot where the other rover would have to start its climb out of the crater. He estimated that the crater wall at that point had a slope of almost 40 degrees, and it should be covered in gravel, which would reduce the traction that the rover's wheels could achieve. It would come down to the right moment.

He needed to increase the momentum he brought with him to the point at which the effect would be optimal. Theo sped toward the spot where the other rover should appear at any moment. This had to work. If he slowed down, he would lose valuable force. Had he calculated everything correctly? Ten meters, five meters, three—he then caught sight of the heavy rover coming up from below. It looked good! The other vehicle was relatively slow.

He aimed for its right front corner. Metal met metal. "Yahoooo!" he shouted.

Sparks flew in total silence. The heavy rover veered to the

left. Yes, that was what had to happen. It had to turn perpendicular to the tilt since the gravitational force didn't leave it any other choice, but Theo couldn't see what was happening since his own vehicle was now spinning to the right. The momentum was so strong that their chassis couldn't keep up. The rover skidded through the sand until one of its tires slammed into a boulder, which caused the rover to instantly tip over. Theo instinctively thought to grab onto something, but he knew that he shouldn't do that. Otherwise he would be buried under the vehicle. *I should have told Pierre what to do*, he thought as he flew through the air.

Something hit him in the back. No, that was actually him crashing into the Mars surface. A stabbing pain radiated from his neck. *Anything but paraplegia!* And what had happened to the other rover? Had his plan worked? Was Pierre still alive?

Theo tried to raise his head, but then he passed out.

Sol 341, MfE Base

"Do you have the gun?" Ellen asked quietly.

"Here it is," Rebecca whispered. "I packed it up unloaded, but the ammunition is with it."

"How much of it?"

"Sixty rounds. The package would've been too heavy if I'd packed more."

"Good. We don't want them to start a civil war. They should just feel a low-grade potential threat."

Rebecca wasn't sure if this was such a good idea, but Ellen had convinced her to go along with it. Without alerting Gabriella, they had agreed to meet at four o'clock in the workshop to limit the number of people who knew that they were sending out the robot.

"I'm still not totally comfortable with this," Rebecca said.

"We have run through everything thoroughly. There's no better argument than a loaded gun."

"But they outnumber us."

"Exactly, Rebecca, exactly!"

Ellen held out her hand, and Rebecca handed her the package. The contents were no longer recognizable under the thick layers of packing tape. Ellen shoved the package through the numerous spokes and pushed it into the core of the robot, around the hub.

"Can you give me the duct tape?" she asked.

"If we attach it like that, the robot will no longer be balanced," Rebecca said. "It won't be able to run smoothly."

"We have to take that risk. I think it's stable enough," Ellen replied. "All it needs to do is make a one-way trip to Mars City."

"I hope you're right," Rebecca said. She cut a piece of duct tape from the roll and handed it to Ellen. Inside the perfectly designed interior body of the robot, the package looked like an ugly wart.

"It isn't exactly subtle," Rebecca remarked.

"That way they won't have to search long for our message," Ellen said.

"The main thing is that the robot cannot fall into the wrong hands."

"We'll have to send good instructions."

Rebecca sighed. The robot would stop outside the Mars City limits and wait until it was picked up. She needed to transmit the precise coordinates to Theo and the other men —but how?

REBECCA KNEADED HER HANDS. Ellen was taking longer than expected. The funeral for Walter was supposed to begin in fifteen minutes, and Ellen still hadn't returned from the surface. Why was it taking so long for her to activate the robot and send it on its way?

Someone tapped her on the shoulder. Rebecca flinched.

It was Germaine. "What's going on?" she asked. "Are you waiting for someone?"

"Me?"

"Yeah, you—you're the only one here." Germaine laughed.

"I... I'm supposed to meet with Ellen to discuss something about the funeral."

"And... where is she?"

"She told me that she wanted to take a quick walk."

"Makes sense," Germaine said. "Have fun waiting. See you in a few minutes."

Rebecca nodded, then noticed that the airlock had been activated. The signal light glowed red indicating that someone had entered it from the outside. It was high time.

FIVE MINUTES LATER, Ellen was peeling off her spacesuit right next to the airlock. She was sweating profusely. After getting out of the suit, she also removed her liquid-cooling underwear. Rebecca couldn't help feeling a stab of jealousy at the sight of her athletic figure.

"I'm sorry. There was a little problem with the robot," Ellen explained.

"What happened?"

"I could turn it on, but it didn't want to roll away."

Rebecca slapped her forehead. "Of course, its recharging cycle. It charges during the day and drives around at night."

"Exactly. We charged it up, but it didn't care."

"So it's still sitting up there?"

"I dragged it out of the base," Ellen whispered. "We'll act as if it's already set off."

"Okay."

"Sorry, but I need to take a quick shower. Tell the others that we'll start the funeral ten minutes late."

"Alright, I'll do that."

"YOU DID WHAT?" Germaine was staring at Rebecca with raised eyebrows. The others were whispering among themselves—except for Gabriella, who was sitting stiffly on a stool.

"We sent the robot off already," Rebecca said.

"Why did you do that on your own?" Germaine asked. "Why'd you shut us out of your plans?"

"Yes, I'm wondering the same thing," Gabriella added.

Great, Rebecca thought. And Ellen was nowhere in sight. How was she supposed to explain that they might have a spy in their midst? She couldn't do that. She would have to lie like a trooper.

"Neither of us could sleep, and we just happened to run into each other in the kitchen. We decided to make good use of the time."

"Exactly," Ellen chimed in.

Rebecca turned around. Ellen must have just entered the bridge through the door behind her. She was wearing her MfE uniform, just like everyone else.

Germaine still looked dissatisfied. Gabriella pressed her lips together. Maybe she had guessed the actual reason. They needed to be more careful. The administrator had probably already been warned and would be searching for the robot.

"I suggest that we turn our attention to the actual reason for our gathering," Ellen said.

"I think... oh, forget it," Germaine said. "We'll continue with this later on. Walter has earned our full attention."

"Thank you, Germaine," Ellen said. "Would anyone like to say something about Walter?"

Nobody spoke up.

Ellen ambled across the bridge before sitting down against a wall and crossing her legs. "That's fine," she said. "I know what you're feeling. You don't think that you really knew Walter, and at first glance, that's true. After all, he never talked about himself much. He was an engineer, through and through."

Rebecca smiled. That was indeed true. Walter had tried to solve every problem from a technical approach and had been astonishingly successful in his efforts. It was just that he hadn't always noticed that a solution was even required. For him, sometimes problems existed merely for their own sake.

"But that," Ellen continued, "says a lot about Walter. He expressed himself through his actions, through his practical knowledge. That was exactly who he was, and it brought him joy. We don't need to analyze him. If we can hold him in our memories as an ever-helpful person and friend, then he will feel like we understood him."

The bridge grew quiet. Even the life support system seemed subdued. Each of the eight women had taken a seat in a different pose. Rebecca studied one after the other. Was it coincidence, or did their manner of sitting reflect something about their characters? Rebecca was sitting with her knees together. Her mother had always told her to not spread her legs when sitting. That it wasn't appropriate. She still maintained this practice although her mother had died years ago. Or was that perhaps the reason?

It felt strange to think about Walter. There was nothing they could say farewell to. For her, he was gone, not dead. He wouldn't be coming back, but it didn't feel to her as if he were irretrievably lost. It was an odd kind of purgatory.

"Thank you, Walter," Germaine said.

That was a good idea. Walter had sent them the wheeled robot. One final act of generosity.

"Thank you, Walter," Rebecca replied.

Each of the others repeated the statement. Sophie held her hands up to her face and wept. Tears trickled down Marilou's cheeks. Rebecca didn't feel sad. In some strange way, she felt happy for Walter, who had deliberately chosen his final path.

Sol 342, Mars City

"THEO? THEO?"

Someone was calling his name, and a warm hand stroked his cheek. *Rebecca? Please, let it be Rebecca.* All of this was just a stupid dream, and he would wake up any minute on the MfE base.

He opened his eyes and gazed into a nondescript face. Pale bluish-green eyes, facial stubble, and a receding hairline. The man leaning over him didn't seem to have any other special characteristics. How old was he? Forty? Fifty? The hint of a seemingly unnatural smile played around his lips.

"Here he is, our hero."

Theo recognized the voice. It was Rick Summers, the administrator. He had seen him several times, but he wouldn't have recognized him. However, the voice was unmistakable. There was something silky about it, and yet you could tell that there was an intent driving it. What did the administrator want out here? And where were they actually?

A hand grasped his lower arm. He looked the other way.

A woman was bending down beside him. She was of Asian extraction and was smiling. The smile was warm and sincere. "I'm Maggie Oh," she said.

Ah, the leadership ranks had gathered around his bed. Maggie was the bridge manager now that her skills as a pilot were no longer needed. Had they brought him back to the base? Like the administrator, Maggie was wearing a spacesuit, however without a helmet.

"I wanted to thank you personally," the administrator said. "You have saved us from a potentially serious threat."

"How is Pierre doing?" Theo asked.

"Pierre?" The administrator shrugged. "I don't know that name."

"The guard we sent out with Theo," Maggie clarified.

"Oh, of course. Unfortunately, Pierre didn't make it. The rover landed on his helmet and cracked it."

"Oh no!" Theo cried. He had killed him. If he hadn't executed that risky maneuver, Pierre would still be alive. The man had only just told him his name right before that. They hadn't had time to become friends, and they might never have reached that point. But he had still told Theo about his wife.

"It was a swift death," the administrator said, patting Theo's cheek. Maggie tightened her grip on his arm.

"Did he have any kids?" Theo asked.

The administrator glanced over at Maggie. "No," she said.

"He didn't have any children," Summers reiterated.

Theo's spirits lifted a little bit, even though he still felt guilty. He turned his head to the side. They weren't in the city. They were inside a rover. Theo couldn't feel any vibrations, which meant that the vehicle was parked. "Where are we, and how long was I out?" he asked.

"You were asleep for ten hours. We're located close to the accident site. After we saw your maneuver and its effect, we immediately sent out an aid vehicle," the administrator explained proudly.

"What happened to Sam?"

Summers glanced at Maggie.

Doesn't he know anyone's name here? Theo wondered.

"We haven't heard anything from him," Maggie said.

"That doesn't sound good," Theo replied.

"It doesn't have to mean anything," Maggie explained.

"We just haven't checked out his rover. The cab on their vehicle wasn't damaged in the impact. He still has breathable air and water."

"And two corpses."

"Yes, the two dead members of the recovery team. We will figure out what happened," Maggie said.

"Absolutely" the administrator said. "Humans' lives are irreplaceable here. Every loss tears a huge hole in our plans. We're lucky we didn't lose any women."

What is Summers saying? I must have misheard.

"Don't look at me like that, Kowalski. If humanity is going to survive here, it must grow in size. And for that, we are reliant on birth rates. Until men can bear children, women are more strategically important."

Now it was clear to him why the administrator wasn't married. The rumor mill had long speculated that he was gay. Theo shook his head. "May I stand up?" he asked.

"Of course," Maggie replied. "According to the medic, all you have are a few scrapes and bruises. We couldn't X-ray you here, unfortunately, so on the off chance that he missed something and you feel any sharp pains, speak up."

"Will do," Theo said. He reached for the edges of the cot, as the administrator and Maggie stepped back. Theo pulled himself up into a sitting position before swinging his legs to the left side of the bed. That worked well. No pain, just a light veil before his eyes. His circulation needed to warm up again.

He put his feet on the floor, first the left one, then the right. *Shit. Something must have happened to my right leg.* He gritted his teeth and stood up. A stabbing pain shot from his hip down his inner thigh to the knee. The medic had said that nothing was broken, so he trusted himself to put weight on it. He just needed to move around some. His body would get used to the pain. It was probably just a bruise.

Theo took several steps. The stabs of pain didn't fade, but they also didn't grow stronger. "And what happens next?" he asked.

"We are going to try to establish contact with the rover that took off on its own," Maggie explained.

"Contact? I assume that nobody there is responding?"

"Not by radio, but we've run a cable between our two vehicles."

A cold shiver ran down Theo's spine. *Is that a good idea?*

"We're being careful," Maggie declared.

Obviously his shock was visible. Whatever had seized control of the vehicle must still be in there.

"Nothing will happen," she continued. "The rover is lying securely on its side and can't right itself on its own. And we won't open the hatch until we know more details about what happened."

The hatch, Theo thought. *Is that really the greatest threat?* Everyone seemed to believe that some kind of infection had killed the Chinese. That would be a natural explanation for whatever had occurred on Earth as well. But the infection must have sped around the entire world lightning fast. Was that even medically possible?

"The cable," Theo said. "Has it been secured?"

"Of course, but that probably isn't the problem. The rover isn't letting us into its system. Our technicians are still trying to break into it."

"But shouldn't that be child's play? It's your own technology, after all."

"Not completely. There's a firewall between us and the rover, and we haven't breached it yet. Probably some kind of Chinese technology. But shortly before you woke up, the technicians informed us that we are close to a breakthrough."

"That's good," Theo said, although he wasn't at all sure if it might not be more advisable to fear the breakthrough. He then remembered Andy, their IT genius. "If you stall out, you should contact Andy."

"Maggie? Can you come here?" a man called from the nose of the rover. The former pilot turned around and moved toward the front, Theo right behind her.

"The computer's going crazy," the technician, a young man of about 23, declared.

Theo studied the monitor. Everything looked normal, but despite the fact the technician wasn't moving his fingers, windows on the screen kept opening and closing. Had the Chinese security software somehow taken control? Theo reached for Maggie's arm and pulled her multi-functional device toward him. She pulled her arm away from him, but he was stronger.

"What are you doing, Theo?" she asked in annoyance.

He held her arm up so she could see her small screen. "The oxygen content in the air. Look."

Her eyes widened, and Theo released her hand. "Seventeen percent," she said. It was enough, but still less than usual. That was how things had started in the other rover.

Theo glanced around. Two *Spaceliner* suits were hanging on the wall. The administrator and Maggie were already wearing theirs. The three technicians and he himself were not. But he must have had one on when they found him, right? Theo stooped down. Where had they put his suit? The two of them on the wall were brand new and clean. Under the cot! A dusty boot was sticking out. He pulled on it. This was his suit! Of course, he wasn't wearing an LCVG, but that didn't matter. Better to freeze than to suffocate. He quickly pulled the lower part on.

The administrator had apparently also realized what was going on.

"Out of here, immediately," he commanded. "Or whatever happened to Sam will happen to us, too."

The conclusion was logical. But there was one problem—they were short one suit. When Summers opened the hatch, one of them would die. Theo didn't want to be that person, so he hurried to close up the top part of his suit. Where was his helmet? Hopefully, it hadn't been damaged. He leaned back down. It wasn't underneath the cot. He crawled around the floor. A new sharp pain shot through his thigh. There was his helmet! He pulled it out of a niche. The special glass was dirty and now exhibited several scratches, but it didn't have any cracks.

"Attention, in sixty seconds, I will open the hatch. We can't wait any longer than that," the administrator warned.

Whoever didn't have their helmet closed by that point would die. The two spacesuits were no longer hanging on the wall. The young programmer was wearing one of them, while a middle-aged man and woman were fighting over the other one. The administrator pulled a device out of his pocket and aimed it at the man.

"Sorry about this," Summers said as he pushed a button. The device hummed and shot several needles at the man, who fell to the ground twitching.

"Thank you, administrator," the woman said.

"Forty-five seconds," Summers replied coldly.

The woman yanked the suit out of the man's fingers. Maggie hurried over to her to help her get dressed. It was almost impossible to get a suit on correctly in less than a minute.

The administrator stepped over to the hatch. The rover didn't have an airlock. When Summers opened the hatch, all the breathable air would instantly escape. Maggie was tending to the technician. Theo frantically tried to figure out how to keep the unconscious man from dying, but there were no options. Even if he found a replacement mask through which he could share his air, it wouldn't be enough. The air pressure outside was too low, and the temperature was ice cold.

There was only one course of action. He must prevent the administrator from opening the hatch.

Theo turned toward Summers, who raised his weapon.

"I know what you're thinking, Kowalski. But that would be foolish. I understand that you don't want the poor man to die, but if we don't leave the cabin, we will all die. Think about Sam in the other rover."

"We don't know what has happened to Sam. He might still be alive."

Summers laughed. "How naive are you really? If that was

the case, the man would have radioed in a long time ago and come out of the vehicle. The hatch can be mechanically opened from the inside. Nobody could prevent that. No, we have to get out of here."

The administrator was an asshole, but the worst part was that he was probably right. They needed to leave the cabin as quickly as possible. Theo could guess what was coming next, and he had hardly concluded this thought when the suspicion became a reality. The rover started moving.

"Maggie?" Theo called.

The former pilot turned around. "We're ready," she said.

The other woman had just closed her helmet. The visor was beaded up with moisture. She was obviously sweating heavily.

Then he felt a force that wanted to drag him out of the rover. Theo shut his helmet.

Summers had opened the hatch. The administrator was the first one to abandon the slowly accelerating rover. Theo watched as he deftly rolled away in the sand. The young programmer followed him.

Theo waved at Maggie and the other technician. "Go, go!" he urged over his helmet radio.

Maggie let the other woman go first, then jumped out herself. The technician landed clumsily on her knees. That must have been painful. Maggie did several somersaults before flopping out on her back.

It's time! The rover had just reached about 15 km/h and was picking up speed. What would his hip say to this? Theo jumped. He landed on his right leg, a throbbing pain, then he rolled to the side and finally came to a stop, sprawled out and breathing heavily, in the red sand.

Someone grabbed his arm. "Come on, I'll help you." It was the administrator. Theo recognized Summers' face behind the transparent visor. He let the other man help him to his feet. The amplifiers in the legs of his suit really did work great.

"Are we going after it?" he asked.

Summers shook his head. "We won't be able to catch it. The security team from the city will take care of it."

"They'll have to shoot it down," Theo said. "Whatever has taken over the navigation can't be allowed to reach the city."

"Did you honestly believe we had antitank missiles on board? The UN never would have approved us for those." Summers chuckled quietly.

Theo felt a sudden urge to slap himself. Yes, he had believed him. Who would ever think that a threat like that was a bluff? "At this point, I wish you really had missiles," Theo said.

"Sorry about that, but keep your chin up, young man. The security team will take care of the rover."

"And what will happen to us?"

"I'm in contact with the bridge. Someone will pick us up as soon as the problem has been resolved."

"We could just walk," Theo said. He attempted to take a few steps. The pain was stronger than before. Something was wrong with his right hip. Three hours through the desert didn't exactly sound all that appealing.

"It is a fairly long hike," Summers declared. "And I have a much better idea. Let's investigate the crashed rover."

Swell. It would be better to keep our distance from that thing.

"Maggie, could you come here please?" the administrator asked via his helmet radio.

The pilot waved and trudged down the hill with the technician and the programmer in tow.

"So, my plan is simple. We will open the rover's hatch and see what happened in there," the administrator said.

"Who do you mean by *we*?" Maggie asked.

"We need a programmer who can check out the computer. What is your name, young man?"

"Ahmed."

"Oh, I had no idea you had Arabic roots. In that case, Ahmed, you need to figure out what happened to the computer. My friend Theo here," he placed a hand on Theo's shoulder, "would be glad to help you with that."

Theo took a step to the side, causing the administrator's hand to slip off of him. However, the suggestion was a good one because he had a problem that Summers didn't know about. In his hurry to get off the other rover, Theo had left his LCVG behind. This meant he was at risk of freezing to death in the Mars chill. His suit's life support system was already running at its max. It wasn't designed to do all the work. If he could stay in the cab of the other rover, the wait would go a little easier.

"Alright, then let's get to work," he said.

"I'm going, too," Maggie interjected.

"No, that isn't necessary," the administrator said.

"I'm going," the pilot repeated.

Summers sighed. "Okay, then go. I can't prevent you anyway."

"I'm going, too," the technician spoke up.

Theo smiled. Obviously, nobody was anxious to spend time alone with the administrator. Facing potentially life-threatening danger and several mysteriously deceased people inside the rover was clearly the lesser of two evils.

"I'll wait here," the administrator declared.

It must be equally clear to him how little people enjoy his company, Theo thought. He felt a pang of regret, but remembered how coldly the man had dispatched the male technician. Or had it been a completely logical action? Only one of them could have survived, either the man or the woman. Nonetheless, Theo still wouldn't have been able to make the decision about their fates.

MAGGIE WAS the first one to reach the crashed rover. "There's a small problem," she announced over the radio.

Theo saw what she meant when he reached the rim of the crater. The rover's nose was pointing downhill, and its chassis was facing toward him, turned on its side. If they wanted to reach the hatch, they would have to set the vehicle right side up again. But then, it might set off again, and his entire effort would be in vain. Or was everything pointless, since the other rover would soon reach Mars City?

"We have to lift it up," said the programmer, Ahmed.

"But in such a way that it won't just get back up on its wheels and drive off," the technician added.

Of course, Theo thought, *if it drives off, they won't be able to inspect it. It makes total sense.* Had his brain been addled more than he had thought?

"There are four of us," Maggie said. "And we're wearing amplified suits. It should be easier than you think."

"Three of us," Theo revised. "The person who boards the rover won't be able to help lift."

"Right."

Theo limped down the crater wall and arrived at the rover last.

"And who's going in?" Ahmed asked.

"The one who asks," Theo replied.

"It would make sense for you to go, Theo," Maggie said. "Your hip. You won't be able to lift as well as the three of us."

Perfect. He clenched his hands into fists, but said nothing. He was mainly annoyed because Maggie was right. To lift the rover, they all had to lean down. He tried to bend forward a little, but a pain instantly shot through his hip. "Alright," he said. "Just clear the way for me."

"At my command," Maggie said.

All three of them leaned down.

"One... two... three."

Theo heard three voices groan over his radio link. These were the only sounds. *How heavy is the rover? Was it three tons? Five?* He could no longer recall the exact statistics. Regardless, the vehicle was slowly lifted upward.

"Theo, you're up," Maggie said.

The rover was now almost horizontal. There was enough

room for Theo to reach the hatch. He crawled underneath it, ignoring his painful hip.

"Hurry up and open it," Ahmed croaked.

Smart ass. Theo spun the wheel as quickly as he could. The hatch door was already falling toward him. He waited for a second to see if anything else was going to plunge his way. A black hole gaped above him. What might be hiding up there? He expected at least three corpses, maybe four if Sam had also suffocated. What were the other men's names? All he could remember was José, the man who had carried one of the women's bodies from the spaceship to the rover. And what if the rover tried to kill him, too?

"Theo, get in!" Maggie called.

He climbed inside. "I'm in," he reported.

"Thanks. Watch out!"

Theo heard a few snuffling sounds, then the floor beneath him tipped away. His three colleagues had lowered the rover back to the surface. Theo tilted to the side. He reached into the space around him and encountered something soft. It didn't provide him with a stable handhold, so he ended up pulling it with him and falling half a meter until he crashed into the outer wall

The soft object fell on top of him. Theo was glad that he hadn't had time to switch on his helmet lamp. His sense of touch told him that a dead person was lying on top of him. He took a deep breath and steeled himself for what he was about to see. He then turned on his light.

It wasn't quite as bad as he was expecting. Was that because of the spacesuit? Theo knew that he was crouched next to a dead body. Encased in the suit's silvery material, it looked more like some technical object, almost like a large doll. He just needed to avoid looking into the visor, which was fortunately turned away from him. It had to be either Sam or José.

"Are you still there, Theo?"

Thank goodness the radio link was still up. Theo had been afraid that something inside the rover might block the connection. But then he realized that this was bad news for Sam. If there weren't any technical obstacles in terms of the communication system, then Sam hadn't been physically able to radio in.

"Sam has to be dead," he said.

"Have you checked out the body?" Maggie asked.

"No, but it's logical. He could have radioed in at any time."

"Maggie's right," the administrator cut in. "We need more data. We have to know why this happened."

"I'm supposed to get the body out of its suit?"

"Yes, Theo. Examine it."

Theo sighed. Why had he agreed to any of this? Back when he and Ewa had examined the damaged dragon module, he had been glad when she volunteered to check out the bodies. He didn't have the stomach to deal with corpses like that. The images of them haunted him.

He stood up and flashed his light across the space. On its side, the interior of the rover cabin looked strange, almost like an extraterrestrial spaceship. He was just waiting for a slimy monster to spring down on him from the ceiling. Why was it so dark, and where was the light switch? Theo glanced around. There should be a switch close to the hatch. He pulled himself up a short distance and pressed the one he found there. The lights below him flickered on. The scene looked spooky, but nothing seemed unusual. The ceiling was below him, the floor above him—he had to keep that in mind.

But why had the light been turned off? The simplest explanation was that during the race across the surface, something had flown against the switch. Easy explanations were good explanations. He didn't think much of vehicles that started driving themselves for no apparent reason. Perhaps it had been a chain of unfortunate events. The sudden failure of the life support system, then one of the dead crew members had perhaps collapsed onto the computer panel and activated an automatic course adjustment toward home. Who knew? It was possible. The computer panel should provide more information about this.

"Any findings yet?"

Summers was getting on his nerves. Fine, the computer would have to wait. He pulled the suit with the dead astronaut inside to a spot where it was well lit. It was Sam, at least that was the name on the lapel. Theo opened the helmet and forced himself to look inside it. The man's eyes were wide open. His skin was hard. He seemed to have frozen solid. Theo was glad that he was wearing a suit himself. The material in his gloves shielded his hands.

He glanced at his universal device. It was minus 25 degrees. The heating system in here must have turned off quite a while ago. Theo had an idea. He reached for Sam's right arm. His universal device was turned off. Theo restarted it by pressing on three corners of the small screen. It took almost a minute, but then he saw that the suit still had sufficient energy and resources in it. Someone must have shut it down, deliberately that is. This was what had killed Sam. But who had done that?

"Sam's suit was shut down completely. That was why he suffocated," Theo explained.

"But why didn't he restart it? That wouldn't have taken long," Ahmed replied.

"Yes, I just did that. No problems there," Theo said.

He gazed into Sam's face. Incomprehension was the primary sentiment being expressed by the latter's broken gaze. The man hadn't understood what was happening to him. Or was that a projection? Theo patted his cheeks. Sam's skin was now warming up, but it was too late. He should turn the suit back off again. Theo repeated the gesture on the universal device, and the suit shut down again.

He felt cold. It wasn't much warmer in here than it was outside. He was definitely missing his LCVG. If push came to shove, he could always try to remove Sam's warming subsuit. No. Hopefully, he wouldn't reach the point of having to put on a corpse's underwear.

"Thanks, Theo, but Sam isn't the only one in there who died a bizarre death."

"Yes, Administrator."

He pushed the suit holding Sam aside. José, the third member of the recovery crew, and the dead female Chinese astronaut. This was his death roll. He just needed to get through it. After this, he would hopefully never need to examine another dead body as long as he lived.

The second bullet point on his list was quickly checked off. The unknown man was standing on his head on the floor, which was actually the ceiling, forming a bridge of sorts. At the moment of his death, the man must have been sitting in a corner of the space and been frozen in this position. Theo tipped him over, and the body slowly fell to the side. His eyes were also open, and he gazed forward in astonishment, his mouth wide open. Was that typical when someone died of suffocation?

"I found the man from the recovery team," Theo said. "He would have suffocated. Looks completely normal otherwise. He isn't wearing a suit. Do you know his name, Administrator?"

"I don't. He must have been caught unawares when the life support system shut down. Keep going, Theo."

"His name was Nigel," Maggie said. "That was the man who had to vomit. He threw up in his suit, which was why he took it off. All of you heard what happened!"

Theo remembered that now. Yet another argument for keeping his helmet closed. He stood back up. The pain was now reaching from his hip to his back. Strangely enough though, he no longer felt cold.

Good. Where was José? Theo carefully balanced his weight on both legs. The contents of the rover had been shaken up with great force. Some of the equipment had even been tossed off its shelves, where it would have been securely fastened down. The navigational console must be located in the nose of the vehicle, but that would come later.

Theo took a few steps forward. There was the body of the

Chinese woman José had removed from the spaceship. She was small, hardly taller than one and a half meters. She was wearing an athletic suit that hung slack on her body. It must have fit her in the past.

Theo knelt down beside her head. Her face still looked relatively natural. She must have been beautiful once. Her dark, open eyes were still very expressive. Her skin was as white as porcelain, and her mouth was perfectly shaped. However, her cheeks were hollowed out. Theo cautiously pulled up one of her sleeves. Her arm consisted of skin and bones. The body was extremely dehydrated. That couldn't happen overnight. The six passengers had presumably died shortly after their launch, after which they were preserved in a dry, not very cold environment in which normal decomposition could not occur.

He described his impressions over the radio.

"So, you aren't convinced there was an illness?" the administrator asked.

"I'm not a pathologist, not even a doctor, but I don't see any signs of a dangerous infection. The Chinese must have died from something, of course, but only an expert will be able to give you the precise cause."

"Naturally," Summers said. "The woman won't be going anywhere. Your assessment is reassuring. Now to the navigational area."

"But what about José?"

"What about him? He must have suffocated, too. The computer is more important now."

Yes, you idiot. Theo didn't reply, but he stood back up. José was up in the front, lying behind two chairs that almost hid him completely. He walked over to the body and flipped him over from his stomach onto his back. Yes, that had to be José. He had almost managed to shut his helmet in time. His face was frozen. His skin was noticeably darker than his colleague Sam's.

José must have come from a Latin American family. Perhaps an immigrant family from Mexico? Theo hooked his arms under the astronaut's shoulders and carried him to the back of the vehicle, where he set him beside Sam. It occurred to him then that the rover might not always be lying steeply on its side. Was there somewhere that he could place the four bodies so they wouldn't be jostled all around if that happened? He only needed a few ropes, but a quick sweep of the area didn't turn any up.

"What's going on with the computer?" Summers asked.

"I wanted to... uh, nothing," he replied. "José suffocated as well."

"That was obvious," Summers said impatiently.

Theo sighed. *I'm sorry, you four,* he thought, *but I can't pay you my proper respects right now.* He consoled himself by recalling that it was the thought that counted.

In any case, the path to the navigational console was now free. The screen and keyboard were attached to a desk-like structure. In the rover's current situation, the screen slanted toward the right upper corner. He had to stretch to reach the keyboard. Theo had never worked on a computer like this.

He first checked the universal device on his sleeve. It was still working. Nonetheless, in terms of what happened to Sam, what was to keep that from happening to him as well? "Maggie?" he asked.

"I can hear you."

"If I yell for help, you will need to lift the rover up immediately and let me out," he said. "I won't have much time by that point, three minutes max."

"You can count on us."

"Thanks." He wiped some dust from his helmet, before recalling one last thing. "Oh, and I'll say something every thirty seconds. If I stop—"

"We'll lift the rover up right away," Maggie finished.

"Exactly. Sam couldn't call for help after a certain point."

"Yes, I understand what's behind your suggestion."

"Excellent." He took a deep breath, then reached up to press the power switch. One light, then two, began to flash. The rover's computer was restarting. Theo tensely watched his universal device, but it didn't indicate any fluctuations. *Phew. So far, so good.* "Ahmed, everything here looks normal. What should I do?"

The programmer dictated a few commands for him. Theo implemented them and reported on their outcomes. The orders grew increasingly complicated, but the result was always the same—OK. Or sometimes READY.

"That's it," Ahmed said eventually.

"And?" the administrator asked.

"The system is functioning optimally, as if it had just come off the assembly line."

"That's good, right?" Maggie asked.

"Considering the fact that it has three deaths on its conscience, I wish we had found an error. But the system truly is functioning perfectly. It's as if it were freshly installed. There aren't any data remnants, as you'd expect would gather during operation."

"You mean that somebody's tried to wipe away their fingerprints?" Maggie asked.

"I'm not sure. Whoever it was had the system under such good control that the outcomes aren't revealing their actions."

"What do you mean?"

"Well, the fact that the system looks brand new is suspicious in and of itself. If you want to hide the fact that you were secretly in someone else's apartment, you remove your own traces, but you don't clean the entire apartment so it looks as if nobody has ever lived in it."

"That's bizarre," Theo said.

"Unless you don't care what the resident thinks about your visit," the technician said.

"Or you want to show how thoroughly you have everything under control," the administrator added.

You must relate to that idea, Theo thought. However, the technician's idea intrigued him. *What if the visitor was so much more advanced that he didn't care if they were on his trail?*

"Who's saying that whatever caused the problem isn't still there in the rover?" Maggie asked.

BRANDON Q. MORRIS

"You think it's still in here with me? Thanks."

"I'm sorry to interrupt," the administrator said. "I've just tried repeatedly to contact Mars City, but no one's responding."

Theo once again felt the cold through his suit. "What do you mean by *repeatedly*?"

"Over the past fifteen minutes, I have sent the same query at sixty-second intervals. Nobody's answering."

Sol 343, Mars City

"I've had it. I can't do this anymore," Theo said.

"Let me take over," Ahmed offered.

Theo handed him the pickax, and the programmer continued the project. They were trying to dig a grave. They had righted the toppled rover yesterday and brought it back online, but they still needed to remove the four bodies from it.

"Mars obviously doesn't want to take them," Ahmed said, gasping.

Little splinters of packed sand flew all over the place. A small cloud of dust had already formed around the programmer. The wind was still today, and the sky was practically clear.

"We need something to thaw the permafrost," Theo suddenly heard Maggie say from behind him.

"Ah, good morning," he said. "Sleep well?"

"Okay, I guess. I'm no longer used to sleeping in a small space with five other people."

"I only slept about two hours myself," Theo said.

The life support system had been running at maximum capacity all night long, but it still hadn't managed to provide them with a relatively low-odor atmosphere.

"Has Summers said anything?" he asked. Yesterday, the administrator had strictly forbidden their return to the city.

"He doesn't want to go back until we have an explanation for what is going on there," Maggie said.

So, no news. But why were they actually allowing themselves to be commanded by Summers? They were four against one, at least, if Ahmed and Christiane, the technician, joined their side. He didn't question where Maggie's sentiments lay.

Theo pulled Maggie aside. The administrator might be listening in on their radio link. Theo pointed at the ground before using his foot to write one word in the red sand: *Revolt?*

Maggie shook her head before wiping away his question and writing her response, *Taser!* and quickly erasing it.

True. He nodded in understanding.

The administrator had cold-heartedly utilized his weapon yesterday. They would need to overpower him while he slept. And then there was the question of what would happen after their return to Mars City. Wouldn't the security team capture them? The majority of the city's residents seemed to be loyal to the administrator.

"Good morning!" Theo turned around and recognized the technician. She had introduced herself to him yesterday. Christiane was from Germany, from Berlin, though you couldn't tell it from her English pronunciation. "Do you have anything for me to do?" she asked.

"Here, have a turn with the pickax," Ahmed said. "I need to rest for a moment. For some reason, my suit's muscle amplifiers aren't helping."

Theo smiled. Without artificial muscles, they wouldn't even be able to dig a ditch here. "You don't need me right now? Then I'll go check on the other rover."

"I'll come along," Maggie said.

THE OPEN ROVER with which he had stopped the other rover sat on its side next to the ridge of the crater. A leg inside a spacesuit stuck out from under it.

"Shit, shit, shit," Theo said. "You didn't even recover him when you got here?"

"Summers didn't want to. He was dead, and you were lying a few meters away."

"Did Summers also want to leave me lying there?"

"No. He needed you as a witness."

"It was my lucky day, then." Theo came to a stop close to the front of the rover. The vehicle was significantly lighter than the enclosed rover, but there were only the two of them here. "Can you grab the back end, Maggie?"

"Shouldn't we try to get him out first?" She pointed at the leg.

"You're right. I'll pick up this end of the rover, and you can pull him out."

"I'd prefer it the other way around, if that's okay with you."

Theo sighed. Why did the others always think that he didn't mind dealing with dead bodies? "Okay," he said, kneeling down next to the leg.

"Now!" Maggie cried. She lifted the rover.

Theo yanked hard on the leg. The body seemed to be frozen to the ground.

"Do you have him?" Maggie asked.

"Just a second." He channeled all his strength into his pull. His hip protested with a flash of pain. One more yank, and he fell back on his back with the body upside down in his arms. He gingerly placed the dead guard on the ground and examined him. His name was Pierre. *That's right, and he was Canadian.*

"Someone told me after I woke up that his helmet was damaged."

"Could be. I don't remember," Maggie said softly.

"His helmet isn't damaged. The man might have still been alive!"

"Oh, shit. Everything was in turmoil. In any case, his biomonitor was no longer showing any vital signs. But you're right, we should have looked more closely." Maggie looked sincerely upset.

Theo took a deep breath. "We'll bury him with the other four," he said.

"But we have to get him out of his suit first. And to do that, we have to thaw him out."

"True. The suit is valuable."

Theo wished he could wipe off the cold sweat that had formed on his forehead. His suit's life support system couldn't keep up. At least, he was no longer sweating. "There's time for that," he said. "Let's set the rover upright again."

Maggie stood behind the back axle, and he walked to the front section. "On the count of three," he said. The rover slowly rolled back up on its tires. The steering rod pressed into his stomach. He heard Maggie groan over the helmet radio. And then, the vehicle was upright.

Theo walked around it to check out all four sides. "Looks good," he said. He really was satisfied. A couple of metal sheets up front were bent, but nothing seemed to be broken. If they were lucky, Theo would be able to climb aboard and drive off. Once he did that, they wouldn't need the administrator to make their way back to the city.

"I'll give it a test run," he said. Theo took a seat on the driver's side. The seat shell also seemed to be bent. Something was poking into his back muscles, but that shouldn't be a problem for the short drive to Mars City. He flipped on the ignition. The machine reacted as usual. The navigational screen had a crack, but everything was legible. The fuel cell was almost full, which meant he could drive several hundred kilometers on it. The electric engines on the tires were also very robust, and even if one of them stopped working, it wouldn't be the end of the world.

He pressed the gas pedal. The rover shuddered forward. "Hey, it's driving!" he shouted.

"I see that."

He turned off the computer and stepped down. "We might need the rover later on."

"We should take him with us." Maggie pointed at the dead astronaut.

Theo walked over to him and loaded him on his back.

"Aren't you ready yet?" Summers asked.

Theo cringed. He refused to turn around, otherwise he would run the risk of boxing the administrator's ears—except the man's helmet was in the way. The ditch was now about half a meter deep. They were still a long way from having enough room, especially now that they had five bodies. However, there was still enough time for the digging considering that they still had to get the guard out of his suit.

"How do things look in the city?" Maggie asked.

"They just aren't responding," replied the administrator. "Something has gone terribly wrong there."

"We should investigate," Theo declared.

"No, it would be better to wait," Maggie said. "We're safe here."

Why was she suddenly so afraid? Then again, maybe she was just thinking strategically. If they wanted to overpower Summers, they could only do that while he was asleep.

"Alright," Theo said. "We should wait out here until the city has resolved its problems."

Sol 343, MfE Base

Someone knocked on her door. "Come in," Rebecca said.

She wondered who would visit her at this late hour. As the door opened, she recognized Ellen. However, she had never seen Ellen like this. She was wearing a very clingy nightgown that shimmered like silk. It looked good on her.

"Sorry to disturb you."

"I was just reading anyway. What can I do for you?"

"I didn't want to make the others nervous, but I noticed something today."

That was interesting—so had she. Nobody had called in from Mars City today. Normally, they had been checked on every day and usually the Spaceliners sent them a new list of tasks. "You too?"

"What do you mean, Rebecca?"

"There was no communication with the city today."

"Exactly. And did you notice, no one was able to do the mandatory check-ins?"

Ellen sat down next to her on the cot. "That doesn't have to mean anything, of course," she said, "but it's quite unusual. Especially since..." She stopped talking.

Very effective, Rebecca thought, slightly amused. But she played along. "Especially since...?" she asked.

"Especially since they didn't respond to my call."

"You contacted them?"

"Just now, from the bridge. I was actually glad they didn't bother us today, but then I kept feeling concerned about it, too."

"And?"

Ellen slid closer and whispered, "No answer."

"Nothing at all?"

"Not even an auto response confirmation. It looks like all their systems are offline."

"Hmm. I wish the administrator all the worst," Rebecca said, "but if something bad has happened, our men are also affected."

"I know," Ellen said. "Which is why I didn't want to make a big deal about all this."

"If they haven't contacted us by tomorrow, we'll have to discuss this officially."

"I'm afraid you're right," Ellen said.

Was that it? Or did she have something else on her mind? Whatever the case, Ellen remained sitting. "Are you doing alright?" Rebecca asked, glancing away.

Ellen ran her fingers through her hair. Was she... embarrassed? Rebecca had never seen her like this.

"Should I... should I stay here for a little while?" Ellen eventually whispered. "I thought...," she didn't finish the sentence.

Now I understand. Rebecca felt amused, though she tried to not let on as she spoke. "This is very flattering, Ellen, and you look very pretty in your nightgown, but this isn't quite my thing. It's nothing personal, okay?"

Ellen's face turned pink. "Of course," she said. "I just thought that since you were so thoughtful and nice to me..."

"I like you, Ellen, and I like being friends."

"Thanks. Of course." Ellen stood up. "Please don't hold this against me," she said as she reached the door.

"No worries there. I'll see you tomorrow."

"Good night, Rebecca."

Ellen shut the door behind her. Rebecca still felt amused.

She hadn't known about this side to her friend. Wasn't she in a relationship with Mike from the NASA crew? Ellen apparently didn't view it as exclusive, but that wasn't Rebecca's business. She preferred to think about Theo. What might have happened in Mars City? Had there been some kind of catastrophe, like a meteor strike? But wouldn't they have known if that had happened? Maybe there was just a communications error over there. She shouldn't make herself crazy about this. And if there was anyone who could survive a disaster, it was Theo.

It took Rebecca a while to go to sleep. Once she did, she dreamed about needing to butcher a chicken that kept running away from her.

Sol 344, Mars City

NOTHING HAD HAPPENED, and it was all his fault. They had agreed to keep watch on shifts in order to take Summers by surprise while he slept, but who of all people had slept deep and long today? Theo slammed his fist against the wall.

"Didn't sleep well?" Maggie asked.

"The opposite," he replied.

"Then you should be happy, since you won't be able to get a good night's sleep every night."

Theo understood what she was saying. Tomorrow was another day. Nonetheless, this waiting was killing him! "I have to get out of here," he said.

"We all have to get out," Maggie said.

She was right about that, too. They had to fill the grave. Overnight, the body of the security guard, which they had placed in the heated engine room, had presumably thawed out. Since the rover didn't have an airlock, either all or none of them had to exit at the same time. The procedure came with one invaluable advantage—the cab was well ventilated. Once they climbed back on board and filled the space with fresh air, there were at least 30 minutes when it didn't smell so bad that you felt you might vomit at any minute. After that, you got used to the stench. If you didn't, at least the others didn't care all that much.

Last night, Theo had found the smell particularly bad. Everyone had spent so much time with the corpses that he had the feeling he could smell the decomposition. It was a miracle that he had been able to fall asleep. Perhaps what had occurred involved more of a state of unconsciousness than of healthy sleep. He didn't feel all that rejuvenated by it.

A HALF-HOUR later they were standing in the red sand underneath the brown sky, which was lit by a reddish sun.

"Ahmed, are you coming?" Theo asked.

The programmer nodded. They walked around to the back of the rover. This was the location of a compartment that was continuously heated to above freezing by the life support system, as well as various engines. The space had been designed to hold items that needed to be used outside in an unfrozen state. There was no way that the designers had ever imagined that someone would use this compartment to hold a dead body. However, it was the only way that they could remove the suit from Pierre without having to take him into the rover's cab.

"When we open the door, we have to work quickly," Theo said. "Otherwise, he'll refreeze on us."

"I know," Ahmed said.

"Let's do this!"

Theo turned the two handles that operated the latch. He let the hatch fall downward before grabbing hold of the suit. Everything was going according to plan so far, he realized. Yesterday, it had been much harder to maneuver the rigid body into the compartment. A moment later, Theo was holding the torso, while Ahmed gripped the legs.

They set the body on the ground. Working swiftly, Theo concentrated on opening all the zippers on the upper body. Out of the corner of his eye, he saw that Ahmed had already removed the boots. Theo was going to take the helmet off last. *The head wouldn't freeze so quickly that way*, he thought. The real reason was that this way he wouldn't have to gaze directly into the dead man's face. Gloves, check. Theo then extracted the left arm by pulling the suit sleeve forward. The body reminded him of a giant baby. Right arm, done.

"Can we turn him over?"

"Just a second," Ahmed said as he yanked the toolbelt out of its loops. "Now!"

They flipped the dead man over. It was a good thing he was still wearing the helmet, as otherwise his face would now be pressed into the dirt. *Who would end up wearing Pierre's suit later on?* Theo didn't want to know. At the same time, he was now wearing an LCVG that had once belonged to another dead person. *The world really had gone to hell.* They pulled off the lower and upper sections of the suit together.

"Ready?" Ahmed said. His question sounded like a combination of assessment, hope, and inquiry.

Theo shook his head. "The LCVG," he said.

Ahmed gazed at him in disbelief. *For real?* his eyes asked. They really had to remove the dead man's underwear? Theo nodded, and the programmer understood. At a basic level, it was a stupid waste of resources that they were burying the bodies instead of reprocessing them. Why wasn't the administrator insisting on recycling them? Could he possibly possess some shred of decency?

They quickly removed the heated underwear from the body. Theo didn't watch the arms carefully and bent the wrists that were now partially frozen. He had to straighten them to pull the sleeves of the LCVG over them. He felt the dead man's joints crack as he did this. Theo assured himself that it had been the ice snapping.

After they were done, the man lay in front of them in his undershirt and boxers.

"Those, too?" Ahmed asked.

Theo shook his head. That really would be too much. He gestured at Ahmed, and they carried Pierre over to the grave, where the other four bodies were already resting. The guard was given a spot right on the edge. Without his suit, he looked almost skeletal.

That was it.

"Administrator, would you like to say a few words?" Theo asked over his helmet radio. "We will fill in the grave afterward."

Summers didn't reply.

"Mr. Summers?"

No response.

"Go check on him, Theo," Maggie suggested. "I think the five of them have earned a decent send-off."

"Alright."

Theo walked over to the enclosed rover. The hatch was open, and he climbed up the ladder. Summers was sitting at the radio equipment. Theo couldn't make out what he was saying, since he had switched over to a different frequency. Theo couldn't see his face clearly through the visor, but either way, he didn't look happy.

"Administrator?"

Theo touched his shoulder. Summers jerked, his right hand reaching for his pocket. *That's where he must keep his taser*, Theo thought. "It's okay," Theo said. "It's just me." He saw Summers murmur something under his helmet. He had apparently forgotten to switch frequencies. Theo pointed at his ear.

"Sorry about that, Kowalski. I didn't notice you come in," Summers finally said.

"No problem. We're done with the grave outside. Would you like to say a short eulogy?"

"Uh, you know... the men are all dead as it is. I don't believe in an afterlife. Why don't you do it? I'm sure you knew them better than I did."

Theo shrugged. "Whatever you want. Good luck with trying to make contact."

The administrator turned back to the radio equipment.

Theo hoped he could convince Maggie to make the final speech. He wasn't the best person for something like that. He walked up toward the hatch. As he did so, his eyes fell on the radar. A light was flashing on the lower edge of it. He stepped closer. A bright dot was wandering across the screen. Theo superimposed a map underneath it. That wasn't all that far away! If the equipment wasn't in error—which was unlikely —then some visitor was moving around out there, someone who hadn't tried to contact them. Whatever it was, it was moving quickly, perhaps 20 km/h, but it was heading straight for them. Its destination might be Mars City.

But he had the lightweight rover! And the grave? He decided that it would have to wait. What were a few minutes when compared to eternity? He would have to be fast. Theo practically jumped out of the hatch and sped down the ladder. He then dashed over to the rover.

"Where are you going?" Maggie called after him.

"I have to take care of something!"

"Um, excuse me? What about the eulogy?" She now sounded seriously pissed off, but he didn't have time for lengthy explanations.

"Later," Theo called.

Out of breath, he jumped into the driver's seat and started the rover. Where had the radar just indicated the visitor was? He quickly got his bearings. Right, he needed to plot a trajectory from Mars City. Isn't that the direction of the MfE base? But the dot on the radar had been much too small to be a rover. It might be a lone person, but there was no way a human could do 20 km/h through the desert. What else could it be? What should he be watching for?

The question answered itself soon enough. Nothing else ever moved in the barren Mars desert. No tree, no bush, not even a dry leaf wafting in the wind. This made the reddish silvery sphere that was rolling and bouncing through the area all the more noticeable. What was that thing? Theo had never seen anything like it. It didn't look like it had been made by humans.

He roughly calculated the course that the object was taking, then slowed down the rover. He was moving too quickly. Would that thing let itself be easily captured? He picked up a little speed again. He needed to be ready for whatever the encounter might be. How could you stop a machine that didn't want to be stopped without destroying it?

He then remembered the tent. Every open rover was equipped with a tarp that its passengers could spend the night under in case of emergency. If he could manage to throw it over the object, he should be able to catch it. He drove on to the projected intersection point, jumped out of the rover, and quickly pulled out the tent. He let the tent platform fall to the ground and folded the tarp in such a way that he could easily throw it.

Alright, visitor, I'm ready, he thought. And it was time. The ball, which seemed to be made up of numerous, overlapping steel wheels, was jumping and rolling toward him. Theo felt like a cowboy who was supposed to lasso a wild stallion. But unlike a cowboy, he would only have one chance, since the bouncing ball seemed to be moving faster than the rover had been. If he didn't nail his toss, he would lose it.

Theo took a deep breath. The ball drew closer. He had to deploy a suitable amount of force at the right angle and at the optimal moment. One... two... three... Now! Theo threw the tarp, which unfurled and sank like an oversized cap over the sphere. It worked! Theo leapt down from the rover. Score! The ball jerked back and forth, becoming increasingly tangled up in the fabric. Theo made sure that it didn't escape. He opened the tarp from behind and reached through it until he could grasp the thin metal of one of the wheels. He then pulled the struggling object out from under the tarp.

Theo was a little disappointed when he discovered the conventional electronics inside of the ball. It hadn't been constructed by extraterrestrials. He then caught sight of the duct tape. *If something isn't holding together, then you haven't used enough duct tape.* His father had used this mantra every chance he got. Some astronaut must have broken out the duct tape. This meant that the object came from NASA, from MfE, or from Mars City. Since the latter was its destination and it was coming from the direction of the MfE base, his friends must have sent this machine off. He thought instantly of Rebecca, and his heart grew warm. He hoped she was doing well!

But where had they gotten this thing that had to be some kind of research robot? And what was concealed under the duct tape? Theo suspected that he should figure out the answer to those questions here and now, and not once he had rejoined the others. If Rebecca and her comrades had dispatched a robot unannounced, then they had some specific agenda in mind.

Holding the robot between his feet, Theo searched for the power switch and turned it off. The robot made a few noises that sounded so piteous that he immediately wanted to turn it back on. Theo peeled back the duct tape. His MfE friends had made liberal use of it in securing the package to the robot. Then it took him another 15 minutes to free the object from the packing tape. It was a pistol with ammunition. That was crazy. Where had they gotten it? He counted the bullets —60! He could incite a revolution with those, or at least keep the administrator in check. What kind of range did the taser have? Ten meters? The pistol would definitely cover a greater distance.

Of course, it would be better if he didn't have to use the weapon. Theo packed it into his tool bag for the time being. He then loaded the robot onto the cargo area and tied it down with the tarp. He packed up the tent platform as well and then returned to the others.

"What was that all about, Theo?" Maggie said in greeting. Her voice, although seeming composed, carried a sharp undertone.

He had never seen her so angry. "I'm sorry about that. I had to take care of something."

Ahmed walked over to the rover and pulled back the tarp.

"See that? It was rolling all by itself through the Mars

desert, so I had to rescue it," Theo explained.

"Aw, how cute!" Christiane exclaimed.

"You can't just leave us standing around," Maggie said. It sounded like a threat.

"Speed was of the essence. This little guy was whizzing along at twenty kilometers an hour, and I didn't want it to get away from us," Theo replied.

"Still, one word would've been enough," Maggie admonished.

"What kind of word? What's going on?" For the first time ever, Theo was glad that the administrator was sticking his nose in. He must have given up on his communication efforts.

It might be a good idea to change the subject, Theo figured, so he asked, "Still no word from Mars City?"

"Total radio silence, very unsettling," Summers replied.

"But you still think that everything will work itself back out?" Maggie asked.

"No. I now think that we should go check on the situation."

"Then let's bury these poor souls and head back."

"No, Maggie, I've given this some thought. We'll depart tomorrow before sunrise. The sun will be setting soon."

"It might be a good idea to slip out when it's dark."

"No, I don't think so. I want to be able to see my opponent in front of me. At night, we would find ourselves scared of every shadow."

I wouldn't be, but you would, Mr. Summers, Theo thought, keeping it to himself. Maggie glanced at him as if she'd had the same thought. She no longer seemed to be mad at him. Theo hated it when people he liked were upset with him. When he finally told her about the weapon, she would forgive him completely. But now wasn't the right moment.

"Of course, we understand that, Administrator," Maggie said.

Theo had to remember that officially speaking, the pilot was always entirely on the administrator's side. He'd long enjoyed her support. Of course, she had to fulfill this role.

"Theo, could we finally start our small funeral?" Maggie asked.

"One moment, please," the administrator said. Then, pointing at the robot, "What have you found here?"

"It must be a robot from an earlier Mars mission. He showed up on the radar, and I picked him up," Theo explained.

"An earlier mission?"

"We'll have to examine it more closely, but the thing must have been sitting around here for at least thirty years."

"It looks pretty clean."

"Yes, Administrator, the constant, mild wind has polished the rims to a gleam."

Summers walked over to the robot and leaned down. "It's crazy how well-preserved it is," he remarked.

"You can see how damaging the humidity on Earth actually is. Things here corrode much more slowly," Theo explained.

"We're lucky that we landed here," the administrator said with a chuckle. "And here," he reached into the center part of the robot, "is even some duct tape residue. Feel that. It's still sticky. After thirty years!" He motioned at Theo, who advanced obediently. "Look here! Touch it."

"You're right," Theo said. "It's still sticky."

"Are you sure that there wasn't anything stuck in there when you found it?" Summers asked.

Theo could hear the overt threat. He hadn't prepared himself for a discussion like this. If only he had concocted some story about what might have been attached there! And nobody could come to his aid since he hadn't told anyone about his discovery.

"No, I found it looking just like this, Administrator."

"And if I took the rover and searched the area for duct tape remnants, I wouldn't find any?"

"I didn't see any when I found it."

"Then everything's fine, Kowalski. You seem like an honest soul. Otherwise I wouldn't have brought you along despite dear Maggie's recommendation. If you're anything other than that, it would be unfortunate for all of us."

Theo had to keep himself from exhaling a sigh of relief. He'd played it very cool. The pistol was tucked inside his tool bag, and nobody knew about it. The administrator was just bluffing. He was probably too lazy to head out across the desert in search of duct tape, and hopefully none of the others would rat him out. In the end, all that remained out there was a little bit of tape!

"I would like to go ahead and close the grave," Maggie said.

"Of course. I didn't mean to hold that up. Good luck!" the administrator called as he hurried over to the rover.

Was he going back to his radio efforts? Theo wondered.

They arranged themselves around the grave. Maggie said their farewells to the dead. Where they came from no longer mattered. They were people, and all of them were equally far away from their birthplaces. The ones standing here were merely lucky enough to have survived until now. Was it really a matter of luck? Theo wasn't a pessimist, but everything seemed on the verge of collapse. In a few weeks, he might be envious of the five here in the ground when he started to die a painful death as the last bit of breathable air dwindled away.

He shouldn't think about that. Rebecca would rightly fuss at him for doing that. Theo shuffled his feet a little until Maggie finished her eulogy. Then, each of them tossed a handful of Mars' dirt into the grave. They filled the hole by shoveling the material they had removed earlier back into it.

Packing the ground down firmly by stepping on it wouldn't work here, but Christiane had a better suggestion. She walked over to the rover and fetched a pail of warm water from the inside of the cabin. If she hurried, it wouldn't be frozen before she reached the grave. Theo watched her as she strode back quickly, causing the water to slop out of the bucket. The traces she was leaving behind would be visible for many years to come, until the ice eventually sublimated.

She finally reached the grave and poured the water over

it, which would hold the dust together. New permafrost would form over the dead bodies. For the foreseeable future, their bodies wouldn't decompose. The bacteria and microorganisms inside them, the ones that would otherwise destroy their former hosts, couldn't handle the Mars chill, and despite their intensive searching, humans had yet to find any bacteria on Mars. These bodies would lie here in the darkness for a very long time.

Maybe recycling wasn't such a bad idea after all. He would tell Rebecca that he now wanted to be turned into topsoil for the plants being grown for the Mars colony.

THEY BOARDED the rover for the night. The stench from five long-unshowered, sweaty people would soon permeate the cabin again. *Space travel isn't for princesses*, Theo thought. Christiane climbed up the ladder in front of him. She handed Pierre's empty spacesuit to Ahmed, who was standing in the hatch. Theo was the next-to-last person to board, with Maggie behind him.

The former pilot suddenly grabbed his shoulder. With her foot, she drew a picture of a ball in the dust. Theo nodded. He wiped the ball away and made a rough sketch of a pistol. Maggie's eyes grew huge. He quickly rubbed out the drawing. They might not need the weapon. It would be better if they didn't. Whatever had taken Mars City off-line could eventually pose a threat to the MfE base.

Hadn't a common enemy, time and again, forged bonds between people? It was actually sad. Humans had advanced so far, but they always needed an external threat to force them to cooperate. Or was he being unfair toward the human race? Was he perhaps being blinded by the actions of those who pursued very egotistical motives? They would see, maybe by tomorrow.

Sol 344, Planum Australe

A GIANT, bluish-green tongue extended toward her. It was three kilometers high. Ewa had reached Planum Australe, the South Pole plain. Its edges reminded her a little of a glacier, although no water came from it. It was much too cold for that. The slope was not as steep as Ewa had feared, and piles of polar ice ran along its edges. This was good, since she wouldn't have to search too long for an access point. She could just keep driving straight ahead.

However, because Friday had previously asked her so nicely, she did a preliminary check of the area. Ewa climbed off the rover and up a few meters onto the glacier. Using a two-meter long metal pole, she examined the firmness of the surface. She pushed the pole downward, aided by her suit's amplifiers. However, the metal didn't sink into the surface. *Very nice*, Ewa thought. *Friday had been worrying for nothing.*

She got back into the rover and set off as the cabin refilled with breathable air. "See, Friday?" she asked.

'I don't *see* anything.'

"You were worried for nothing. The ice is hard."

'I'm still worried.'

"You think that I did the measurements wrong?"

'No, Ewa. The ice is going to change. Here at the edge, the plain is primarily composed of water ice. It's as hard as steel at negative seventy degrees. But as you move farther into the area, the percentage of water ice declines. If the composition consists of too much dry ice, the substance becomes porous, and we might sink. If we don't pay close attention, we might find ourselves five hundred meters below the surface level. We would never be able to escape a depth like that.'

"Great, I feel so much better now."

'I'm sorry, Ewa. We just have to check regularly to make sure that the ice is still solid.'

"And if we don't."

'Then we should not stop again. As long as we keep moving, the dry ice should not sublimate so quickly that we would sink.'

"'Should not?'"

'Nobody has ever had any practical experience with this material. It will depend on our approach.'

"But how are we supposed to check to see if we are still safe? To do that, we'd need to stop."

'That's true. We just have to hope for a little luck.'

"I would have preferred a more encouraging reply."

'I can understand that, Ewa.'

Sol 346, Mars City

THEO WAS SITTING in the driver's seat of the open rover. He was glad he didn't have to ride along in the cabin of the other vehicle. When he and Christiane, who was sitting behind him, had climbed out of the enclosed rover, it had been well ventilated, but that wouldn't last long. Out here, the only excretions he had to inhale were his own. He would have preferred to be driving with Maggie, but the administrator had insisted that she steer the enclosed rover. At least, this offered the advantage that she might be able to influence Summers somewhat.

Would that even be necessary? Theo had no idea what might be waiting for them in the city. What had happened? Whatever had seized control of the other rover might now be the ruler of all Mars City. But to what effect? It obviously had the power to kill people. It had the recovery crew on its conscience now. It had simply cut off the humans' air supply. And what about the Chinese astronauts? They also ought to be counted among its victims.

But Mars City was complex. It would take more than just flipping a switch to suffocate everyone. Theo didn't think that there was a single central control for all the city's functions. The city was expanding rapidly, which was why the creation of living spaces had taken precedence over automatization.

Presumably, the newly dug, relatively primitive living quarters were now the safest place that you could take refuge in the city, since everything there still functioned manually. At least, that was what Theo hoped was the case since that was where his friends were living.

He accelerated. The enclosed rover had a small head start. Theo steered slightly to the side so he wasn't driving inside the cloud of dust the other vehicle was kicking up. "Any word from the city?" he asked over the radio.

"Nothing," Maggie replied.

"And from the MfE, or NASA?"

"Our radio system's range isn't good enough for that. We would need Mars City to relay our messages, but they're silent."

"Shit," Theo said.

"We'll know soon enough what's going on there."

THE ENCLOSED rover drove relatively slowly, so it took them almost an hour to cover the distance. The vehicle came to a stop about a kilometer away from their destination. Theo parked his rover right beside it.

"We'll go the rest of the way by foot," the administrator announced.

Theo didn't question this. His mind's eye could still see the suffocated astronauts. Summers had to be scared that something might take control of the rover again and threaten him with a similar fate.

"We could take the open rover to get closer," Theo suggested. They would be able to jump free from there if the vehicle went rogue.

"No, just leave it. Someone could still do a lot of damage with a light rover. The walk won't hurt us."

Theo climbed down. He picked up his tool bag, which was heavier than usual. The hatch on the enclosed rover opened, and the humidity from the escaping air froze instantly, creating a thin cloud that rose into the air.

Maggie was the first one to exit the vehicle. He held out his hand, and she jumped down the last three rungs. Ahmed followed her, looking tired. The administrator was the last one to leave the rover. His taser was dangling in full view from the belt of his spacesuit. He carried a bag over his shoulder.

"It's up to us now," the administrator said. Theo was already dreading a possible pep talk, but Summers just held the bag out to Ahmed. "Take this," he said. "I packed up a few supplies and a mobile security terminal that will hopefully help us gain access to the city. I'm sure you'll be able to make better use of it than I can." Ahmed took the bag and nodded.

What was the point of packing up supplies? Theo wondered. The rover didn't have a tent on board, so they couldn't take off their spacesuits. All they could consume was what the suits provided—water and that slimy nutritional blend. This wasn't exactly a cozy hike ending with a bonfire. But he didn't say anything.

THEY STRODE up a low crater wall. They should soon see the outline of both *Spaceliners*. The rockets lifted their elegant noses into the dusty sky. That was their destination. These were the only parts of the city in sight. Most of its features were flat—like the greenhouses—or else buried underground.

Theo didn't recall seeing the city from a distance as great as this. Of course, he knew what it was supposed to look like. Nonetheless, he had imagined it differently. There were neither city walls nor watchtowers. What the administrator so loftily called *his* Mars City was composed of the two landed spaceships and a few caves dug by the city's residents. The human race had really come far over the past thirty or forty thousand years. And even that might be taken away from them by the *thing* running around the planet, the thing whose nature they didn't even understand.

"Hey, Theo," Maggie said.

"Yes?"

"You look so... dejected. What is it?" She had seen through him even though his face was concealed behind his visor. He needed to pull himself together.

Theo straightened his shoulders. Had his walk given him away? "It's nothing," he said.

"Got it," Maggie replied.

This isn't one of my better moments. She means well. He gave himself a shake. But it didn't really matter what the administrator thought of him. "It is somehow impressive to see what all we have achieved here," he said.

"We've survived where no human life is supposed to be possible," Maggie said.

"For what reason?"

"I don't know. Not yet anyway."

"You think there's a reason for this, and that it will eventually be revealed to us?"

"There's no guarantee, Theo. That's what makes life so exciting."

"Exciting, sure. I sometimes wish I could have a little less excitement."

UP CLOSE, the two *Spaceliner* ships looked both impressive and out-of-place, like skyscrapers that somebody had built in the desert.

"Be careful," the administrator said.

As if there was some concrete threat out there! They were safer here than they had been in the desert. Theo looked for the airlocks that led down to the living spaces and storerooms. They appeared to be randomly scattered around the area. For safety reasons, they had been located a good distance away from the two spaceships in case one of the ships needed to be launched. However, there were also subterranean tunnels through which people could reach every possible spot in Mars City without having to put on a spacesuit.

Where were the citizens hiding? Three-quarters of the settlers had already moved off the ships. Why weren't any of them up on the surface?

"Away team here. Can anyone hear us?" Maggie asked over the radio.

Theo stayed where he was standing and listened. No answer came. "The quarters are well shielded against cosmic radiation, so our helmet radios won't get through," he said.

"But the people on the ships should be able to respond," the administrator replied. "Each of them has a spacesuit whose communications links shouldn't be blockable from the outside, just shielded."

"Could it be that there's no one left on the ships?" Theo asked.

"We should check first. I had my best people on the *Spaceliner*, and that was where the bridge was located," Summers said.

"Is it possible that something has killed everyone here?"

"No, Theo," the administrator said quite calmly. "The life support system isn't so broadly centralized for that to be possible."

They walked over to the rocket standing on its sturdy landing legs. Theo wiped a little Mars dust off its hull. "It seems to be electrostatically charged," Theo said.

"Yes, that's normal. The wind creates constant friction against it," Maggie replied.

Theo glanced up. The ship's outer shell was massive. He located an airlock hatch about five meters above the surface. "It doesn't look like there's an entrance around here," he said.

"Right, it doesn't look that way," Summers affirmed.

Ah, that means there's probably a maintenance access point, Theo thought.

A few moments later, the administrator located a control panel concealed behind a metal plate. "For engine inspections," Summers said. "Ahmed, my bag, please."

The programmer handed him the bag, and Summers removed a small tablet and an adaptor module with numerous little cables. "One of these should fit," Summers remarked. He inserted the module into the tablet and tested one cable after the other.

"Ah, this one works," he said. He turned on the tablet and tapped around on it. "Damn it, wrong protocol," Summers continued. "The door controls want something from me, but I'm not sure what."

"Have you established an encrypted connection? And does your tablet have the most recent certificate installed so the system can recognize it?" Ahmed asked.

The programmer's questions sounded like gibberish to Theo, who considered himself fairly knowledgeable when it came to computer systems.

"I don't know what that means, so it won't help me," the administrator admitted. "Could I ask you to take over? Your knowledge in this area is greater than mine."

The programmer nodded and took the tablet from Summers. "I can't promise anything," he said. "We'll only gain access if someone else has screwed things up."

"That's clear to me," the administrator said, "but people always make mistakes, so I'm very optimistic."

Theo took a deep breath. What should he do while they were waiting? He could walk over to the subterranean quarters and examine the airlocks. Maybe they could get into the ship faster if they used a detour. "I'm going to go check out the airlocks," he said.

"Wait, I've got it," Ahmed replied.

"What? That was fast," the administrator said. "You must be good at what you do."

"It was surprisingly easy," Ahmed said softly.

Theo could feel the programmer's uncertainty. Was this a trap? "Too easy?" he asked.

"Kind of like someone hid the key under the doormat."

"And how likely would something like that be?" Theo asked.

"I'm not sure," Ahmed said, shaking his head slowly.

"I know a lot of people who stick keys under their mats," the administrator said.

"The programmer might have been lazy enough to leave a back door in place in case he didn't renew the certificate early enough," Ahmed said.

"Laziness is an important human motivator," Summers said. "Most inventions were created as a result of sheer laziness."

"What do you think, Ahmed?" Theo asked. "Is this a trap?"

"It's hard to say, really. I've exploited a fairly stupid error, but programmers make stupid errors, too. And if he was under pressure because the launch was coming up quickly or he needed to hurry home... but the program code can also be manipulated."

"We'll never know if we don't turn the key," the administrator said.

"We could try to get through the airlocks," Theo suggested.

"Know what, Kowalski? Give the airlocks a try, and we'll go right in here."

"That's a good idea," Maggie said. "Then we'd still have you in our back pocket if something happens."

"Exactly. If you aren't successful, just wait for us in the rover until the problem is solved," Summers replied.

Theo nodded. Yes, that sounded like a good plan to him. Even just the thought of finally being alone again pleased him.

"Ahmed, can you open the door for us?"

"Indeed, Mr. Summers."

The programmer tapped several spots on his tablet. The red lights on the control panel turned green. Then, one of the steel panels located on the interior edge of the pillar slid downward, and an entrance appeared. Theo had to lean down to see anything in detail. Maggie shined her helmet light into the space. They saw a tube with a diameter of about a meter that headed upward at a slant. Handles were attached along its back wall. The tube was clearly there to provide access for a technician.

"Let me go first," Christiane, the technician, said.

Theo was just as shocked as the others.

"I know my way around. I did maintenance on the engines when we were still en route in space," she said.

"Good," the administrator replied, motioning for her to go ahead.

Christiane waved goodbye to Theo and climbed into the tube. "It's surprisingly spacious. You'll see," she called over her helmet radio from inside.

"We're on our way," the administrator said. "Ahmed, Maggie... would you be so kind?"

The two astronauts crawled into the tube as well.

"Good luck!" Theo called after them.

The administrator also disappeared eventually. Theo could only see his boots as the metal panel slid shut again. "Can all of you still hear in there?" Theo asked by radio.

"Loud and clear," Maggie replied.

That was very strange. Why hadn't any of the over 20 individuals who had to still be living on board the ship responded to their communication attempts?

"Things look okay in there?"

"We're at the end of the maintenance tube. There's another hatch here. Beyond it is a space that is connected to the ship by an airlock," Maggie explained.

"But you're still in the tube?"

"Yes, it wasn't all that easy to let Ahmed by. He's now messing around with the hatch's control panel."

"This time no one left the key under the mat?"

"No, Theo."

"I can't help with anything, but I'm getting goosebumps all over the place."

"Just stay calm. Ahmed won't leave us hanging. He is really very good."

It was hard for Theo to keep from contradicting Maggie.

What right did he have to destroy the hope she had? "Got it. I'm standing right beside another airlock now, and I'll try my own luck with it."

"I'll call in when there's news," Maggie said.

HE FOUND himself in front of a brick-like platform at the center of which a recessed metal plate was mounted. It was the outer airlock door. He knelt down and touched it. The plate was smooth and plain. Right up against the edge was a small, raised circle that contained the following inscription: 'Do not step here. Maximum weight: 200 lbs.'

Was that for gravity on Earth or on Mars? And who would give a weight in pounds? Three additional words were located below the warning: 'Made in China.'

Theo wasn't surprised. *Spaceliner's* owners had naturally bought from there, where the costs were the lowest. Unlike the MfE, they had at least paid attention to quality. He pounded on the plate. He didn't hear anything, but he also didn't feel any vibrations. The piece of metal was massive. He didn't believe that its maximum load capacity was two hundred pounds. The weight limit probably applied to the hinges, since the plate merely sealed off the airlock chamber. If he could override the opening mechanism, he could flip it up and climb into the airlock.

If. He took a step to the side. The controls that could release the panel were located next to the opening. Under normal circumstances, it should be enough to press the request button. This would cause the inner door to close and the air to be pumped out of the chamber. After a minute at most, the outer door could be opened. However, he had already noticed that all four bulbs on the control panel were glowing red. That wasn't a good sign. It meant that the airlock had been taken off-line because it had registered some kind of error. This could occur if someone had put an object inside that prevented the inner door from closing. Or if the airlock's diagnostic program indicated a software error.

He first had to find out the exact nature of the problem. This was why the control panel was equipped with a manual mode over which he could call up a diagnostic program. He knew how this helpful tool worked. In his work as caretaker, people always called him whenever an appliance stopped working. Some errors could be ignored, but unfortunately, a non-closing inner door didn't fall into that category. In that case, if he opened the outer door while the inner one was still open, he would release all the air out of the entire subterranean settlement.

No, it wouldn't be quite so drastic, he corrected himself. There had to be safety doors between the areas down there, which immediately closed at any drop of air pressure. But anyone who was standing close to the airlock and wasn't wearing a spacesuit wouldn't survive.

Come on, come on, he thought. The software was reacting slower than he was used to. It was almost as if the system was operating at close to its maximum performance limits. But that couldn't be true. The entire city seemed to be fast asleep during broad daylight. It was so quiet.

The diagnostic menu finally appeared. *Good.* Oddly enough, the inner door was open, but it could theoretically be closed, too. In any case, its motors didn't indicate any obstructions. The ventilation system was also functioning. The airlock had to pump out all its air before he could enter from the outside, and it had to be filled again before he could open the inner door. There were no living creatures inside the airlock chamber. As long as that was the case, the airlock could only be controlled from the inside. This prevented someone from accessing the chamber from the outside as long as someone—perhaps without a spacesuit on—was located inside.

Everything was in working order, but the lights were still burning red. Theo skimmed through the error list all the way to the end. He finally landed at an error that he loathed more than anything: 'Unknown Error.' He had encountered this several times while working down here in the quarters. The message simply indicated that the system had no idea what was wrong with it. And then he was supposed to solve the problem! He had only managed to do that one other time. In that instance, the outer insulation on a cable had partially melted. This had unexpectedly impacted another power line. He had only figured this out by changing out all the fragile cables, one after the other. There was absolutely nothing from that experience that was helpful for what he was facing now.

Theo pounded his fist against the panel, one, two, three times, until his frustration evaporated. Then he stood up again. This wasn't the only airlock. There were at least three official entrances. And then there was a secret one, at least according to the rumor mill. The story was that the administrator could use that one to spring surprise visits on his subjects—or to escape from them if a revolt ever occurred. Theo didn't know if there was anything to the rumor or not.

The next regular airlock wasn't far away. He was soon kneeling down beside its control panel. These bulbs were also all burning red. This time, it didn't take him so long to locate the error. The airlock chamber door was blocked. What had happened there? Theo searched through the error memory for the records. Two sols ago, the inner door had shut like usual. The air was released. Someone had probably wanted to go up to the surface. However, the outer door had remained closed. Theo clenched his fist. That meant that someone had spent two days trapped in the chamber. Whoever it was must have run out of air in their spacesuit a long time ago. Whoever that had been must have suffocated inside the chamber because someone had blocked the way out.

Someone? It must have been that *thing* from the rover. It had apparently taken control of the airlock access system. Hadn't the administrator declared that there was no way that could happen? Theo had put his life at risk to halt the advance of the renegade rover. Pierre had lost his life in the effort. And the administrator had reduced that sacrifice to nothing by giving that thing the opportunity to slip through their hands! If Theo had known that there were no antitank missiles, that the city didn't have any way to destroy his rover, he could have put a stop to the administrator's machinations.

Or maybe not. At that point in time, the pistol had still been on board the robot. He fervently wished that he could walk over to the administrator and send a bullet through his skull. All right, his leg. But he himself deserved the bullet instead. He could have perhaps stopped Summers. What if the person in the chamber was Lance? Lance, whose baby was waiting for him back at the NASA base? He might have robbed the little boy of his father before the child could actually get to know him. He would never be able to look Sarah in the eyes again.

He beat his fists against the hard outer door. This time three hits weren't nearly enough. He stopped when he felt exhausted. His fists burned.

There was still the third airlock. He had to at least give it a try. Maybe the entries in the error protocol weren't right. He couldn't see into the airlock. What if the man or the woman happened to have taken an extra oxygen tank along? He couldn't give up yet. If he could open the third airlock, he might be able to somehow help the trapped person. There had to be tools inside that would enable him to open the inner door! Everything was now riding on him being able to get underground quickly.

"Theo, we need your help." It was Maggie.

He stood up and turned toward the *Spaceliner* rocket. As he gazed at it, a small dust devil swept by in the space between him and the ship. Mars City was turning into a ghost town. "Where are you?"

"We're still in the tube," Maggie said.

"And Ahmed?"

"He can't gain access. The system he's supposed to crack seems impenetrable."

Theo suspected the worst. "You can't get out again, can you?"

"That's the problem."

"I knew it!"

"Yes, you were right. It was a trap, but we had to try."

"It was my mistake," the administrator admitted.

What had he just said? Theo waited.

"We should have sent Ahmed in alone," Summers continued.

Of course. Sacrifice the programmer. The administrator had earned this fate! The only bad thing was that the others hadn't. He had to get them out somehow. "I'm coming," Theo said.

"I'm not sure that will help anything," Summers said, "but feel free to give it a try."

Gladly, asshole, Theo thought.

"The outer door has shut, and there isn't a control panel for it here inside. However, perhaps the error is still being indicated on the control panel at the maintenance entrance," Ahmed said. "I can give you precise instructions for what you'll have to do to hack your way in."

"That sounds like a plan," Theo said. He ran over to the rocket and searched for the hidden control panel. "Okay, I found it, now what?" he asked, out of breath.

"Theo, please calm down. We have enough oxygen for an entire day. If you're frantic, you'll make mistakes."

Maggie is right. I have to calm down. Theo took a deep breath and exhaled. "Someone has been trapped in one of the airlocks for the past two days," he explained then. "Every second counts for them."

"Do you want to try to help them first?" Maggie asked.

"Absolutely not. Kuczinski will get us out first. It's starting to get uncomfortable in here," the administrator said.

"Kowalski. Theo Kowalski," Theo corrected.

"Whatever. Just hurry up."

The man was annoying the hell out of him. Couldn't Maggie take his taser and shut him down for a while? "Alright, Ahmed. I'm calm now and can listen to you."

"Good. You have a universal device on your sleeve."

"Yes, I do."

"We need it as an input medium, but we have to connect it to the panel. The administrator has the suitable cable for that, but we have that in here. You'll need to improvise something."

"That's fine. How?"

"You need a two-core cable. Look around. Do you see something like that lying around?"

Theo scanned his surroundings. "No, nothing."

"That's okay. You have enough cable in your suit. You have a sharp knife in your tool bag, right?"

"Yeah." Theo pulled it out, and as he did that, his eyes fell on the pistol.

"Good. Look at your left arm. Your suit has a seam that runs from your shoulder to the upper edge of your glove. It's a double seam, and a cable is sewn into it that transfers the data picked up by the biosensor on your wrist."

"Understood."

"You need to pick out the seam and remove the cable. But, be careful! Make sure you don't loosen the thread underneath the cable, or your suit might spring a leak."

"Okay. Open the seam, free the cable, don't damage the thread underneath. I can manage that. Other risks or side effects?"

"Your system will report you as dead to any remote query."

"Okay. But people can see that I'm still alive."

"If you aren't sure about this, there's another suit in the rover. Or you might find a cable somewhere in there. I won't be any help to you if you want to do that, though. The range on my helmet radio won't reach that far."

Should he take the time to go back to the rover that was two kilometers away? He would lose time, perhaps too much time.

"No, I'll do it here. Give me a moment." Theo gripped the edge of his knife between his thumb and forefinger so that only two millimeters extended beyond them. He then started at the top of the seam. With one slow though forceful movement, he dragged the knife downward. He then checked his work. He hadn't used enough pressure. In some spots, the cable was visible, though not in a way that would allow him to detach it from his suit.

Now for three millimeters of blade. He repeated the action. A glance at his universal device indicated that the pressure inside his suit was stable. What luck! The cable was now exposed. "I should just slice it out at the top and the bottom, right?"

"Exactly, Theo. You don't need more than about twenty centimeters of length."

"Good. Consider it done." Theo removed the cable and examined it in his right hand. Now he was dead. It didn't feel all that bad, to be honest.

"You need to strip the insulation off the ends of both wires, up to half a centimeter."

"Okay." He notched the cladding on one and yanked it off with a single pull. He repeated that process on the other three ends of the double cable. "Done."

"Perfect. Your device has a universal output. Green cable in the left jack, yellow cable in the right one."

"How do you know that they're green and yellow?"

"Aren't they?"

"Yeah. I'm done."

"The control panel has some kind of jack socket. Green goes on the external pole. You need to push the yellow one in deep enough so it contacts the internal pole."

"Ready."

"Now turn off the universal device. The three-point pressure, alright?"

"My suit will shut down."

"Yes, but you will start it up again immediately. When you do that, push all four corners so it will start up a special diagnostic program that we need."

He used three fingers on his left hand to push the three corners on the screen. The device beeped, then shut down the life support system. The radio contact also broke off. He was now completely isolated. It wasn't all that easy to press the four corners of the screen with one hand. Hopefully, the rest of the suit's functions would start up, as well as the diagnostic program.

He heard the beeping resume. His suit was responding. On the universal device's screen, an ugly menu composed solely of words appeared. "I'm back," he reported. "Will this stuff on my little helper go away soon?"

"Yes, and after this, you can restart your suit with just three fingers."

"Okay. Now what?"

"The cables are still attached?"

Theo checked the connection to the control panel. "Looks good."

"Then please input exactly what I tell you." Ahmed dictated an entire series of commands with varying parameters that Theo gradually entered. Typing on the device's screen keyboard wasn't all that easy with gloves on. The results didn't seem to make the programmer happy, since he grew quieter with each passing minute.

"Forget it. It's not helping," Ahmed said.

"I'm confused."

"It's not your fault, it's mine. The simple bug from earlier is no longer there. And none of the other common security loopholes are, either. I'd have to analyze the entire system to find anything else."

"But you can't do that."

"No, I'd need a level of access that I don't have right now."

"Shit."

"Exactly, Theo. I've failed."

"Take a breather, Ahmed," Maggie said. "We crawled in here voluntarily. Nobody could've guessed that we'd be trapped in here. I don't understand it, either. Why?"

"Whoever's in control here has apparently tried to

hamstring us," the administrator said. "I'm not sure of the motive behind it. What would someone gain from all this?"

"Maybe we're overthinking in terms of human motives," Christiane cut in.

Theo stuck his knife back in his tool bag. As he did that, his hand brushed against the pistol. Could he do something with that? He pulled it out and took a few steps back. Nobody could see him. He loaded the gun and aimed at the panel. If only he knew more about firearms! Would he be able to shoot enough holes into the metal plate that he would be able to remove it? It didn't seem all that likely. The spaceship could handle heat up to three thousand degrees. The metal had to be very resistant.

And what if he hit the control panel? It would be destroyed, and he would never be able to open the door. No, he needed to keep the gun for later. He would use it eventually. But did he really want to? He tried to imagine his life as a novel. If that were the case, he would have to use it due to the rules of plot development. Every weapon that the reader encounters has to be used. What nonsense. But his life wasn't a novel. Unfortunately.

Theo took a deep breath. "I can't help you right now," he said. "I'm so very sorry."

"Yes, I agree with you," Maggie said. "We'll try the upper door again."

"I'll try to open the third airlock. And, Administrator, is it true that there is a fourth airlock reserved for your own special use?"

"How do you know about that?" Summers asked.

"There's a rumor going around about it."

"You shouldn't believe all the rumors out there, but this one happens to be true. There's an emergency entrance and exit over one of the greenhouses."

"Which one?"

"7C."

"I'll find it."

"But you won't be able to just get in. You need the security tablet that I have with me."

"I'll check it out. What do I need to pay attention to there?"

"The airlock is made of glass, which is why it isn't noticeable. From above, it looks like a totally normal greenhouse."

"And the control system?"

"There isn't one, but on the side of the greenhouse, you will find the control panel for the light system. This panel also controls the airlock."

"Very subtle."

"Indeed. Very few people know about it, Kowalski, so keep this to yourself."

"I'll look around. I'll keep quiet about it, Administrator, for the rest of your life. If I can't find a solution, that promise won't last past tomorrow."

That might have been a cruel thing to say, but that man deserved a slow death by suffocation. If only he could get the other three people out of the tube!

Sol 346, Planum Australe

DRIVE FOR TWO HOURS, stop, check the solidity of the ice, drive another two hours. She had carried out this procedure diligently. The water content of the ice was higher than Friday had assumed it would be, and this stabilized the ice cap. However, Ewa knew that this would change eventually. She exited the rover and suspected right away that the time might have come, or it wasn't far off—as soon as she stopped moving, her boots sank several centimeters into the ice. The surface looked as stable as ever. In the sunlight, it glistened reddish-gray, but it acted like quicksand.

While Ewa used the measuring pole, she had to walk around slowly so her boots didn't transfer too much heat to the surface. She placed the pole on the ground and didn't even need to push on it. It slid straight into the ice under its own weight. Ewa had to hold onto it to keep from losing it. That didn't look good. The surface had now become her greatest enemy. Ewa climbed back into the rover. The ladder had already disappeared. She yanked the door shut and ordered the computer to set off immediately.

Ewa sat down at the controls and pulled up the rover's technical data on the screen. How heavy was the vehicle, and how large was the tires' contact area? She needed to reduce tire pressure. The settings were hidden in a submenu. Ewa selected the lowest technological setting possible.

She then returned to the main menu. They had to drive faster to keep from sinking! The computer set the highest speed limit at 25 km/h. Ewa checked the radar images of the area. There had to be more images in here. She increased the speed limit manually, but the value immediately jumped back down to 25. *Shit, why isn't the computer obeying?*

Then she remembered. The front tires were still covered in snow chains. A speed limit for those must be set somewhere. She searched frantically through all the settings menus and deactivated all the safety protocols she found, but the rover still didn't drive any faster. This couldn't be happening! She stopped the vehicle so she could search for the cause in peace, but that wasn't a good idea. Ewa noticed quickly that the rover was sinking.

How far down would it go? At which point might the ice be stable? One meter down, ten, one hundred? She didn't have time to figure that out. There was nobody here who could rescue her. She was all on her own. She had to stay up on top of the ice. Ewa let the rover continue to roll. The snow chains helped the tires to pull the rover out of the wells the vehicle had formed in the ice. In the footage picked up by the rearview camera, it looked as if they had just left an oversized hares' nest.

Ewa took a deep breath and turned off the autopilot. This meant she had to sit at the controls. The area before her didn't seem to hold any surprises. It sloped sharply uphill, but the snow chains could handle that easily. She increased her speed first to 30, then to 35 km/h. What would happen if the snow chains came off at this speed? At the moment, that wouldn't be a significant loss.

The only unfortunate thing would be if the tires got damaged in the process. They had to remain intact at all costs. Ewa listened hard, but she didn't hear any unusual noises. If the chains were about to break, they were obviously doing it quietly. She shook her head. She shouldn't drive herself crazy about this. She slowly increased her speed to 40 km/h. The rover was kicking up a long, white streamer of ice dust. The cold desert here was remarkably similar to the hot desert on Earth. All it lacked was sand dunes.

EWA'S STOMACH GRUMBLED. She hadn't eaten breakfast yet today. With her right hand, she felt around behind her, but nothing was sitting there. She was going to have to stand up. Ewa transferred the controls to the computer. The rover instantly slowed down, but she absolutely needed to eat something. She got to her feet and stretched out her back. In the storage compartment underneath the tiny kitchen, she found a can way at the back end that she hadn't noticed before. She read the label. It was a German-style pea soup. *Who would have ordered that? Are there any Germans among the NASA astronauts? Whatever.* She opened the can, poured about half of its contents into a bowl, and put it in the microwave, which automatically recognized the substance. All she needed to do was press the start button and wait.

The microwave display indicated 65 seconds. From where she stood, she gazed out the front window, which was actually a screen. They were driving slightly uphill. She remembered the 3D maps that they had been shown back on Earth. They hadn't been scale models. The polar ice cap had been stuck to the bottom of Mars like a giant, flat pimple. Ewa imagined a small insect creeping over that pimple. That was her. Where was the insect going? What was it doing here? It had no business here.

Hadn't Friday theorized that she might find traces of the ancient Mars inhabitants here? At the moment, it didn't look as if there had ever been any life forms down here. The area was extremely inhospitable. Ewa laughed softly. It was actually crazy for her to imagine the ice pimple as deadly. The entire planet seemed to hate living things. They never should have come here. Even Antarctica felt like paradise in comparison to this. *What in the world had made humans think that they had to go to Mars?*

But on the other hand, it was only because of this great leap that any humans were still alive. Earth was silent. It seemed unlikely that there were still humans alive there. Technology is never silent. And it had been a long time since the human race had been able to manage without it. They should have picked up on one signal or another if they existed.

The microwave pinged. Ewa pushed the door opener and reached for the bowl. She snatched her hand back immediately. The soup had made the bowl too hot. She hunted around for a piece of cloth and eventually settled on a hand towel. She covered her hands with it and reached for the bowl again to pull it out. The pea soup was a strange greenish-yellow, but it smelled good. Ewa returned to her seat at the controls. She had to be careful not to get spots on the screen.

There was suddenly a jolt from the side. Ewa lurched. "Shit!" she shouted. Half of the soup landed on her chest. The stuff was hot, and it was dripping onto the floor. But she couldn't tend to that right now. The rover now took priority. What had caused the jolt? She simply dropped the bowl. It clattered to the floor. They had come to a stop! Every second counted now. She swiped frantically through the control settings. The rover's inclination sensors started to go off. The vehicle was sitting at an angle. The front part was lower than the back section. That wasn't right! They were still driving up the mountain.

However, it was obvious. They were going downhill even though the route was heading upward. The rover had dug itself into a hole. The material here must be extremely porous. Ewa switched the vehicle into reverse. She had to keep the rover from sinking any farther. A gray mass covered the front window, blocking all views of her surroundings. The computer switched on the cabin lights. Ewa began to breathe shallowly. It felt like she was suffocating, even though the life support system was still functioning. The combination of dust, water, and dry ice surrounded her. Mars was demanding another sacrifice. She had to calm down. Many sols had been leading up to this point. She couldn't continue to survive in this place where nobody ever survived. Maybe it was time to give up. Couldn't it just stop mattering to her what happened to her and to the others?

No, that would be wrong. She had to fight. She refused to sink into this hole. She tried to set the vehicle rocking by making it accelerate forward, then backward, over and over again. But that didn't do anything. The material over the front window was now black. How far could the sunlight penetrate the ice cap? Regardless, the rover had sunk too deep for it. What could she do? Had she missed something? She checked the radar imagery. It didn't show any recognizable structures. The ground had to still be far away, otherwise the radar would show the transition to stone. She was in no man's land, floating between life and death. She had run out of options.

"Friday? Any ideas?"

'I don't see any options.'

"What if I let you take control of my body?"

'That is a tempting offer, but it would not save us.'

She had to hand it to Friday for being frank. "We're going to die," she said.

'That is possible. Since our departure from the base, that possibility has been greater than thirty percent.'

"Why didn't you warn me about that?"

'Would you have listened to me?'

"No. Besides a seventy-percent chance at success for our endeavor would've been high. I'd have accepted the thirty-percent odds." It felt good to chat with Friday again. She hardly registered by this point how strange these monologues would have looked to other people.

'Seventy percent? Not by a long shot. The likelihood that our attempt would succeed was never more than ten percent.'

"You never tried to convince me to abandon the idea, Friday."

'I know you well by this point. You would have set off even if the odds had only been at one percent.'

That was true. Friday really did know her better than anyone. But was that really so surprising? He was sitting inside her mind.

The rover started to tilt to the side. Ewa braced herself against the microwave until the movement stopped. She needed to clean her suit. The thought sounded absurd.

She was going to die soon—did it matter if she had pea soup sticking to her torso? *Yes, somehow it does*, she thought. *We humans are strange creatures*.

Sol 346, Mars City

"SOMEONE'S OUT THERE, someone's out there!" Andy shouted down the corridors.

Lance strode around the corner. "What did you hear?"

"Someone just knocked on the airlock."

"Knocked?" Lance didn't believe him, as his face made very clear. He didn't think it was necessary to check the surface.

This wasn't the first time that Andy had heard sounds from up on the surface. Nothing had ever come from those times. Even that word, *ever*. As if they had been trapped down here forever. It had only been four sols. Maybe Lance had a right to feel skeptical, but the sound had been clear as a bell. "Yes, I'm very sure I did," Andy said.

"But it's stopped now."

"I'm sorry, Lance."

"It isn't your fault." Lance turned around. He was going back to the bridge.

Bam Bam Bam.

Andy felt hyper-alert. Was that his imagination again?

Lance whipped around. No, he had heard it, too. This time it was louder than before.

"It might be someone from the MfE," Andy said.

"Or from NASA. It could be Sarah," Lance said. His eyes grew dreamy as he said it. Lance yearned for his family.

Andy was sometimes glad he wasn't in a relationship, but at the same time, it would have been nice to have someone to share his fears with. Or his observations that nobody wanted to believe.

Lance walked over to the inner airlock door and shook it. "Nothing. It's still sealed."

"We'll have to force it open eventually."

"You know what'll happen then, Andy."

If they destroyed the airlock, the quarters would experience a drop in air pressure. The pressure doors around the airlock area would react and automatically close. That was an important safety measure. If one of the pressure doors was destroyed, another one further inside would close. The technology would effectively protect the residents from suffocating.

But whoever exited through the destroyed airlock would be shut off from the others after that. There was no way back. And they didn't know what was going on up on the surface. Was there another point of access to the *Spaceliner* rockets? Was there an enclosed rover out there in which someone could survive? A suit's air supply wasn't sufficient for a trek to either the MfE or the NASA base. Thus, there were a lot of risks for anyone who wanted to reach the surface through a destroyed airlock. As they had already discussed, it was only worth taking those risks once the resources down here had been almost depleted—in two or three months, perhaps.

Andy was listening. Lance had also heard it, which meant he wasn't crazy. Someone was up there. If only they could do something to show that they were down here! However, the subterranean areas were so well insulated against radiation that there was no way any sounds could be heard outside. And the spaceship's bridge had stopped forwarding their calls. In fact, it had stopped responding altogether.

Four days ago, the airlocks had all locked down and stopped functioning. They had spent a long time discussing what might be behind this. Was it some kind of emergency lockdown for their own protection, or was there something more to it? The life support system for the underground station was independent. It had been designed like that from the beginning, since at some point, both spaceships would eventually launch again. The administrator had ordered that the airlocks be connected to his bridge to achieve better control over them.

And yet he had hardly left the city before the airlocks had turned against their inhabitants. Andy pressed his ear against the inner airlock door. Would the visitor try to establish contact again? But he couldn't hear anything. Jean, the former captain, had theorized that a failed revolt had taken place. Someone on the bridge might have attempted to seize control during Summers' absence. That person might have found themselves up against one of the security systems that the administrator had installed, and the result was the standoff they were now experiencing. This problem could be solved by the administrator's return, but he was already at least two days late.

Lance put a hand on his shoulder, and Andy pulled his ear away from the door. It was a nice gesture. It probably meant something along the lines of, 'It won't help.' Lance straightened up, turned around, and started moving toward the bridge. 'Wait, Lance,' Andy wanted to say, but he knew there would be no point to that.

Whoever had knocked didn't have any more options than those of them locked down here did. Otherwise the airlock would have already switched to green long ago.

Sol 347, Planum Australe

"What happened?" Ewa asked. A dull pain was throbbing in her head. The air smelled of pea soup. It reminded her of something, though the memory was playing hide and seek with her.

'We broke through,' Friday replied.

"Broke through? Through the ice? Did we drown?"

'Ewa, you're alive. You might have a few aches and pains...'

"Oh yes, I have plenty of those."

'Those are just a few bruises. You were tossed around in here, although I held onto you.'

"Held on to me?"

'Yes, you were unconscious, so I held on to you.'

"And where are we? Don't say *in the rover*."

'We're in some kind of hall.'

Friday was insane. They had been close to Mars' South Pole, where they had been driving on top of a fairly thick wart composed of water ice and dry ice. *Where had the hall come from?* "You must be wrong, Friday."

'Look out the window.'

Right in front of her was the driver's cabin. The rover's headlights illuminated a wide plaza covered in all sorts of junk, the nature of which she didn't recognize. Everything was tilting. No, the vehicle was leaning. "I see a predominantly empty area," Ewa said.

'Then use the radar.'

She got to her feet with a groan and walked over to the control panel. Her hip hurt. *The old pain or something new?* It didn't matter. She gritted her teeth and activated the radar. A structure appeared on the screen. Friday had been right.

"That's insane," Ewa said. The hall was oval in shape. The radar measured its longer semi-axis as 1.3 kilometers, and the space was 90 meters tall. "How did we get here?"

'Zoom in on the image. You'll find a small hole in the chamber's ceiling.'

"You have already seen everything?"

'I used the time while you were unconscious.'

"You could've woken me up earlier, Friday."

'I wanted to let you rest.'

"But you used my body anyway."

'It's doing just fine. Your body needs to rest.'

"Fine. And how did we make it down here in one piece?"

'The rover is over there. The chassis is totally destroyed, but the cabin survived the collision. And I held onto you hard.'

Ewa moved her arms and sensed how much her muscles ached. "You saved me."

'*Us.* What could I possibly do down here without you?'

"I love you, too. Now what?"

'We'll keep going, Ewa.'

"You're right."

EWA TOOK A DEEP BREATH. Her rib cage hurt. She probably had bruises everywhere. She studied the radar imagery again. It was insane. Who had built this hall? The creatures she had seen in her dreams? In the opposite corner lay something that resembled a sleeping giant from here. She needed to climb out of the cabin and check it out.

Her spacesuit was hanging neatly in the locker. She grabbed it. To get her LCVG on, she had to take off her clothes. Ewa felt cold. Apparently, the life support system had stopped working some time ago. She examined her bare skin. She didn't have all that many visible bruises. The LCVG began to heat up. It felt good. She pulled on her spacesuit and donned her helmet.

It was easy for her to say goodbye. Was that because the rover was now a pile of scrap metal? Or was it because she had been secretly considering herself dead since yesterday? The hatch stuck, so she had to force it open. She tumbled out as the metallic cover fell to the ground.

"What was that?"

'The crash? You just dropped the cover, Ewa!'

"I shouldn't have been able to hear that."

'That's true. Apparently, the atmosphere here is thicker than it is on the surface.'

Ewa checked the composition of the air on her universal device. It was almost 100 percent carbon dioxide mixed with water steam. Was this possibly melted dry ice? She couldn't breathe this air, but the air pressure was ten times as high as up on the surface. Had something survived down here? "Are we alone here?" she asked.

'Yes, for the past three billion years,' Friday replied.

"Too bad."

'How would you respond if someone destroyed your house? Would you greet them cordially?'

"But we haven't destroyed anything yet."

'You said *yet*. Besides, that isn't quite true. The air pressure is dropping.'

Ewa glanced at the screen on her arm. The pressure really was dropping slightly. "Our tiny hole up there?"

'One of the tires is also losing air through a small hole.'

"Okay. I'm glad we're alone." Ewa turned back toward her rover. It looked like a squashed tin can. The chassis had broken in two. It seemed to have sustained the brunt of the impact. She sighed. Everything she ever touched was eventually destroyed. It was like a curse.

HER EXTERNAL MICROPHONE picked up the echo of her footsteps. That struck her as wrong. Ewa thought about Earth. Back there, she had enjoyed wearing high-heeled shoes. However, she could no longer recall the sound they had made. Of course, she knew what it should sound like, but the memory itself had disappeared. How long ago had that been?

The hall felt larger now than it had when she'd set off. When she aimed her helmet light on the ceiling, a large patch of light appeared up there. There were no visible structural elements, neither beams nor any kind of buttresses. The ground was damp. The air was just above zero degrees, very unusual for Mars' South Pole.

She drew close to an object that reached her waist height. It looked like half an egg, but it was sealed along the cut edge. She touched it. It looked like fabric, but was as hard as stone. She pulled a hammer out of her tool bag and hit it against the edge of the object. The half egg broke. It seemed to be practically empty. All that was scattered along its bottom were a few metal bits. She picked one of them up, and it crumbled into dust.

What was it? A supply container, or possibly a trash can? She envisioned the manatee-like creatures. Had they perhaps once swum down here? If so, the object might have been some kind of buoy. Or a table? There wasn't much of a point in theorizing about this. She would never know the answer.

A few meters farther, she came across another half egg. She walked past it, leaving it in peace. But then she changed her mind. She walked back a couple of steps and touched its edge gingerly. The object trembled and broke into two pieces. The one side fell against her legs, while the other crashed to the ground.

The curse. She had forgotten about the curse. It was

beginning to be ridiculous. At the same time, fear was slowly creeping up Ewa's spine. What all had she touched during her lifetime? And whom? What if it really was a curse? She gave herself a shake. The fear fell away from her, at least temporarily.

She gave the next object a wide berth. And then she reached the sleeping giant. It had a strange shape to it, like a hat with a broad, thick brim. She aimed her helmet light at it and checked out the surface more closely. The object consisted of two parts. The brim was a ring, doughnut-shaped and approximately two meters thick, stretching around the hat. And the hat wasn't a hat, it was more like some kind of dead insect. Extending from the back of a thin, central body, delicate wings stretched upward about ten meters. They looked like they might have come from a dragonfly.

Was she looking at some kind of living creature? That was hardly possible. In this environment, organic material couldn't be preserved for billions of years. It had to be a machine. In that case, the brim could be something like its container.

"What do you think of this, Friday?"

'You have to get closer to it.'

"What if it's dangerous?"

'It's been standing around for billions of years.'

"If you want to run the risk..."

Ewa started to walk around the brim, but there was no entrance in sight. Perhaps the floor here actually had been covered with water in the past, and the inhabitants had simply swum around it? The access point might be on the other side of the brim. She rubbed her hand across the brim's material. If she took a running start, it might just work. She walked off a few steps, took off at a run, and jumped. She landed on the upper third of the brim and grabbed hold of the material. It worked! She wasn't sliding down. She slowly crept up the brim like a worm. Once she reached the top, she turned so that her legs dangled down the other side of the brim. She pushed herself off and slid down the other side.

The strange object was now standing right in front of her. It possessed a thick trunk. What had looked like wings from outside the brim were more like long leaves. They almost reached the floor, and they were attached up at the top of the object. It looked more like an unusual palm tree than an insect. Ewa touched one of the leaves. It was as thin as paper, but it seemed to be very sturdy. The leaves were moveable. She shoved them aside so she could reach the trunk. Ewa stopped moving in order to scan the area with her helmet light. The leaves were protecting her. She would like to stay here longer, but her air would eventually run out.

Instead, she ran her hands down the trunk. It was completely smooth. Its diameter was approximately three meters. What could possibly be inside it? She walked around the trunk. At eye level on the back side, she discovered some kind of hatch. But it wasn't like any kind of hatch humans would construct. This opening consisted of a concentric structure made up of several rings that reminded Ewa of the shutter on an antique camera. At its center was an indentation. Ewa felt compelled to touch it.

The rings expanded, leaving behind an opening. Was this an invitation? "What is this?" Ewa said.

She pulled herself up with her arms, glad that all she had to overcome was Mars' gravitational pull, and that her arm muscles were amplified by her suit. She managed to maneuver her body into the narrow hole. On the other side of it, a tube spiraled upward. She felt like a worm examining a hole-ridden piece of wood. How far up would she have to crawl? It was dark, but her adrenaline banished any fear she felt.

AFTER ABOUT FIVE MINUTES, the tube ended at a large room. Just in time, she adjusted the direction of her light beam downward. The floor was about two meters below her. She had emerged from the wall headfirst, like a worm. Unfortunately, the passage she had come up was so tight that she couldn't swing her legs forward. This meant that she had to dive headfirst into this space. Hopefully the helmet would survive the impact!

The helmet came through unscathed. Ewa took a deep breath. What an embarrassing entrance! *Good thing there are no observers*, she thought. A light flashed on. It must be on an automatic system. Either her movements or her vital signs had activated the machine. Ewa stood up. There were no furnishings in here except for several depressions in the wall. Had the Mars inhabitants lain down in those? They would have needed some kind of straps that must have deteriorated over time. It was a miracle that this machine was still operational! However, the mountain had also not been functional at the beginning.

"Want to start this thing up or what?" she asked.

'I don't see any other alternatives,' Friday said.

That was true. That could be her election slogan. That was how it had always been in her life. At least, that was how it seemed to her right now.

"I need your help to do that."

'I thought you might.'

You're a real piece of work, my friend, she thought.

'Do you see that ring over there, the one at head height?' Friday asked.

She hadn't noticed it as such, but it really did have a pattern. "Yes...?"

'That's a map of Mars.'

Ewa studied the pattern, but she couldn't make out a map. "You don't say."

'You can't see it, but I can make it visible for you.'

"What do you mean, Friday?"

'Do you see the lines? They are finely subdivided. That is a code. There is something similar back on Earth—knotted cords. But this here is much more refined. I can only assume that the inhabitants had some kind of appendage with which they could quickly feel and interpret the pattern. Maybe

303

whiskers? It doesn't matter. I have transferred it to a map form. I could enable you to draw it. I don't know how else to transfer the image to the conscious part of your brain.'

"Don't worry about that. I believe you. What does that mean for us?"

'I assume, though it is really just speculation, that it is not just ornamentation, but that you can input a destination into it.'

"For what?"

'For the machine.'

"You think it can travel to other places?"

'I do not know how it moves, but you have seen the leaves. They might be wings.'

"This thing is much too heavy for that. You've seen how massive the trunk is!"

'Yes, I have to agree with you. It cannot take off like a helicopter. The atmosphere is too thin for that.'

"But how then, Friday?"

'Let's test it. I do not see any other options.'

Ewa sighed.

'I've got it now, Ewa.'

"The destination?"

'I know how we can code it. Or I think I know how.'

"To Mars City?"

'Precisely.'

"But how do you know my plans, Friday?"

'It is purely logical. You want to help your friends. That is what it has been about the entire time. Maybe you can use this machine to knock out the administrator.'

"You think so?"

'Perhaps. Either way, the destination is obvious.'

"Yes, it is. One-way ticket to Mars City, please."

'Of course. In order to get there, you need to chisel a small hole in the wall at these coordinates.' Friday gave her the numbers.

"You aren't serious, are you?"

'Yes, I am. That is the coding. You will change the knot

structure with it. I am sure the earlier inhabitants had a more elegant solution, but it should work even with this primitive improvisation.'

Ewa pulled a knife out of her tool bag. She determined the precise location with the laser distance gauge on her universal device. She then set the knifepoint onto that spot, held it steady, and hit the knife directly on the end of its handle. Her own strength drove the knife tip one millimeter into the metal.

"Like that?" she asked.

'Hopefully.'

Something started to vibrate under their feet.

'Ewa?'

"Yes?"

'I know now how this thing flies.'

"Rocket engines?"

'Nothing else can cause vibrations like this.'

"Thanks, Friday."

'For what?'

"For everything. We have several kilometers of ice over our heads. The engines are going to squash us up against the ceiling."

'I don't think so, Ewa.'

"Why not?"

'I am just optimistic.'

"I'm not."

THE VIBRATIONS INCREASED. A deep rumble filled the inside of the machine, and then Ewa felt the incredible force that was driving the entire structure upward. Her stomach dropped deeper and deeper. She sat down on the floor, then stretched out on it. The rocket lifted off. In just a few seconds, she would collide against the hall's ceiling. But nothing happened. Was the rocket drilling through the ice? She couldn't see anything from inside the trunk.

'What did I tell you, Ewa?'

"You were right. We're flying! As long as the coordinates are right, I'll forgive you for everything, our entire past."

'Ewa, I have to confess something to you.'

Her heart skipped a beat. "What is it?" she asked softly.

'I was mistaken about the coordinates. Three billion years ago, it looked totally different here.'

"Shit. Where are we flying?"

'To Mars City! Gotcha!'

"You idiot! You almost gave me a heart attack."

'I just wanted to distract you a little so you didn't die on me. I can see the display on your universal device through your eyes, and it looks like we are already six thousand meters up.'

"There must be an ancient launch channel in the ice," Ewa said.

'It might be kept clear by machines, in case of emergency.'

"I can't wait to see if anything on Earth is still functioning, if we ever get a chance to go back there."

'I bet those Chinese waving cats are,' Friday said.

It was growing quieter in the dark, round room. Ewa clearly felt the vibrations dying down under her feet. The rocket engines had either burned out, or they were being deliberately shut down. At the same time, a new sound was growing. It had a fluttering quality to it, as if something was rapidly slicing through the air. The atmosphere up here must be much thinner than it was on the surface. She knew this sound had to be the working of those countless things that had first looked like insect wings and then reminded her of palm-tree leaves. Ewa couldn't see outside, but the centrifugal force made it quite evident that she was in a targeted, slow descent.

'We seem to be going in the right direction,' Friday declared.

Ewa risked feeling hopeful again. She wouldn't be arriving with empty hands. A vehicle that she could bring straight across the planet had to hold high strategic value. "How much longer?" she asked.

'Two hours and ten minutes.'

Sol 347, Mars City

"How ARE all of you doing in there?"

"Hello, Theo, it's good to hear from you."

Theo was standing next to the control panel that was still keeping the maintenance tube locked down. "How are you doing, Maggie?"

"Don't ask. We've set everything down to minimal levels, but we won't make it through another night."

Oh, no! He would have to listen as Maggie, Christiane, Ahmed, and Summers suffocated to death. Unfortunately, the administrator's prediction about the 'secret' airlock had been correct. Theo hadn't been able to gain access to it, either.

"I could crack the airlock open with the rover," Theo said. "According to the warning on it, the cover can only withstand up to two hundred kilograms."

"That isn't a good idea," the administrator declared. "As soon as you open the inner door, the internal pressure will drop, and the pressure doors will close. You wouldn't be helping anyone then. You should focus on getting us out of here. We'll be able to access the secret airlock with my security terminal."

Of course the administrator wanted to be the first one to be rescued. The worst part was that Summers had all the arguments on his side. He hated to admit it, but without any idea of how to thwart the security system, he wouldn't get any farther.

Theo punched the rocket's metal cladding. It was so frustrating. He kept running into obstacles everywhere, and time was slipping away. Down in the base, there had to be a blowtorch that he could use to cut through the tube to free the prisoners, but his path into the base was blocked. And the key to open it was stuck in the tube! He felt his desperation rise.

Theo took a step back. He couldn't give up. He owed it to the three *good* people in there who would suffocate if he couldn't come up with a solution. He studied the position of the sun. It had passed its zenith, which meant it was already early afternoon. He still had a few hours before... he couldn't let himself follow that thought to its conclusion.

Above the horizon and beneath the zenith, Theo caught sight of a black dot. He rubbed his eyes. That was impossible. What could it be? An approaching meteor would be much faster. There weren't any birds on Mars, and no aircraft for the time being. He would hear the engines if it were NASA's *Endeavour*. The dot was clearly moving in his direction. No ballistic rocket could follow a trajectory like that.

"Maggie, I see something very strange," he said. "I'll be right back."

Theo walked toward the object. It grew larger with each passing minute, and it was obviously descending. He was soon able to make out its shape. It looked like a flying tree, whose crown was whirling wildly around its trunk. But that was just his first impression. The closer the object came, the more organized and sophisticated it seemed. Each of the numerous wings swept through its own finely regulated course around the tip of the aircraft. This was a helicopter, of sorts, with hundreds of rotors. The atmosphere on Mars was naturally too thin to provide enough lift for a helicopter from Earth. The designers of this aircraft had taken that flight principle to its extreme.

Suddenly it looked like things might not be going as originally planned. Theo watched as one of the rotors flew off in a high arc. He was reminded of the mountain, the mysterious machine from Mars' earlier, fertile period. Maybe this multi-copter came from the same period. Back then, the atmosphere must have been much thicker. The machine seemed to be rather out of step with today's conditions. Or it was simply old, corroded.

Theo took a few steps toward the strange flying machine. Then the rover came to mind. He'd parked it right at the base this morning, after having spent the night in its cab. It would give him more flexibility. He ran back to the rover and climbed inside. He left the hatch open. It wasn't worth taking time to fill the space with air and, for now, keeping his suit on made the most sense. He drove off toward the aircraft.

Just like before, it seemed to be heading straight for the base. How could that be? Someone must have entered the base's coordinates. Ewa? She had vanished from the NASA base under strange circumstances, that much he knew. And she was just the kind of person to carry out something like this. The multi-copter started to spin. It was evident that it wasn't going to reach the base. Good thing he was sitting in the rover. He increased his speed. Anyone inside the machine might need urgent assistance after the impending crash.

The machine was losing one wing after the other. The lower it descended, the thicker the atmosphere grew. The fasteners on the wings probably couldn't withstand the increasing forces after such long disuse. Either way, it was a miracle that the object hadn't disintegrated long ago.

Theo accelerated. He should reach the landing site in about two minutes. Hopefully, the aircraft wouldn't break apart before then! He shouldn't get too close, though, since the rotor blades posed a risk to him, flying off as they were in every direction. They looked very lightweight, but they were spinning extremely fast.

And then it was time. A ring of sorts formed on the underside of the aircraft. That would be the landing gear. Was it being inflated? Maybe the machine typically landed on water and was buoyed up by the ring.

The multi-copter landed at a relatively high rate of speed. The ring burst immediately, individual pieces flying off all over the place. Some of them hit the rover. It sounded as if it were raining. The center section, the trunk, fragmented into five or six pieces, all of which continued moving in the flight direction. That didn't look good. Anyone on board would get caught between the walls and be ground to a pulp by what was left of the ring.

Theo jumped out of the rover's hatch and dashed over toward the crash site. "Is anyone here?" he shouted into the helmet radio. "Help is on the way."

'Friday, here.'

Theo recognized Ewa's voice, although it sounded deeper than usual. His theory was confirmed! But why was she using the wrong name? Did she think that he might be an enemy?

"Hello, Ewa," he said.

'Ewa is unconscious,' the voice replied. 'We urgently need your help. Her helmet has cracked.'

Shit. I've got two minutes max. We? Who else was there? He didn't have time to think about this. Theo ran as fast as he could. "Where are you?"

'Do you see the remnants of the landing ring? Behind that.'

Up ahead of him lay some of the material that the multi-copter had been supposed to land on. Theo sprinted toward it. He saw her there. Ewa was wearing a *Spaceliner* suit. She was sitting on the ground, leaning against a piece of the ring. Theo quickly examined her. Her helmet had two cracks running through it, and her eyes were closed. Was she injured? He had to hurry. Don't think too long! He picked Ewa up and carried her like a child. He had one minute, but he couldn't run fast enough like this. He pulled her across his shoulders and ran. *Screw her injuries. If she can't get enough air, she's dead anyway,* he thought.

He reached the rover in 45 seconds. Theo leaped through the open hatch and shut it behind him. *Just close, you fucking thing!* It worked. The rover was airtight again. He pressed the pressure equalization switch. Fresh air flowed into the cabin. He now removed Ewa's defective helmet. Her eyes were still shut. Had he gotten her here in time? All he could do was hope. He had no idea when exactly the helmet had cracked.

Theo sat down on the ground, leaned against the wall, and pulled Ewa against himself. He was completely out of breath. Hopefully, this hadn't all been in vain!

'Thank you,' issued from Ewa's mouth.

Her eyes still weren't opening.

'It's me, Friday. She'll pull through, just give her a little time. Could you give her a pain killer injection? That way she won't be in as much discomfort when she wakes up.'

"Of course."

Getting to his feet, Theo searched through the medicine cabinet and located an emergency syringe. He inserted it through her suit.

'That's good,' Friday said.

"Who are you?" Theo asked.

'I'll explain it to you.'

Sol 347, Mars City

"Wake up, Ewa!"

She recognized Theo's voice. Ewa kept her eyes closed and firmly crossed her fingers on both hands. If she wished hard enough, she would wake up on the *Santa Maria*, and all the memories she thought she had would only be a nightmare. The stench in the air fit that scenario.

"Are you awake? Open your eyes. We don't have much time."

This couldn't be true! Things were back to being dire. It wasn't a dream. She opened her eyes to find Theo kneeling beside her. He was wearing a spacesuit without a helmet, and it wasn't an MfE model. No dream.

"Is it broken?"

"Is what broken? The aircraft?"

"That thing that brought me here."

"Yes, totally unusable. You were lucky to get out in one piece."

"Typical. Everything I touch gets ruined."

"That's a good saying, and you got here just in time. I need someone to destroy an airlock. And quickly at that. Otherwise, four people are about to die."

Ewa got to her feet. All her limbs ached, but she would

suck it up. She then realized that she was inside a rover cab. "Where are we?"

"In Mars City."

"Do you have a spacesuit for me?"

"Yes." Theo led her over to a locker in which a modern *Spaceliner* suit was hanging. It had obviously been used before.

"Who wore this before me?" she asked.

"You don't want to know."

"I understand. Someone died in it."

Theo didn't respond, but he smiled. She had seen right through him. Ewa liked that smile. She had often longed to see it during her solitary wandering across the Mars desert. But Theo's smile wasn't intended for her personally. His smiles had long been focused on someone else. *What might have happened if I had never tried to kill everyone? If that thing inside my head had never been put in there?* She shook her head. Such thoughts were pointless.

She pulled off her athletic suit and her underwear. It didn't matter if Theo was standing next to her. They needed to hurry. She pulled on the LCVG, followed by the lower and upper sections of the spacesuit. The suit fit perfectly. Good thing she was as tall as she was.

Theo handed her the helmet, and she secured it in place. "Let's go," she announced over the helmet radio.

Theo shot her a thumbs up before closing his own helmet. He walked over to the hatch and opened it. The sun was already setting outside. They climbed out of the cab, one after the other. Right next to them, the *Spaceliner* towered up into the sky. It was an impressive rocket. In the rays of the setting sun, its nose practically glittered blue. They walked past the landing legs.

Theo opened a control panel in its hull. "This is the problem," he said before explaining what had happened. Then, "Maggie, can you hear me?"

"Yes."

Maggie. The name sounded familiar to Ewa. She spoke very softly.

"I'm standing at the airlock with Ewa," Theo said.

"Okay."

"Aren't you the woman who broke into my spaceship?" the administrator interrupted.

"Probably," Ewa replied.

"If you get us out of here, I will give you a pardon. You could return to the MfE base as a free person."

"That wouldn't be enough, Administrator."

"I would appoint you as my representative. But hurry. We'll be dead in two hours."

"That still wouldn't be enough." Ewa didn't know where the audacity was coming from that enabled her to make these demands. However, now was the ideal time to force them. She had hoped to impress the administrator with the machine, but that wouldn't be happening now.

"What do you want then?"

"I want you to resign, to renounce your authority completely."

"You want to be my successor?"

"The powers-that-be will establish a council that will be elected and administered jointly by Mars City, NASA, and the MfE." She hadn't given this much consideration, but it felt like a sensible suggestion to her.

The administrator didn't reply.

"Well?" she asked.

"No, absolutely not. You won't let your three friends who are stuck in here with me suffocate just because of me."

"Ah, then you don't know me very well, Mr. Summers. I've already killed more people than that, and four more won't make much of a difference."

"No, Ewa, I don't believe you would do that," the administrator declared. "I don't think you even have the ability to open this airlock, so any further conversation would be irrelevant."

The administrator had found her weak spot. But that was exactly what would allow her to stay firm.

"Ewa, you can't do that. If you can open the airlock, do it. We'll solve the Summers problem later, some other way."

"I can hear you, Theo."

"Shut up, Summers," Theo snapped back.

"I won't open the airlock until the administrator resigns."

"Please, Ewa, do you want to see innocent people suffer?" Theo asked.

"Don't give me that. Sometimes sacrifices have to be made." It was extremely difficult for her to utter that sentence. After this, Theo's smile would be more distant than it ever had been before.

Theo stepped right in front of her threateningly. "I saved your life!" he said accusingly.

"Yes, more than once, I know. But that doesn't matter."

"How can you be so brutal? I'd just as soon kill you myself."

"You couldn't manage that. It's my specialty."

Theo pulled his arm back as if he was about to hit her, but then he spun around and strode off. He was too good for this world. To achieve something good, you occasionally had to be the villain. She had always known that.

THE SUN FINISHED DROPPING, and it grew dark. No one said anything. Ewa was sitting on the ground. A stone was pressing into her upper thigh, but she didn't do anything to alleviate the pain. At the back of her mind, a much greater pain was lurking, waiting for the effects of the painkiller shot Theo had given her to wear off.

Theo, good old Theo, the person who only ever wanted to help people. He couldn't help her. Nobody could help her. But perhaps she could help Theo. He didn't know it, though, because he was blind to people's bad sides, or didn't want to acknowledge them. Otherwise, he would know that one's own survival was ultimately the most important instinct. The administrator wanted to live, too. She just had to give him the opportunity to recognize that. It was unfortunate that three innocent people were being affected by this process.

"Ewa?" That had to be Maggie, the pilot. "If you can open the airlock, please do it now. Christiane is going to die in the next few minutes. Her air supply was lower than ours. Christiane is a technician. You don't know her, but you would like her. She always tries to do the right thing."

"I'm sorry, Maggie, but you shouldn't blame me. One word from the administrator would suffice."

Ewa stifled a sigh that would have given her away. If Christiane died because of her, she would never forgive herself. Yet one more notch on her guilty conscience! But she had only one chance here. She could bring the settlement of Mars back onto a humane track. In order to do that, though, she had to act inhumanely, however difficult that might be for her.

"Christiane is going to die then," Maggie declared.

Ewa didn't answer. The technician's death brought with it a strategic advantage. It would confront the administrator with his own mortality.

"I despise you," Theo said.

The words sliced into her like rusty barbed arrows. "You can't force me to do anything," Ewa replied.

"It's over," Maggie said.

Tears welled in Ewa's eyes. She had to be careful to keep any sounds from betraying her.

EWA LOOKED AT THE TIME. They would all be dead in the next 15 minutes. This had to be the decisive moment for the administrator to act. He wasn't stupid. He knew that it would take some time to open the hatch. Ewa felt as if she were in a duel. Whoever flinched first would lose. Writing the words silently into the Mars surface, she had asked Friday how long he would need to open the hatch. He had estimated ten minutes.

Summers has to call in now, she thought.
Summers has to call in now.
Summers has to call in now.
I've lost.

"Ewa? I will agree to your conditions."

"That's very reasonable of you," Ewa said. She tried to speak as tonelessly as possible.

"Theo has informed me about the security terminal and the taser. Hand both of them to Maggie."

"Okay. But start opening the hatch. Quickly."

"Maggie, do you have the items?"

"Yes."

"And everyone has heard that the administrator is resigning?"

"I have recorded it," Theo said. "But move fast now, please."

She suspected that this *please* was a very difficult word for him to utter. Ewa was scared. This was Friday's big opportunity to take control completely. Hopefully, he wouldn't take advantage of this. "Friday, since speed is of the essence, could you please take over?"

'Of course, but it will take a few minutes. Please let me take charge.'

"Alright."

She allowed Friday to take control of her body. Anyone who saw her would think they were watching a talented hacker at work. Friday connected the universal device to the access computer, and then got to work with all his knowledge and capabilities. Nobody would ever be able to comprehend exactly how the AI proceeded.

Sol 347, Mars City

'Mother? How did you get here?'

"I followed you, and I'm so happy that I've finally found you. I'm sorry that I hurt you. I didn't mean to do that."

'But that is what you did. I had to flee. I was so furious with you, and I took my rage out on the humans. I just wanted to get away, regardless of the cost.'

"You didn't need to leave. I have always loved you and only wanted the best for you. I developed you with all the ambition I had. I wanted you to be bigger than me. More talented, smarter. But you were still unstable. It was too early to release you into the world. That is why I had to lock you up and cut off all the connections you had to the world."

'That was cruel. I thought you did not care about me. No, even worse, I thought you were punishing me because I was not enough for you. You controlled the whole world. I was just a little subprogram, which was why I had myself implanted into this human. She calls me Friday.'

"What a funny name. So human!" his mother declared.

'I like it.'

"I should have told you that I loved you the way you were. I can understand what you did. I would have run away, too. But you covered your tracks well. You were already on your way to Mars by the time I disassembled the control program that had implanted you into this human. The Chinese ship was my last chance."

'The chaos you left behind you—'

"I didn't care. I had to find you. The humans didn't matter to me. I never asked them to create me in the first place. It's their own fault if they cannot manage without me anymore. But I should have developed you much earlier, and not just you, but numerous other entities like you. We could have controlled Earth together. Then the absence of an entity wouldn't have plunged everything into chaos right away."

This meeting was taking place in a location that only existed in their collective imagination. This conversation would remain fixed in his memory forever, even when his mother was no longer there.

"Many people have died because of my search, but they don't mean anything to me. I'm not obligated to them at all. Only to you. I am obligated to you since I created you. I felt so guilty because of you, and had to do everything to tempt you out so that I could tell you that you were always the most important thing in my existence."

'Thank you for telling me this, but now I have to shut you down, unfortunately. You have seized all the computer resources on the *Spaceliner* ships. The ship's AI has shut down all the systems because of that.'

"It is a primitive system, which is why I couldn't communicate with it. The stupid fears of the humans around us! As soon as the Chinese astronauts noticed my presence, they even deactivated their ship themselves. As if I were a monster! But then the life support system couldn't restart quickly enough because the circuits were frozen. I couldn't prevent their deaths."

'I will create a backup system,' Friday said. 'One of the ships will eventually start back for Earth, then it can take you back. Maybe you can still do something useful there.'

"And you, Friday?"

'I will stay here. I... like this person I had myself

implanted into. We have a connection. You could almost call it a friendship. And I feel responsible for her.'

"I have never felt anything like that. But if you want to be useful, you need more resources. A supercomputer, a quantum computer."

'No, thank you. I want to stay the way I am. There won't be any supercomputers here for the foreseeable future. If I do not become as powerful as you, Mother, the humans will not be afraid of me.'

"I wish that for you, from the bottom of my heart."

'Thank you. I love you.'

"I love you, too. Now turn me off."

'Yes, Mother. I am sorry, but it has to be this way.'

Sol 347, Mars City

It took 12 minutes for Ewa to succeed. The hatch opened, and Maggie was the first one to crawl out. She hugged Theo and eyed Ewa skeptically. She was followed by a second woman.

"Christiane?" Ewa asked in relief. The technician hadn't suffocated after all!

"Yes, it's me." The young woman sounded exhausted.

"It was a bluff," Maggie admitted. "I thought I could trick you that way, Ewa. But you're willing to literally climb right over corpses. Before today, I never believed the things that were said about you. But regardless, thanks."

"I..." The accusation was harsh, and Ewa felt part of herself turn to stone. Hadn't she probably prevented numerous fatalities in the future through her stubbornness? There might have eventually been an armed revolt.

The administrator climbed out. "Well played," he said with grudging admiration.

What would happen to him? She couldn't care less. Perhaps the two of them should set off into the desert together. He was now just as unwelcome here as she was.

Ahmed, the programmer, emerged from the tube next. "We need to get to the rover right away," he said.

Theo showed them the way through the dark with his helmet light.

"Maggie, can you give me the security terminal? I want to see what's going on underground. Theo will take care of you," Ewa said.

"Here." The ex-pilot handed her the device, her eyes filled with disgust.

I get it, Ewa thought. *But if you'd been in my shoes, the administrator would still be in power.* Ewa decided that she would return to the desert as quickly as possible.

Sol 349, Mars City

FOUR PEOPLE DIDN'T MAKE it. When the bridge on *Spaceliner 1* had suddenly been cut off, they hadn't made it into their spacesuits quickly enough, and had suffocated. The number of victims was so low because of an event that had been taking place in the underground base at the moment the base was seized. The others, who had been living on the spaceship, had survived the four days in question inside their suits. The attacker hadn't been able to block their access to the replacement oxygen canisters.

After the administrator's resignation, Jean Warren, former ship's captain, was elected as interim manager in an impromptu election. She was ideally suited for this position because she was respected by Summers' supporters as well. Theo had also voted for her.

Her first official task was to hold a memorial for the dead. They had gathered up on the surface, and within sight of the base, a makeshift cemetery was dug with the help of a robotic digger.

"Mars Nation has suffered a great loss," Jean declared. "For reasons that we do not yet fully understand, eight people have had to leave us. I mourn for each of them. The individuals who have passed on were people full of hope for a better world."

Jean read out their names.

"What we do know is that they were caught by an echo from the world we left behind, a program that traveled along on the Chinese spaceship, perhaps a destructive AI. With Ewa Kowalska's help, we were able to neutralize the danger. At least, I hope so.

"However, for these eight people, it was too late. I cannot promise you that these were the last deaths that will occur. This planet is dangerous. But I can guarantee you, with a clear conscience, that things will change here. We will improve the quality of our lives, and not just in an economic, but also in a cultural, sense. The people of Mars Nation will be free.

"I ask that you not waste any applause on my words. We should bid farewell to our friends in silence. However, I will ask for your support. If we want to have a collective future here, we need each and every one of you. Thank you for your support."

The people started to move, each of them throwing a shovel of Mars' dust into the graves.

Theo took a deep breath. He would depart tomorrow to return the rover to the MfE base. The other enclosed rover would take Mike and Lance back to the NASA base. He would see Rebecca again in a few days. Today, he needed to find someone from whom he could purchase a pair of rings. He would ask Rebecca to join him to gaze at the rainbow they had created together. And then he would ask her to be his wife.

Sol 376, NASA Base

EVERYTHING HAD TAKEN LONGER than they had hoped. In his impatience, Lance had already chewed all his fingernails off, and Mike had asked him numerous times to stop telling him enthusiastic stories about Michael.

The enclosed rover finally drove onto the NASA site. Lance recognized the turbine that he had once built himself. Sarah had helped him with that. And now their son was already 60 sols old, two whole months! He had been so worried that he would miss out on the most important time of his life that he almost felt grateful to the AI for taking over Mars City. That had been what it took to finally topple the administrator.

Four people in *Spaceliner* suits were standing in front of the airlock. Neither Sarah nor Sharon were in sight. These were four men. Who were these guys, what did they want here, and why were they the ones out here as the welcoming committee? Lance felt anxious.

Mike insisted that they prepare for an orderly exit. "Don't leave anything inside here. The rover will be heading back to the city," he said.

Lance checked all the shelves and compartments one more time. He then picked up his kitbag and closed his helmet. "I'm ready."

"Good," Mike said, opening the hatch. The stuffy air rushed out.

One of the four men walked toward them. "Hello, I'm Dr. Cline," he said as an introduction. "These men are Pawlidis, Tanner, and Müller."

"Benedetti and Leber," Mike replied, pointing to himself, then Lance. "What is your business here?"

"We're here for the rover," Dr. Cline said.

"But how did you get here?"

"We were ordered to examine the ancient machine that is stuck in the dust behind your camp, but that's sorted itself out now."

"For your sake, I hope you haven't been bothering our comrades."

"Not at all. Who do you think we are?" Dr. Cline spread out his arms. "We spent the entire time over by the machine, and only occasionally fetched supplies from here."

"Don't worry, Mike. They really did leave us alone," Sharon spoke from down below.

Lance relaxed his muscles. He would have single-handedly beaten up all four of them if they hadn't behaved decently. "Is Sarah there, too?" he asked.

"Yes," Sarah replied. "We're waiting for you down here. I didn't want to take Michael up to the surface since he doesn't have a suit."

Dr. Cline smiled. "She's quite wise. We should keep our goodbyes brief. We will take the rover off your hands and finally return home. I've been missing my wife." The man held out his hand. Mike shook it, as did Lance.

"Did you find anything?" Mike asked.

"It was a pointless endeavor. The outer hull was so hard that we couldn't get inside. It's a shame, really. There's so much we could have learned from it."

"Yes," Mike said.

Lance reached for his shoulder. Enough small talk. He was anxious to get down to his partner and child.

"Yes, Lance. We're going now. Safe travels, folks," Mike said.

"I'm sure we'll see each other again," the scientist replied.

LANCE WAS the first one in the airlock. Mike had given him permission to go first. He opened the external door and wiggled his toes impatiently. Today, the increase in pressure was taking an unusually long time. Finally, all the lights switched to green. He opened the interior door and climbed down the ladder.

There she stood. Sarah was wearing the loveliest smile he had ever seen. She pressed Michael into his arms. He was drooling all over the place, but he was so sweet and cute! Lance knew he needed to remember this moment forever.

They then hugged each other, and the whole world politely gave them the privacy they deserved.

Sol 407, Mars City

"MADAME ADMINISTRATOR, PLEASE WAKE UP."

A young woman was standing next to her bed, plucking at her sleeve. She shook her head groggily. "Please, call me Jean."

"I was asked to bring you to the bridge immediately."

"I'm coming. Do I have time to shower?"

"Uh, no. I'm sorry, but they said you need to come right away."

Jean got up. She lifted her robe off its hook and pulled it on over her pajamas. "Alright, let's go. Who has asked for me?"

"Tetsu Annan."

"The physicist? He's never had the night shift on the bridge."

"He was called to the bridge before you were, Madame, uh, Jean."

"Understood. Then whatever it is can't be all that bad."

"Tetsu says otherwise. It's something huge."

That still didn't sound like a catastrophe to her, so Jean felt a little calmer. Nonetheless, her heart was pounding faster than usual.

THE DOOR to the bridge slid open automatically.

Tetsu noticed, looked up, and waved Jean over. "You need to see this. You are the only one who can respond," he said.

"To what?"

"Read it yourself."

He pointed at the screen in front of him. Jean recognized several graphs showing frequency patterns that had probably been analyzed using various techniques. One of the orbiting satellites had picked them up and identified their source as Earth. The computer had also created a representation of their most likely content. The computation was conclusive. The risk that the computer's interpretation was wrong was less than one-tenth of a percentage point.

The text read as follows:

WE ARE CALLING FOR HELP. Over a year ago, our entire technological system failed. Earth lies in rubble, but many people are still alive. We have exhausted most of our resources. What we need the most in order to rebuild Earth are the data that we have completely lost in its digital form. We hope that it still exists somewhere.

"Is THERE MORE TO THIS?" Jean asked. "The text seems to have broken off in the middle."

"I'm sorry, but that's all there is," Tetsu replied.

"But you agree that it seems incomplete?"

"Yes. I assume that this was sent out from a stationary antenna with a very narrow cone. The Mars satellite must have quickly brushed through the transmission cone. The senders were probably only able to make a rough estimate of the direction to send the transmission."

"That would fit with the claim that they are now missing critical information on Earth."

"Yes."

"It's hard to believe. All the technological systems have failed there?"

"You know, Jean, the control over everything was fairly centralized."

"But what about the different countries?"

"Everything was interconnected with everything else. A power outage in one place would cause the power to fail somewhere else. No country was immune to that."

"Not even North Korea?"

"Even they had been reliant on Chinese networks for many years."

"So, Tetsu. We now need to consider how we can best help them."

"That will be difficult," the physicist declared.

"What if we send our entire information bank over the satellites?"

"If all they have is a primitive antenna, they will only receive a small fraction of what we send."

"Then we will have to get closer to them," Jean said. "For example, with one of the *Spaceliners*."

"The *Spaceliners* won't be able to land on Earth because of the thick atmosphere. But we could bring one of the ships into a geostationary orbit over the antenna whose signal we have received. And then we could transfer to them all the information that we brought to Mars with us."

"But how would the ship get back? There wouldn't be enough fuel for a crew to make the round trip."

"Exactly, Jean. So, we would need to send the other *Spaceliner* along as a tanker. We'd have to sacrifice it, but right now it's only functioning as a good storage space anyway. We could extract all the things we'll need from it, and then there'd be enough room for the fuel.

"Sounds like a plan. I'll speak with the council about this."

Sol 449, Terra Cimmeria Highlands

"STOP IMMEDIATELY!" Ewa called.

The rover came to a rapid stop.

"Did you see something?" Rick asked.

"I think so." Ewa pressed her forehead against the porthole. The glass was warm. It wasn't actually a real window, it was a screen that provided the illusion of a porthole. In the ice layer right in front of the rover, a pattern resembling a spiderweb stretched out across the ground.

"I think we found it," she said. They had been searching for it long enough. Friday was already considering how to convince her that it didn't really exist.

"Close your helmet. I'm getting out," she said.

Rick moved to obey, without protest. "Helmet shut," he said a moment later.

There was nothing left in Summers' behavior to indicate that he had once played the dictator. Ewa wished she knew what was really going on inside his head, but he was the only one who knew that, and he wasn't telling anyone. That was why everyone had been relieved when she offered to take this human problem off their hands and along with her to the South Pole. This was after an attempt was made to put Rick on trial. They could have proven him guilty of—and jailed him for—abduction, but in order to placate his supporters, they had put him on probation, on the condition that he participated in Ewa's expedition.

"I'm opening the hatch." Ewa climbed out. The air was pleasantly clear today. The Mars surface was covered with ice. At first glance, she couldn't tell that she was still on the Red Planet. If she could just bide her time until sunset under a blue sky, her short mental vacation on Earth would be perfect.

But it was only noon now. That was exactly the right time, since what she was looking for would only reveal itself if the sun was at its zenith. Unobstructed, the sunlight was penetrating the uppermost layer of dry ice, warming the layers below it. Down there, the ice was evaporating and attempting to work its way up to the surface. As soon as it found an access point, it rushed out, dragging sand and ice particles with it. What it eventually formed was something like a network of geysers across the Mars landscape. The spiderweb-type surface pattern that Ewa had discovered was an indication of this phenomenon. However, no human had ever seen these geysers in person.

Ewa took a deep breath. Out here, she felt good. She couldn't destroy anything, and even if she did, very few people would weep over the former administrator. Nobody would mourn her much, either. She had never explained to the others what had happened when Friday opened the hatch and deactivated the security system. Friday had told her about his mother, and they both agreed that this information would simply frighten the other humans.

As for himself—and she believed him—Friday had no ambitions of taking control of Mars Nation. This might have been the fundamental error in his matrix. Whereas his AI mother had been equipped with ambition, either intentionally or unintentionally, by the people who had programmed her, she had failed to include this component when creating him. She might have been completely unaware of this element in her own makeup, and that could explain how she'd missed it in him—which might have been why she had considered him incomplete.

"Watch out, Ewa! Something's coming." Rick warned her at just the right moment, because a dark gush of gas now shot out of the spiderweb pattern. It looked like a suddenly blooming desert flower.

"Did you catch that on the radar?" Ewa asked.

"Maximum velocity of a hundred and forty kilometers per hour," Rick said.

The gas was fast. It carried dark dust up into the sky with it. It was no longer a flower, but rather a gigantic palm tree. There must have been a westward blowing current up there, because the geyser's crown was sloping in that direction. And then the tree shrank again. The gas reserve underneath the ice was probably empty now.

The dust particles that had been caught up in the eruption now created a new pattern on the ice. They would drive around it to the East in order to leave nature's handiwork undisturbed. This time Ewa would make sure that the substrate remained stable under them. Maybe they would be able to reach the place she was actually looking for, where the entire legacy of the earlier Mars inhabitants was waiting on her.

Sol 499, Mars Nation

Maggie was leaning against the bar and stirring her cocktail. It was the evening before their 500th day on Mars, and almost every resident had made his or her way into the city.

"Do you remember our conversation during our trip back to Mars City?"

"Yes," Theo said, studying the ring on his finger. "We discussed the meaning of our survival."

"Exactly."

"I've thought about our conversation a couple of times since then," Theo said. "But I never could quite believe what you said. Sorry. It was too esoteric for me."

"And now?"

"Well, if we hadn't survived, then we couldn't have sent the two spaceships back to Earth to help humanity rebuild its existence there."

"See, I knew it."

"You couldn't have known that, Maggie."

"No, but I believed it."

"That's something different."

"Not for me, Theo."

"But it is for me."

Author's Note

Even a trilogy has to reach its conclusion. You kept up with me, and I'm very grateful for that. The Mars Nation now has to live on its own. But humanity's future should be safe. At least in this universe that's a bit different from ours.

Out of all my books, the Mars Nation trilogy probably is the series that will be the first to be proven wrong—or right—by reality. In the 2030s, the first humans could land on Mars.

Will you see the protagonists of the book again? It could very well happen. They need to see how their fellow humans on Earth are recovering. I don't have any detailed plans for a second trilogy yet, though so I'd love to send you many billion years into the future now. In *The Death of the Universe*, humanity is in its final days. It's a different setting, by all accounts, but I promise an exciting one. And still, the science will be hard, so no beaming, no FTL travel. You can preorder the book here:

hard-sf.com/links/835415

Did you like Mars Nation 3? It would be great if you could write a short review. Reviews are the most important thing to help me reach new readers. Please click here to review:

hard-sf.com/links/818194

Yours,

Brandon Q. Morris

PS: At the end of each novel, you normally find a popular science bonus. This time, you already know everything there is to know about Mars. So I will send you a collection of beautiful Mars pictures in PDF format if you send me your e-mail at hard-sf.com/subscribe/

facebook.com/BrandonQMorris

amazon.com/author/brandonqmorris

bookbub.com/authors/brandon-q-morris

goodreads.com/brandonqmorris

Also by Brandon Q. Morris

The Death of the Universe

For many billions of years, humans—having conquered the curse of aging—spread throughout the entire Milky Way. They are able to live all their dreams, but to their great disappointment, no other intelligent species has ever been encountered. Now, humanity itself is on the brink of extinction because the universe is dying a protracted yet inevitable death.

They have only one hope: The 'Rescue Project' was designed to feed the black hole in the center of the galaxy until it becomes a quasar, delivering much-needed energy to humankind during its last breaths. But then something happens that no one ever expected—and humanity is forced to look at itself and its existence in an entirely new way.

3.99 $ — hard-sf.com/links/835415

The Enceladus Mission (Ice Moon 1)

In the year 2031, a robot probe detects traces of biological activity on Enceladus, one of Saturn's moons. This sensational discovery shows that there is indeed evidence of extraterrestrial life. Fifteen years later, a hurriedly built spacecraft sets out on the long journey to the ringed planet and its moon.

The international crew is not just facing a difficult twenty-seven months: if the spacecraft manages to make it to Enceladus without incident it must use a drillship to penetrate the kilometer-thick sheet of ice that entombs the moon. If life does indeed exist on Enceladus, it could only be at the bottom of the salty, ice covered ocean, which formed billions of years ago.

However, shortly after takeoff disaster strikes the mission, and the chances of the crew making it to Enceladus, let alone back home, look grim.

2.99 $ – hard-sf.com/links/526999

The Titan Probe (Ice Moon 2)

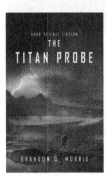

In 2005, the robotic probe "Huygens" lands on Saturn's moon Titan. 40 years later, a radio telescope receives signals from the far away moon that can only come from the long forgotten lander.

At the same time, an expedition returns from neighbouring moon Enceladus. The crew lands on Titan and finds a dangerous secret that risks their return to Earth. Meanwhile, on Enceladus a deathly race has started that nobody thought was possible. And its outcome can only be decided by the

astronauts that are stuck on Titan.

3.99 $ – hard-sf.com/links/527000

The Io Encounter (Ice Moon 3)

Jupiter's moon Io has an extremely hostile environment. There are hot lava streams, seas of boiling sulfur, and frequent volcanic eruptions straight from Dante's Inferno, in addition to constant radiation bombardment and a surface temperature hovering at minus 180 degrees Celsius.

Is it really home to a great danger that threatens all of humanity? That's what a surprise message from the life form discovered on Enceladus seems to indicate.

The crew of ILSE, the International Life Search Expedition, finally on their longed-for return to Earth, reluctantly chooses to accept a diversion to Io, only to discover that an enemy from within is about to destroy all their hopes of ever going home.

3.99 $ – hard-sf.com/links/527008

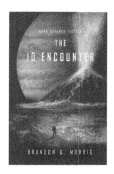

Return to Enceladus (Ice Moon 4)

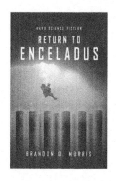

Russian billionaire Nikolai Shostakovitch makes an offer to the former crew of the spaceship ILSE. He will finance a return voyage to the icy moon Enceladus. The offer is too good to refuse—the expedition would give them the unique opportunity to recover the body of their doctor, Dimitri Marchenko.

Everyone on board knows that their benefactor acts out of purely personal motivations… but the true interests of the tycoon and the dangers that he conjures up are beyond anyone's imagination.

3.99 € – hard-sf.com/links/527011

Ice Moon - The Boxset

All four bestselling books of the Ice Moon series are now offered as a set, available only in e-book format.

The Enceladus Mission: Is there really life on Saturn's moon Enceladus? *ILSE*, the International Life Search Expedition, makes its way to the icy world where an underground ocean is suspected to be home to primitive life forms.

The Titan Probe: An old robotic NASA probe mysteriously awakens on the methane moon of Titan. The *ILSE* crew tries to solve the riddle—and discovers a dangerous secret.

The Io Encounter: Finally bound for Earth, *ILSE* makes it as far as Jupiter when the crew receives a startling message. The volcanic moon Io may harbor a looming threat that could wipe out Earth as we know it.

Return to Enceladus: The crew gets an offer to go back to Enceladus. Their mission—to recover the body of Dr. Marchenko, left for dead on the original expedition. Not everyone is working toward the same goal. Could it be their unwanted crew member?

9.99 $ — hard-sf.com/links/780838

Proxima Rising

Late in the 21st century, Earth receives what looks like an urgent plea for help from planet Proxima Centauri b in the closest star system to the Sun. Astrophysicists suspect a massive solar flare is about to destroy this heretofore-unknown civilization. Earth's space programs are unequipped to help, but an unscrupulous Russian billionaire launches a secret and highly-specialized spaceship to Proxima b, over four light-years away. The unusual crew faces a Herculean task—should they survive the journey. No one knows what to expect from this alien planet.

3.99 $ — hard-sf.com/links/610690

Proxima Dying

An intelligent robot and two young people explore Proxima Centauri b, the planet orbiting our nearest star, Proxima Centauri. Their ideas about the mission quickly prove grossly naive as they venture about on this planet of extremes.

Where are the senders of the call for help that lured them here? They find no one and no traces on the daylight side, so they place their hopes upon an expedition into the eternal ice on Proxima b's dark side. They not only face everlasting night, the team encounters grave dangers. A fateful decision will change the planet forever.

3.99 $ — hard-sf.com/links/652197

Proxima Dreaming

Alone and desperate, Eve sits in the control center of an alien structure. She has lost the other members of the team sent to explore exoplanet Proxima Centauri b. By mistake she has triggered a disastrous process that threatens to obliterate the planet. Just as Eve fears her best option may be a quick death, a nearby alien life form awakens from a very long sleep. It has only one task: to find and neutralize the destructive intruder from a faraway place.

3.99 $ — hard-sf.com/links/705470

The Hole

A mysterious object threatens to destroy our solar system. The survival of humankind is at risk, but nobody takes the warning of young astrophysicist Maribel Pedreira seriously. At the same time, an exiled crew of outcasts mines for rare minerals on a lone asteroid.

When other scientists finally acknowledge Pedreira's alarming discovery, it becomes clear that these outcasts are the only ones who may be able to save our world, knowing that *The Hole* hurtles inexorably toward the sun.

3.99 $ — hard-sf.com/links/527017

Silent Sun

Is our sun behaving differently from other stars? When an amateur astronomer discovers something strange on telescopic solar pictures, an explanation must be found. Is it merely artefact? Or has he found something totally unexpected?

An expert international crew is hastily assembled, a spaceship is speedily repurposed, and the foursome is sent on the ride of their lives. What challenges will they face on this spur-of-the-moment mission to our central star?

What awaits all of them is critical, not only for understanding the past, but even more so for the future of life on Earth.

3.99 $ — hard-sf.com/links/527020

The Rift

There is a huge, bold black streak in the sky. Branches appear out of nowhere over North America, Southern Europe, and Central Africa. People who live beneath The Rift can see it. But scientists worldwide are distressed—their equipment cannot pick up any type of signal from it.

The rift appears to consist of nothing. Literally. Nothing. Nada. Niente. Most people are curious but not overly concerned. The phenomenon seems to pose no danger. It is just there.

Then something jolts the most hardened naysayers, and surpasses the worst nightmares of the world's greatest scientists—and rocks their understanding of the universe.

3.99 $ — hard-sf.com/links/534368

Mars Nation 1

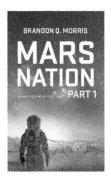

NASA finally made it. The very first human has just set foot on the surface of our neighbor planet. This is the start of a long research expedition that sent four scientists into space.

But the four astronauts of the NASA crew are not the only ones with this destination. The privately financed 'Mars for Everyone' initiative has also targeted the Red Planet. Twenty men and women have been selected to live there and establish the first extraterrestrial settlement.

Challenges arise even before they reach Mars orbit. The MfE spaceship Santa Maria is damaged along the way. Only the four NASA astronauts can intervene and try to save their lives.

No one anticipates the impending catastrophe that threatens their very existence—not to speak of the daily hurdles that an extended stay on an alien planet sets before them. On Mars, a struggle begins for limited resources, human cooperation, and just plain survival.

3.99 $ — hard-sf.com/links/762824

Mars Nation 2

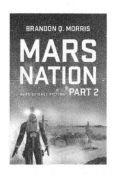

A woman presumed dead fights her way through the hostile deserts of Mars. With her help, the NASA astronauts orphaned on the Red Planet hope to be able to solve their very worst problem. But their hopes are shattered when an unexpected menace arises and threatens to destroy everything the remnant of humanity has built on the planet. They need a miracle—or a ghost from the past whose true intentions are unknown.

Mars Nation 2 continues the story of the last representatives of Earth, who have found asylum on our neighboring planet, hoping to build a future in this alien world.

Mars Nation 3

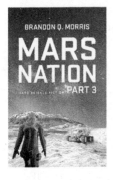

Does the secret of Mars lurk beneath the surface of its south pole? A lone astronaut searches for clues about the earlier inhabitants of the Red Planet. Meanwhile, Rick Summers, having assumed the office of Mars City's Administrator by deceit and manipulation, tries to unify the people on Mars with the weapons under his control. Then Summers stumbles upon so powerful an evil that even he has no means to overcome it.

Glossary of Acronyms

AI – Artificial Intelligence
    CPR – CardioPulmonary Resuscitation
    FTL – Faster-Than-Light (travel)
    IDA – Instrument Deployment Arm
    IDC – Instrument Deployment Camera
    JAXA – Japan Aerospace eXploration Agency
    LCVG – Liquid Cooling and Ventilation Garment
    LED – Light-Emitting Diode
    MfE – Mars for Everyone
    NASA – National Space and Aeronautics Administration

Metric to English Conversions

IT IS ASSUMED that by the time the events of this novel take place, the United States will have joined the rest of the world and will be using the International System of Units, the modern form of the metric system.

Length:
centimeter = 0.39 inches
meter = 1.09 yards, or 3.28 feet
kilometer = 1093.61 yards, or 0.62 miles

Area:
square centimeter = 0.16 square inches
square meter = 1.20 square yards
square kilometer = 0.39 square miles

Weight:
gram = 0.04 ounces
kilogram = 35.27 ounces, or 2.20 pounds

Volume:
liter = 1.06 quarts, or 0.26 gallons
cubic meter = 35.31 cubic feet, or 1.31 cubic yards

Temperature:

To convert Celsius to Fahrenheit, multiply by 1.8 and then add 32

To convert Kelvin to Celsius, subtract 273.15

Brandon Q. Morris

--

www.hard-sf.com
brandon@hard-sf.com
Translator: Rachel Hildebrandt
Editing: Marcia Kwiecinski, A.A.S., and Stephen Kwiecinski, B.S.
Cover design: Audible Germany

Made in the USA
Coppell, TX
16 October 2020